U0095787

新理念大学英语
泛读教程

（第二册）

总 主 编：梁为祥　肖　辉

副总主编：吕　晔　蔡　斌　韩　英　杨　华

主　　编：吕　晔

副 主 编：白新芳　王玉明

编　　者：高　菲　胡　燕　李海军　王莲生
王宇涯　徐　斌　徐惠良　周　琳

东南大学出版社

·南京·

图书在版编目(CIP)数据

新理念大学英语泛读教程:全4册 / 梁为祥,肖辉主编.—南京:东南大学出版社,2011.8

ISBN 978-7-5641-2934-7

Ⅰ.①新… Ⅱ.①梁… ②肖… Ⅲ.①英语—阅读教学—高等学校—教材 Ⅳ.①H319.4

中国版本图书馆 CIP 数据核字(2011)第166630号

新理念大学英语泛读教程(第二册)

出版发行:东南大学出版社
社　　址:南京市四牌楼2号　邮编:210096
出 版 人:江建中
责任编辑:史建农
网　　址:http://www.seupress.com
电子邮箱:press@seupress.com
经　　销:全国各地新华书店
印　　刷:南京新洲印刷有限公司
开　　本:787mm×1092mm　1/16
总 印 张:48.75
总 字 数:1186千字
版　　次:2011年8月第1版
印　　次:2011年8月第1次印刷
书　　号:ISBN 978-7-5641-2934-7
总 定 价:98.00元(共4册)

前 言

《新理念大学英语泛读教程》是英语教学不可缺少的教学内容，也是英语其他课程的一个重要补充。本“教程”内容是围绕提高学生的英语能力所设计的。为了达到这个目的，根据“泛读教程”的教学特点和要求，在编写过程中着重强调了如下几个方面的内容：

一、为了扩大学生的英语词汇量，拓宽知识范围，获得更多的知识信息，丰富学生的语言知识，本教材注重选材范围，力求涵盖社会科学、人文科学以及自然科学等方面的内容。一、二册着重选择适用英语，如：电子商务、经济、贸易、金融、证券交易等方面的文章；三、四册侧重于选择社会科学和人文科学以及自然学科等方面的文章。本教材的教学目的是要求学生以自学为主，故文章的篇幅不宜太长。一、二册的文章250～300个单词，三、四册的文章350～400个单词。文章由易到难，便于学生阅读、理解和掌握，从而提高学生的阅读兴趣和学习效果。

二、为了帮助学生在学习过程中更好地理解和掌握文中的语言词汇知识，课文后列出了文中的词语和词组，并针对重点常用词语和词组设计了10个句子为填空题，帮助学生掌握这些词语和词组的用法。

三、每篇文章设计5个理解题，每道题含有4个选项，选项中包括对词组、段落以及全文的理解，从中选择最佳答案，提高学生的理解力。

本教材适用于专科院校和本科院校的学生阅读教学，包括英语专业学生和公共英语的学生。为了使本教程更具有适用性、针对性，编写组特邀请了东南大学、河海大学、新疆医科大学、安徽农业大学、湖州师范学院、江阴职业技术学院、无锡科技职业技术学院等院校的教师参加了集体编写工作，由东南大学外国语学院教授、浙江越秀外国语学院聘用教授梁为祥先生以及南京财经大学肖辉教授担任总主编，并审阅了全部书稿。在编写过程中，史建农编辑给予了大力支持与协作。书中如有谬误之处，欢迎读者给予指正。

编 者

2011.8

Contents

Passage 1

On the day Marco Polo was born in Venice in 1254, his father Nicolo Polo and his uncle Maffeo had just left the city. They had gone on a trading journey.

Venice was a great seaport in the thirteenth century. Her warships controlled the eastern Mediterranean Sea and protected her merchant ships. Her trade in goods from Asia for resale in Europe was the most important source of her wealth. We would call it today a luxury trade. Goods which had traveled thousands of miles by caravan to a Mediterranean port were not for the common people's markets. Silk cloth from Cathay (now called China), precious stones from India, spices from south-east Asia — these were for the rich people of Europe, the nobles and the new merchant classes.

Nicolo Polo was one of the great merchant princes of Venice. The purpose of his journey was to make contacts at the sources of supply of his goods. Too many merchants had to make a profit from the goods before he could buy them in the markets of the eastern Mediterranean ports. Perhaps he hoped to cut out some of those middlemen or to make other improvements in the quality of the goods or the way of getting them to Venice. The heads of big trading houses make journeys for similar purposes today, but the similarity ends there. We can scarcely compare the modern executive's luxurious travel by air-conditioned jet plane with Nicolo's months of courageous traveling by ship, on horseback, on foot, and by camel caravan to the court of Kublai Khan.

Ⅰ. New Words and Expressions

Venice	[vɪnɪs]	(*n.*)威尼斯(意)
seaport	[ˈsiːpɔːt]	(*n.*)海港
Mediterranean Sea	[medɪtəˈreɪnjən siː]	地中海
Nicolo Polo		尼可罗·波罗(人名)
Marco Polo		马可·波罗(人名)
warship	[ˈwɔːʃɪp]	(*n.*)军舰
source	[sɔːs]	(*n.*)来源
resale	[ˈriːseɪl]	(*n.*)零售
luxury	[ˈlʌkʃərɪ]	(*n.*)奢侈,豪华
Cathay	[kæˈθeɪ]	(*n.*)[古语,诗歌用语]中国
noble	[ˈnəubl]	(*n.*)贵族

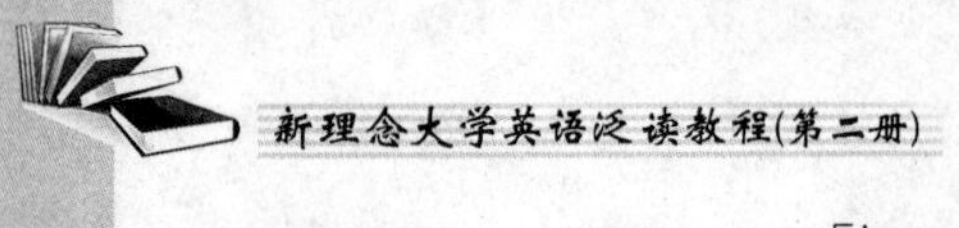

caravan	[ˈkærəvæn]	(*n.*)(在沙漠或危险地区结伴而行的)旅行队,商队
spice	[spaɪs]	(*n.*)香料,调味品
prince	[prɪns]	(*n.*)名家,王子
south-east Asia	[saʊθ-iːstˈeɪʃə]	东南亚
merchant	[ˈmɜːtʃənt]	(*n.*)商人,国际贸易批发商
class	[klɑːs]	(*n.*)阶级,阶层,类
similarity	[sɪmɪˈlærɪtɪ]	(*n.*)类似,相似
scarcely	[ˈskeəslɪ]	(*adv.*)稀少地,罕见地
executive	[ɪgˈzekjʊtɪv]	(*n.*)决策人,董事会,行政官
air-conditioned	[ˈeə-kənˈdɪʃənd]	(*a.*)空调的
jet plane	[dʒet pleɪn]	喷气式飞机
be born in		出生在……
luxury trade		利润丰厚的贸易
by caravan		通过商队
make contact		保持联系
make a profit from		从……获利
cut out		谋得,剪去,开出
on horseback		在马背上
on foot		步行
by camel caravan		靠骆驼运输

Ⅱ. Fill in the blanks in the following sentences with the listed words or expressions.

control	precious	make contact	make a profit from
cut out	get... to	in the quality of	compare
courageous	similarity		

1. The project is complete as far as ________ the river is concerned.
2. He likes to ________ with wealthy people.
3. This canned soup can't ________ to homemade.
4. It was ________ of him to oppose his chief.
5. I'll cut down my smoking, maybe ________ it ________ entirely.
6. He tries to ________ trade.
7. They have lost ________ working time.
8. When did you ________ those goods ________ Qingdao?
9. There is a great ________ between all her children.
10. There is a great improvement ________ these products.

Ⅲ. There are four choices marked A. B. C. and D. in the following questions. You should decide on the best choice and mark the corresponding letter with a circle.

1. Nicolo Polo and Maffeo left Venice ________.

   A. in 1264　　B. in 1254

   C. in 1234　　D. in 1274

2. Nicolo Polo and Maffeo _______ a trading journey after they had left Venice.

   A. carried out　　B. conducted

   C. carried on　　D. went out

3. "A luxury trade" in the passage maybe means "_______".

   A. glad business　　B. pleased business

   C. joyful trade　　D. enjoyable trade

4. His purpose of doing business was _______.

   A. for the people's necessities of Europe

   B. for a part of people's necessities

   C. for all the upper classes of Europe

   D. for all wealthy people and the new merchant classes

5. "Cut out" in the passage maybe means "_______".

   A. cut about　　B. omit

   C. press　　D. cut off

Marketing Research involves the use of surveys, tests, and statistical studies to analyze consumer trends and to forecast the quantity and locale of a market favorable to the profitable sale of products or services. The social sciences are increasingly utilized in customer research. Psychology and sociology, for example, by providing clues to people's activities, circumstances, wants, desires, and general motivations, are keys to understanding the various behavioral patterns of consumers.

Coupled with applications from the social sciences has been the introduction of modern measuring methods when surveys are made to determine the extent of markets for a particular product. These methods include the use of statistics and the utilization of computers to determine trends in consumers' desires for various products. Scientific analysis is being used in such areas as product development, particularly in evaluating the sales potential of new product ideas. For example, use is made of mathematical models, that is, theory-based projections of social behavior in a particular social relationship. Sales projections become the basis for many important marketing decisions, including those relating to the type and extent of advertising, the allocation of salespeople, and the number and location of warehouses.

Ⅰ. New Words and Expressions

statistical	[stəˈtɪstɪkəl]	(*a.*) 统计的
forecast	[ˈfɔːkɑːst]	(*v.*) 预测,预报
quantity	[ˈkwɒntətɪ]	(*n.*) 数量,大量
favorable	[ˈfeɪvərəbl]	(*a.*) 有利的,适宜的,赞同的
profitable	[ˈprɒfɪtəbl]	(*a.*) 可获利的
utilize	[ˈjuːtɪlaɪz]	(*v.*) 利用,使用
psychology	[psaɪˈkɒlədʒ]	(*n.*) 心理学
sociology	[ˌsəusɪˈɒlədʒɪ]	(*n.*) 社会学
motivation	[ˌməʊtɪˈveɪʃən]	(*n.*) 刺激,积极性,兴趣,动力
pattern	[ˈpætən]	(*n.*) 模式,方式
couple	[ˈkʌpl]	(*v.*) 联结,结合
extent	[ɪksˈtænt]	(*n.*) 广度,程度

development	[dɪˈveləpmənt]	(n.)开发
evaluate	[ɪˈvæljueɪt]	(v.)估价,评价
mathematical	[ˌmæθɪˈmætɪkəl]	(a.)数学的
model	[ˈmɒdl]	(n.)模式
projection	[prəʊˈdʒekʃən]	(n.)预测,预示,计划
market	[ˈmɑːkɪt]	(v.)市场运作
clue	[kluː]	(n.)线索,暗示
provide clue to		为……提供线索
key to		……关键
couple with		同……联接,结合
relate to		与……有联系,有关联

Ⅱ. Fill in the blanks in the following sentences with the listed words or expressions.

forecast	quantity	favorable	utilize	motivation
pattern	couple with	development	evaluate	relate to

1. Teachers should ________ studying ________ teaching.
2. We live in a new suburban housing ________.
3. The weatherman ________ good weather for tomorrow.
4. The situation will develop in a direction ________ to the people.
5. It was too early to ________ fairly his performance.
6. ________ was at a very high level, and the students did not have to be prodded (督促).
7. This is a question of ________, not quality.
8. The stress ________ may vary with the situation or context.
9. We are interested in what ________ ourselves.
10. All the households should try to ________ solar energy for saving the source of energy.

Ⅲ. There are four choices marked A. B. C. and D. in the following questions. You should decide on the best choice and mark the corresponding letter with a circle.

1. When "market" is used as "verb", it means ________.
   A. buying or selling at the marketplace
   B. controlling the locale
   C. displaying at the marketplace
   D. managing the market

2. Making research on customers may be classified to _______.
   A. psychological science　　B. social science
   C. humanity science　　D. natural science
3. The various behavioral patterns of customers can be known _______.
   A. through the various surveys
   B. through paying a visit to customers
   C. through buying and selling models
   D. through psychological and sociological science
4. The extent of markets for a special product can be determined _______.
   A. by the estimation of market
   B. by the surveys of market
   C. by the evaluation of market
   D. by the sales of market
5. The trends in customers' desire for various products can be determined _______.
   A. by the utilization of statistics and computers
   B. by the purchase and sales at market
   C. by the quantity of sales
   D. by the service after sales

Passage 3

People invest because they want their savings to show growth. Growth is the increase in dollar value of an investment over a period of time. Suppose you buy 5 acres of land for \$500 an acre and at a later date its value goes up to \$700 an acre. The land has increased in value, so your investment has provided growth.

An investment that provides growth, however, always involves risk, because there is always the possibility that the dollar value of the investment may decrease instead of increase. To see how this happens, let's again use the example of owning land. Suppose that when you wanted to sell the 5 acres of land, you could get only \$300 an acre. The dollar value of your land has decreased.

Some people will not put their savings into high-risk investments. They do not want to risk the chance that the dollar value of their investment will decrease. Other people, however, prefer this kind of investment. They seek a much greater return on their money in the form of the difference which is called capital gain. Usually, an investment with more growth potential is also a higher risk investment.

Investing can be done in several ways. The most common ways are savings accounts, savings bonds, stocks and corporate bonds, real estate, and objects of value such as rare coins.

By far the most popular form of investing is the savings account. The reasons for its popularity are clear. The money in a savings account is safe. There is little risk that the dollar value of your savings account will decrease. The savings can be converted to cash quickly; therefore, it can be used easily in case of an emergency in which you might need cash. Also, since there are many financial institutions that offer savings accounts, it is usually easy to find one that is nearby and convenient.

Ⅰ. New Words and Expressions

invest	[ɪnˈvest]	(*v*.) 投资
savings	[ˈsevɪŋz]	(*n*.) 存款,储蓄金
suppose	[səˈpəʊz]	(*v*.) 认定,猜想
acre	[ˈeɪkə]	(*n*.) 英亩

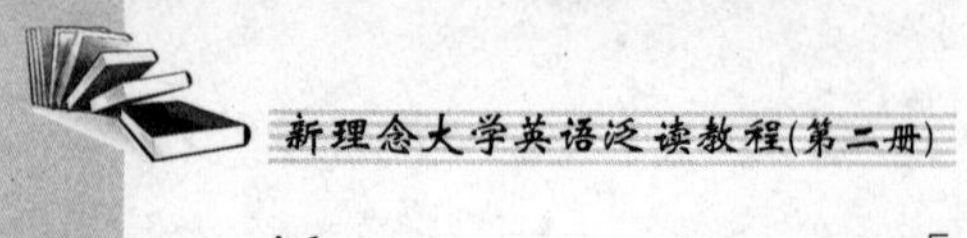

risk	[rɪsk]	(*n*.) 风险,危险
own	[əʊn]	(*v*.) 拥有,占有
decrease	[diːˈkriːs]	(*v*.) 减少
high-risk	[haɪ-rɪsk]	(*n*.) 高风险
prefer	[prɪˈfɜː]	(*v*.) 喜欢,愿意
return	[rɪˈtɜːn]	(*n*.) 收益,利润
gain	[geɪn]	(*n*.) 利润
potential	[pəʊˈtenʃəl]	(*n*.) 潜力
convert	[kənˈvɜːt]	(*v*.) 转变,转化
cash	[kæʃ]	(*n*.) 现金
emergency	[ɪˈmɜːdʒənsɪ]	(*n*.) 紧急情况
nearby	[ˈnɪəbaɪ]	(*a*.) 附近的,邻近的
convenient	[kənˈviːnjənt]	(*a*.) 方便的
dollar value	[dɔːlə væljʊ]	货币价值,美元价值
over a period of time		超过一段时间
at a later date		以后的时间
go up		上涨,上升
instead of		而不
put… into		把……投入到
in the form of		以……形式
capital gain		资本利得
savings accounts		储蓄账户
savings bonds		储蓄公债
stock and corporate bonds		公司债券
rare coins		稀有钱币
financial institutions		金融机构
real estate		房地产

Ⅱ. Fill in the blanks in the following sentences with the listed words or expressions.

invest	suppose	risk	own	decrease
return	gain	convert	go up	put... into

1. National income will ________ by 6.9 percent next year.
2. More new buses are to be ________ service.
3. He has a good cash ________ from his writings.
4. ________ he is absent, what shall we do?
5. Has ________ of war died down in the Middle East?

6. Many underdeveloped countries _______ their natural resources.
7. The _______ in sales was almost 20 percent.
8. Everyone would _______ by it.
9. He _______ his $100,000 in a business enterprise.
10. These engineers _______ the oil revenues into other forms of wealth.

Ⅲ. There are four choices marked A. B. C. and D. in the following questions. You should decide on the best choice and mark the corresponding letter with a circle.

1. The purpose which people invest is _______.
   A. to show their fortune
   B. to develop national economy
   C. to gain economic profits
   D. to keep the financial value
2. The risk of investment means _______.
   A. the economy comes down
   B. the dollar value may decrease
   C. the enterprises break down
   D. the economic crisis
3. "Return" in the passage means "_______".
   A. gain B. money C. cash D. reply
4. Investment can be done _______.
   A. in 3 ways B. in 5 ways
   C. in 6 ways D. in 4 ways
5. The most popular form of investment is the savings account, because _______.
   A. the investment is valuable
   B. the money in bank can't lose
   C. the money in a savings account is not risky
   D. the money keeps in bank

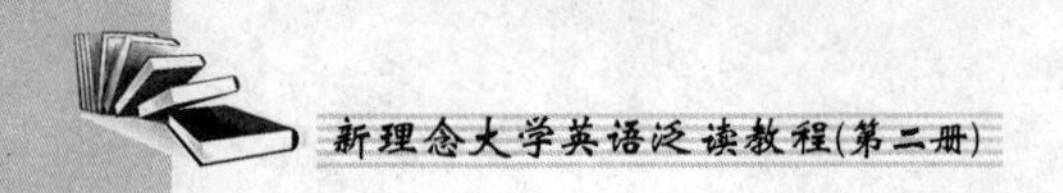

Passage 4

Culture is one of the most challenging elements of the international marketplace. This system of learned behavior patterns characteristic of the members of a given society is constantly shaped by a set of dynamic variables: language, religion, values and attitudes, manners and customs, aesthetics, technology, education, and social institutions. To cope with this system, an international manager needs both factual and interpretive knowledge of culture. To some extent, the factual knowledge can be learned but its interpretation comes only through experience.

The most complicated problems in dealing with the cultural environment stem from the fact that one cannot learn culture — one has to live it. Two schools of thought exist in the business world on how to deal with cultural diversity. One is that business is business the world around, following the model of Pepsi and McDonald's. In some cases, globalization is a fact of life; however, cultural differences are still far from converging.

The other school proposes that companies must tailor business approaches to individual cultures. Setting up policies and procedures in each country has been compared to an organ transplant; the critical question centers around acceptance or rejection. The major challenge to the international manager is to make sure that rejection is not a result of cultural myopia or even blindness.

Fortune examined the international performance of a dozen large companies that earn 20 percent or more of their revenue overseas. The internationally successful companies all share an important quality: patience. They have not rushed into situations but rather built their operations carefully by following the most basic business principles. These principles are to know your adversary, know your audience, and know your customer.

Ⅰ. New Words and Expressions

challenge	[ˈtʃælɪndʒ]	(*v.*) 挑战
marketplace	[ˈmɑːkɪtpleɪs]	(*n.*) 市场,集市,商界
dynamic	[daɪˈnæmɪk]	(*a.*) 动力的,有活力的
variable	[ˈveəriəbl]	(*n.*) 可变的事物
aesthetic	[iːsˈθetɪk]	(*a.*) 美感的,有审美力的
institution	[ˌɪnstɪˈtjuːʃən]	(*n.*) 机构

factual	[ˈfæktʃʊəl]	(*a*.) 实际的，事实的
interpretive	[ɪnˈtɜːprətɪv]	(*a*.) 解释的
stem	[stem]	(*v*.) 起源于
diversity	[daɪˈvɜːsɪtɪ]	(*n*.) 多样，不同，千变万化
globalization	[ˌgləʊbəlaɪˈzeɪʃən]	(*n*.) 全球化
converge	[kənˈvɜːdʒ]	(*v*.) 会聚，集中，互相靠拢
tailor	[ˈteɪlə]	(*v*.) 缝制，配合，适应
procedure	[prəˈsiːdʒə]	(*n*.) 程序，工序，过程
organ	[ˈɔːgən]	(*n*.) 机构
transplant	[trænsˈplɑːnt]	(*n*.) 移植，移种
critical	[ˈkrɪtɪkəl]	(*a*.) 苛求的，严重的，评论的
rejection	[rɪˈdʒekʃən]	(*n*.) 拒绝，反对
myopia	[maɪˈəʊpɪə]	(*n*.) 近视
blindness	[ˈblaɪndnɪs]	(*n*.) 盲目，文盲
revenue	[ˈrevɪnjuː]	(*n*.) 国家的税收
adversary	[ˈædvəsərɪ]	(*a*.) 对手，敌手
cope with		对付，处理
to some extent		在某种程度上
deal with		处理，解决
in some cases		在某种情况下
be far from		远离
make sure		确信
rush into		碰上，遇到，进入

Ⅱ. Fill in the blanks in the following sentences with the listed words or expressions.

challenge	variable	converge	procedure	tailor
critical	rejection	cope with	deal with	in some cases

1. Have you taken all the ________ into account in your calculations?
2. The first step in the ________ for making a kite is to build the frame.
3. We ________ (改革) bus services to meet the needs of suburbs.
4. He keeps applying for jobs but constant ________ have discouraged him.
5. Our school ________ the local champion team to a football match.
6. Thousands of spectators ________ on the city for the horse race.
7. There was more work than I could ________.
8. It takes years to develop one's ________ ability.
9. The book ________ reading, writing and speaking.

10. He can control his own emotion ________.

Ⅲ. There are four choices marked A. B. C. and D. in the following questions. You should decide on the best choice and mark the corresponding letter with a circle.

1. According to the passage, which of the following is true?
   A. All international managers can learn culture.
   B. Business diversity is not necessary.
   C. Views differ on how to treat culture in business world.
   D. Most people do not know foreign culture well.
2. According to the author, the model of Pepsi ________.
   A. is in line with the theories of the school advocating the business is business the world around
   B. is different from the model of McDonald's
   C. shows the reverse of globalization
   D. has converged cultural differences
3. The two schools of thought ________.
   A. both propose that companies should tailor business approaches to individual cultures
   B. both advocate that different policies be set up in different countries
   C. admit the existence of cultural diversity in business world
   D. both A and B
4. This article is supposed to be most useful for those ________.
   A. who are interested in researching the topic of cultural diversity
   B. who have connections to more than one type of culture
   C. who want to travel abroad
   D. who want to run business on international scale
5. According to *Fortune*, successful international companies ________.
   A. earn 20 percent or more of their revenue overseas
   B. all have the quality of patience
   C. will follow the overseas local cultures
   D. adopt the policy of internationalization

Among all the fast growing science and technology, the research of human genes, or biological engineering as people call it, is drawing more and more attention now. Sometimes it is a hot topic discussed by people.

The greatest thing that gene technology can do is to cure serious diseases that doctors at present can almost do noting with, such as cancer and heart disease. Every year, millions of people are murdered by these two killers. And to date, doctors have not found an effective way to cure them. But if the gene technology is applied, not only can these two diseases be cured completely, bringing happiness and more living days to the patients, but also the great amount of money people spend on curing their diseases can be saved, therefore it benefits the economy as well. In addition, human life span (寿命) can be prolonged.

Gene technology can help people to give birth to more healthy and clever children. Some families, with the English imperial family being a good example, have hereditary diseases. This means their children will for sure have the family disease, which is a great trouble for these families. In the past, doctors could do nothing about hereditary diseases. But gene technology can solve this problem perfectly. The scientist just need to find the wrong gene and correct it, and a healthy child will be born.

Some people are worrying that the gene research can be used to manufacture human beings in large quantities. In the past few years, scientists have succeeded in cloning a sheep, therefore these people predict that human babies would soon be cloned. But I believe cloned babies will not come out in large quantities, for most couples in the world can have babies in very normal way. Of course, the governments must take care to control gene technology.

Ⅰ. New Word and Expressions

gene	[dʒiːn]	(*n*.) 基因
biological	[ˌbaɪəˈlɒdʒɪkəl]	(*a*.) 生物的
cure	[kjʊə]	(*v*.) 治疗，治愈
imperial	[ɪmˈpɪərɪəl]	(*a*.) 帝王的，英制的
hereditary	[hɪˈredɪtərɪ]	(*a*.) 遗传的，世袭的
predict	[prɪˈdɪkt]	(*v*.) 预测，预言，预示

clone	[kləun]	(v.)克隆
draw attention		吸引注意力
do nothing with		对……什么也没有做
as well		也,还
in addition		此外
give birth		出生,生孩子
for sure		一定,肯定
in the past		过去
in large quantities		大量地
succeed in (doing sth.)		做……取得成功
come out		出现
in very normal way		以正常的方式
take care		小心,注意

Ⅱ. Fill in the blanks in the following sentences with the listed words or expressions.

care	at present	predict	bring... to	succeed in
solve	take care	do nothing with	span	come out

1. Now, there are a few students with ill-behavior whose teachers at present can nearly ________.
2. You must ________ when crossing these busy streets at the rush hours.
3. There are few remaining diseases that these modern drugs cannot ________.
4. What I had ________ fortnight (两星期) ago had happened far sooner than I had anticipated.
5. I am very anxious for him to ________ all he undertakes.
6. We ________ all our energies ________ bear on the compilation of this dictionary.
7. However, I thought the thing out ________ the mystery.
8. ________, there are two thousand workers in our company.
9. The builders spared no effort to finish ________ the river before the deadline.
10. The stars ________ as soon as it was dark.

Ⅲ. There are four choices marked A. B. C. and D. in the following questions. You should decide on the best choice and mark the corresponding letter with a circle.

1. The phrase "these two killers" in the second paragraph refer to ________.
   A. some hard diseases to be cured
   B. the two diseases of cancer and heart disease

C. hereditary family diseases

D. these two murders

2. Some English imperial families hold ________.

A. all kinds of diseases

B. not difficult diseases to be cured

C. hereditary diseases

D. some infectious diseases

3. Gene technology can help to cure hereditary diseases because ________.

A. scientists finds the wrong gene and correct it

B. human babies can be cloned by it

C. some people with hereditary diseases can have more living days by it

D. doctors can not cure cancer and heart diseases by it

4. The main purpose of the author writing the passage is ________.

A. to tell us that Gene technology will cure cancer and heart diseases

B. to tell us that Gene technology can be used to clone

C. to tell us that these two killers are dangerous

D. to tell readers that Gene technology is useful

5. The attitude of the author on cloning human beings in large quantities is ________.

A. positive

B. passive

C. negative

D. indifferent

Passage 6

In recent years many countries of the world have been faced with the problem of how to make their workers more productive. Some experts claim the answer is to make jobs more varied. But do more varied jobs lead to greater productivity? There is evidence to suggest that while variety certainly makes the worker's life more enjoyable, it does not actually make him work harder. As far as increasing productivity is concerned, then, variety is not an important factor.

Other experts feel that giving the worker freedom to do his job in his own way is important, and there is no doubt that this is true. The problem is that this kind of freedom cannot easily be given in the modern factory with its complicated machinery which must be used in a fixed way. Thus while freedom of choice may be important, there is usually very little that can be done to create it.

Another important consideration is how much each worker contributes to the product he is making. In most factories the worker sees only one small part of the product. Some car factories are now experimenting with having many small production lines rather than one large one, so that each worker contributes more to the production of the cars on his line. It would seem that not only is degree of workers' contribution an important factor, therefore, but it is also one we can do something about.

To what extent does more money lead to greater productivity? The workers themselves certainly think this is important. But perhaps they want more money only because the work they do is so boring. Money just lets them enjoy their spare time more. A similar argument may explain demands for shorter working hours. Perhaps if we succeed in making their jobs more interesting, they will neither want more money, nor will shorter working hours be so important to them.

Ⅰ. New Words and Expressions

productive	[prəˈdʌktɪv]	(*a.*) 生产的,有成效的,多产的
claim	[kleɪm]	(*v.*) 要求,请求,主张,声称,断言
varied	[ˈveərɪd]	(*a.*) 各种各样的
productivity	[ˌprɒdʌkˈtɪvɪtɪ]	(*n.*) 生产率,生产力

enjoyable	[ɪn'dʒɔɪəbl]	(*a*.) 有趣的,愉快的
complicated	['kɒmplɪkeɪtɪd]	(*a*.) 复杂难懂的,结构复杂的
consideration	[kənsɪdə'reɪʃən]	(*n*.) 考虑,体贴,考虑因素,敬重,意见
contribute	[kən'trɪbjuːt]	(*v*.) 捐助,投稿
experiment	[ɪks'perɪmənt]	(*v*.) 尝试,做实验

Ⅱ. Fill in the blanks in the following sentences with the listed words or expressions.

contribute to	face with	rather than	lead to
as far as... concerned	experiment with	no doubt	claim
succeed in	neither... nor		

1. We ________ a lot of problems but we'll win through in the end.
2. She ________ she was qualified for the job and we took her on trust.
3. The discussion ________ unanimous approval of the plan.
4. She's the equal of her brother ________ intelligence ________.
5. Honesty and hard work ________ success and happiness.
6. He was never weary of ________ different ways of planting his crops.
7. We will have the meeting in the classroom ________ in the great hall.
8. Hard graft is the only way to ________ business.
9. He has ________ prepared his lesson ________ gone to bed.
10. There is ________ that we will be successful.

Ⅲ. There are four choices marked A. B. C. and D. in the following questions. You should decide on the best choice and mark the corresponding letter with a circle.

1. Which of these possible factors leading to greater productivity is NOT true?
   A. To make jobs more varied.
   B. To give the worker freedom to do his job in his own way.
   C. Degree of workers' contribution.
   D. More money and shorter working hours.
2. Why is it hardly possible to give workers freedom to choose their own way of doing jobs in a modern factory?
   A. Because the machines in the factory are complicated and should not be operated at will.
   B. Because this kind of freedom will make the administration of the factory a tough job.
   C. Because the workers usually doubt this freedom of choice.
   D. Because the management think this freedom for workers not important.

3. The last sentence in this passage means that if we succeed in making workers jobs more interesting, ________.
   A. they will want more money
   B. they will demand shorter working hours
   C. more money and shorter working hours are important factors
   D. more money and shorter working hours will not be so important to them
4. What is the main idea of the passage?
   A. The problems in production.
   B. The possible factors leading to greater efficiency.
   C. To what extent more money leads to greater productivity.
   D. How to make workers more productive.
5. The author of this passage may be a ________.
   A. financier B. worker C. manager D. psychologist

Passage 7

Large companies need a way to reach the savings of the public at large. The same problem, on a smaller scale, faces practically every company trying to develop new products and create new jobs. There can be little prospect of raising the sort of sums needed from friends and people we know, and while banks may agree to provide short-term finance, they are generally unwilling to provide money on a permanent basis for long-term projects. So companies turn to the public, inviting people to lend them money, or take a share in the business in exchange for a share in future profits. They do this by issuing stocks and shares in the business through the Stock Exchange. By doing so, they can put into circulation the savings of individuals and institutions, both at home and overseas.

When the saver needs his money back, he does not have to go to the company with whom he originally placed it. Instead, he sells his shares through a stockbroker to some other saver who is seeking to invest his money.

Many of the services needed both by industry and by each of us are provided by the Government or by local authorities. Without hospitals, roads, electricity, telephones, railways, this country could not function. All these require continuous spending on new equipment and new development if they are to serve us properly, requiring more money than is raised through taxes alone. The Government, local authorities, and nationalized industries therefore frequently need to borrow money to finance major capital spending, and they, too, come to the Stock Exchange.

There is hardly a man or woman in this country whose job or whose standard of living does not depend on the ability of his or her employers to raise money to finance new development. In one way to another, this new money must come from the savings of the country. The Stock Exchange exists to provide a channel through which these savings can reach those who need finance.

Ⅰ. New Words and Expressions

practically	[ˈpræktɪkəlɪ]	(*adv*.) 实际上,几乎,简直
create	[krɪˈeɪt]	(*v*.) 创造,造成
prospect	[ˈprɒspekt]	(*n*.) 希望,前景,景色
permanent	[ˈpɜːmənənt]	(*a*.) 永久的,持久的

share	[ʃeə]	(*n*.) 一份,股份
stock	[stɒk]	(*n*.) 股票
the Stock Exchange		股票交易所
circulation	[ˌsɜːkjʊˈleɪʃən]	(*n*.) 流通,循环,发行量,消息传播
stockbroker	[ˈstɒkˌbrəʊkə]	(*n*.) 股票经纪人
authorities	[ɔːˈθɒrɪtɪ]	(*n*.) 当局,官方
channel	[ˈtʃænl]	(*n*.) (消息)渠道

Ⅱ. Fill in the blanks in the following sentences with the listed words or expressions.

on a smaller scale	come from	agree to	depend on	seek to
be unwilling to	develop	create	come to	at large

1. Correct ideas ________ social practice.
2. When we talk about the world, we mean the world ________.
3. Don't ask me any more. They are friends of mine and I ________ tell tales out of school.
4. The project is being undertaken ________.
5. Everybody can ________ this school, without respect to class, race, or sex.
6. France is one of the ________ countries.
7. That would ________ a wrong impression.
8. Most of the parents ________ forbid their children to smoke.
9. States ________ become stronger through alliance.
10. But that all ________ the specific circumstances.

Ⅲ. There are four choices marked A. B. C. and D. in the following questions. You should decide on the best choice and mark the corresponding letter with a circle.

1. Almost all companies involved in new production and development must ________.
   A. rely on their own financial resources
   B. persuade banks to provide long-term finance
   C. borrow large sums of money from friends and people they know
   D. depend on the population as a whole for finance
2. The money which enables these companies to go ahead with their projects is ________.
   A. repaid to its original owners as soon as possible
   B. raised by the selling of shares of the companies
   C. exchanged for a part of ownership in the Stock Exchange
   D. invested in different companies in the Stock Exchange

3. When the savers want their money back they ________.

   A. ask another company to obtain their money for them

   B. look for other people to borrow money

   C. put their shares of the company back in the market

   D. transfer their money to a more successful company

4. All the essential services on which we depend are ________.

   A. run by the Government or our local authorities

   B. in constant need of financial support

   C. financed wholly by rates and taxes

   D. unable to meet the needs of the population

5. The Stock Exchange makes it possible for the Government, local authorities and nationalized industries ________.

   A. to borrow as much as they wish

   B. to make certain everybody saves money

   C. to raise money to finance new developments

   D. to make certain everybody lends money to them

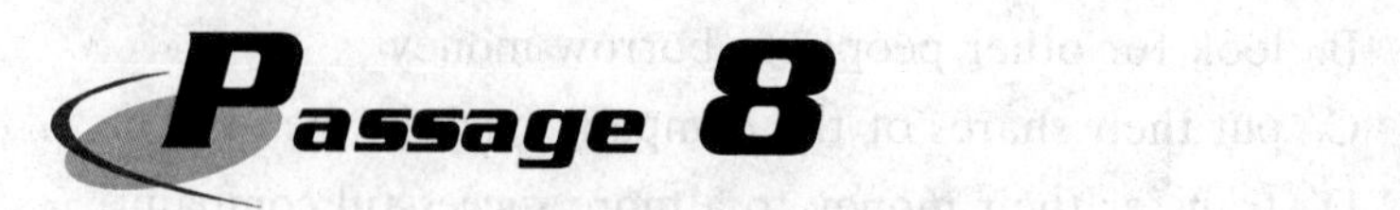

Passage 8

Anyone can buy the shares of a quoted company. They are freely bought and sold in a special market — the Stock Exchange. When a company wishes to be quoted, it applies to the Stock Exchange for a quotation, which is a statement of the share price. If the application is successful, the Stock Exchange deals in its shares and publishes their price each day.

There are three main reasons why companies obtain a quotation. First, many companies need to raise money to expand their businesses. For example, they want to build a bigger factory or produce a new range of goods. To finance this, they could try to get the money from a bank. But perhaps they have already borrowed heavily, so they don't want to increase their debt.

Secondly, there are companies which have been built up by their owners over the years. As the owner gets older, he does not want all his money to be tied up in the business. Therefore he sells part of the company to the public.

Finally, there is the type of business which started many years ago. It has now become a large company and its shares are spread among various members of a family. Some may have interest in the company, while others have different ideas about how to run it. Shareholders disagree strongly, so it becomes difficult to run the company properly. In such a case, the only solution may be to obtain a quotation on the Stock Exchange.

There is one reason why the owners of a company may not wish to obtain a quotation. If the directors are the only shareholders — or have very large shareholdings — in their company, they may be getting substantial benefits from it. For example, the business may own things like the directors' houses, their cars and even their wives' cars. It pays perhaps for their petrol and holidays, which are business expenses. In this case, it may be better not to become a quoted company.

Ⅰ. New Words and Expressions

quoted company		上市公司
quotation	[kwəʊˈteɪʃən]	(*n.*) 报价,报价单
the share price		股价
application	[ˌæplɪˈkeɪʃən]	(*n.*) 申请
expand	[ɪksˈpænd]	(*v.*) 扩张,增加

a range of 一套，一系列

increase [ˈɪnkriːs] (*v.*)增加，提高

spread [spred] (*v.*)传播，展开，散布

director [dɪˈrektə] (*n.*)董事

substantial [səbˈstænʃəl] (*a.*)大量的，实质的，可观的

Ⅱ. Fill in the blanks in the following sentences with the listed words or expressions.

a range of	spread	try to	build up	for example
in this case	deal in	expand	apply to	be tied up

1. The rules of safe driving ________ everyone.
2. The facts added together to ________ an indisputable theory.
3. We cannot assume anything ________.
4. The store ________ secondhand clothes.
5. Our firm ________ with an American company.
6. A factory must ________ diversify for further development.
7. ________, London is the capital of Britain.
8. Moreover, under normal circumstances, monetary policy can boost growth in ________ ways.
9. The news soon ________ to the farthest corner.
10. The company is eager to ________ into new markets.

Ⅲ. There are four choices marked A. B. C. and D. in the following questions. You should decide on the best choice and mark the corresponding letter with a circle.

1. Some companies prefer not to ask the bank to finance their expansion because ________.
   A. no bank is willing to lend loans to them
   B. it is impossible to borrow the amount of money they need from the bank
   C. they don't want to be deeper in debt
   D. banks ask for a high interest on their loans
2. According to Para. 3, if several members of a family have shareholdings in a company, ________.
   A. the company will be run more efficiently
   B. the company will be more difficult to manage
   C. all the shareholders want to obtain a quotation
   D. problems may arise because each of the members wants to hold more shares
3. Some company owners don't want to obtain a quotation because ________.
   A. as the only shareholders, they can dominate the companies

B. as they have very large shareholdings in their companies, they can run the companies as they please

C. they can use company houses and cars when they want to

D. as large or sole shareholders, they can benefit a lot from their companies

4. Which of the following can NOT be learned from the passage?

A. To obtain a quotation in the Stock Exchange is a better way to raise fund.

B. A quotation is a statement of the share price.

C. Some company owners sell part of their company shares to the public because they don't want all their money tied up in the business.

D. In order to be quoted, a company must apply to the Stock Exchange.

5. What can we learn from the passage?

A. Shares of a company can be bought by anyone.

B. Shares are freely bought and sold in the Stock Exchange.

C. Share price remains stable.

D. Share price is decided by the Stock Exchange.

Passage 9

The expression "benchmarking" has become one of the fashionable words in current management discussion. The term first appeared in the United States in the 1970s but has now gained world-wide recognition. But what exactly does it mean and should your company be practicing it?

One straightforward definition of "benchmarking" comes from Chris Tether, managing director of a New Zealand-based consultancy firm specializing in this area. "Benchmarking involves learning about your own practices, learning about the best practices of others, and then making changes for improvement that will enable you to meet or beat the best in the world." The essential element is not simply imitating what other companies do but being able to adapt the best of other firms' practices to your own situation.

Instead of aiming to improve only against previous performance and scores, companies can use benchmarking to inject an element of imagination and common sense into their search for progress. It is a process which forces companies to look closely at those activities which they may have been taking for granted and comparing them with the actives of other world-beating companies. Self-criticism is at the heart of the process although in some cases this may upset managers who are reluctant to question long established practices.

The process of identifying best practice in other companies does not just mean looking closely at your competitors. It might also include studying companies which use similar processes to your own, even though they are producing different goods. The point is to look at the process rather than the product. For example, Italian computer company Arita wanted to improve the quality of its technical manuals and handbooks. Instead of looking at manuals produced by other computer companies, Arita turned to a publisher of popular handbooks such as cookery books, railway timetables and car repair manuals. As Arita's Technical Director Claudio Benclii says, "All of these handbooks are communicating complex information in a simple way — exactly what we are aiming to do. And in many cases they succeed far better than any computer company."

Ⅰ. New Words and Expressions

benchmarking ['bentʃˌmɑːkɪŋ] (*n.*) 基准调查，基本标准调查，基准检测

recognition	[ˌrekəgˈnɪʃən]	(*n.*) 承认,认出,赏识
straightforward	[ˌstreɪtˈfɔːwəd]	(*a.*) 易懂的,笔直的,坦率的
definition	[ˌdefɪˈnɪʃən]	(*n.*) 定义,阐释,清晰度
consultancy	[kənˈsʌltənsɪ]	(*n.*) 咨询,顾问的工作,咨询公司
imitate	[ˈɪmɪteɪt]	(*v.*) 仿效,仿制,模仿
adapt	[əˈdæpt]	(*v.*) 改编,使适应
inject	[ɪnˈdʒekt]	(*v.*) 注射,注入,引入,插入
competitor	[kəmˈpetɪtə]	(*n.*) 竞争者,对手
manual	[ˈmænjʊəl]	(*n.*) 指南,手册,键盘
publisher	[ˈpʌblɪʃə]	(*n.*) 出版者,出版社,发行人
cookery	[ˈkʊkərɪ]	(*n.*) 烹调法,烹调术

Ⅱ. Fill in the blanks in the following sentences with the listed words or expressions.

specialize in	adapt	at the heart of	instead of
take for granted	compare with	imitate	learn about
turn to	gain wide recognition		

1. He ________ in the field of tropical medicine.
2. The company began by ________ radios but has now decided to branch out into computers.
3. I want ________ your new policy on investment.
4. I would recommend that you buy a DVD player ________ a VCR.
5. It ________ that everyone is equal before the law.
6. Teacher takes Shelley ________ Keats mutually.
7. What he said struck ________ the problem.
8. We can ________ him for help.
9. James can ________ his teacher's speech perfectly.
10. He doesn't think he can ________ himself to the hot climate.

Ⅲ. There are four choices marked A. B. C. and D. in the following questions. You should decide on the best choice and mark the corresponding letter with a circle.

1. According to the writer, benchmarking must always involve ________.
   A. changing your activities on the basis of new information
   B. copying exactly what your competitors do
   C. identifying the best company in your market
   D. collaborating with other companies in the same field

2. Some managers may resist benchmarking because ________.
   A. it takes their activities for granted
   B. it makes them examine the way they work
   C. it makes others question their efficiency
   D. it gives them a lot of extra work
3. What sort of companies should you compare yours with?
   A. Those producing similar goods.
   B. Those communicating most effectively.
   C. Those using similar processes.
   D. Those leading the domestic market.
4. Anita found that a publishing company could ________.
   A. make more money than a computer firm
   B. produce technical manuals for them
   C. show them how to improve their own manuals
   D. help them move into new markets
5. What is the writer's purpose in writing this article?
   A. to recommend the process of benchmarking
   B. to criticize firms that do not carry out benchmarking
   C. to give tactual information about benchmarking
   D. to explain why benchmarking does not suit every firm

Passage 10

First off, you need to know what an ecommerce solution is. An ecommerce solution can be defined in many ways. An ecommerce solution is a way to define electronic shopping carts. An ecommerce solution is used for businesses that sell things on the web. An ecommerce solution makes it possible for any sale or transaction to be made. They enable the use of credit cards and other forms of payment to be used right on your website. It is used for large companies like Ebay or Amazon. But now an ecommerce solution is for small companies and businesses as well.

There are other aspects and definitions of this subject. An ecommerce solution can also be defined as software that allows you to do business on the web. It is also a software that designs websites that are used just for selling products or services on the web. An ecommerce solution can also be defined as a company that hosts websites. Either way you look at it, an ecommerce solution is for anyone doing business on the web.

An ecommerce solution does many things, as you can now tell. Finding a good ecommerce solution can be a tedious task. The best thing to do is to go online and use a search engine. Type in ecommerce solution and look at the top websites listed that offer this. There are many ecommerce solution stores that offer free trials. Many often guarantee ease of set up, customizable solutions, and guaranteed results with powerful marketing tools and affiliate programs. All of this is included in a set price.

When looking for an ecommerce solution, shop around and see which one offers you the best deal. Most offer a set yearly fee. This can be anywhere from $300 to $800 a year. There are some ecommerce solution stores that offer a month to month contract, however. These are usually $55 to $100 a month. Many offer a 30 day money back guarantee if you are not happy with the results of the ecommerce solution and its software.

With all of this in mind, you are that much closer to finding a great ecommerce solution. There are many options out there, so do your research. For anyone who wants to do business on the web, it is an absolute necessity. Soon you will be on your way to a profitable and successful web based business!

Ⅰ. New Words and Expressions

ecommerce [ˈiːˈkɒməːs] (*n.*) 电子商务

transaction	[træn'zækʃən]	(n.)交易,办理,处理,事务
website	['webˌsaɪt]	(n.)网站
Ebay	['iː'beɪ]	(n.)易趣(一知名网上购物网站)
Amazon	['æməzən]	(n.)亚马逊(美国的一家网络电子商务公司)
tedious	['tiːdjəs]	(a.)单调乏味的,沉闷的
guarantee	[ˌgærən'tiː]	(v.)保证,担保
ease	[iːz]	(n.)容易,悠闲,安逸,自在
customizable	['kʌstəmaɪzəbəl]	(a.)可定制的
affiliate	[ə'fɪlɪeɪt]	(n.)分公司,附属机构
contract	['kɒntrækt]	(n.)合同,合约,契约
profitable	['prɒfɪtəbl]	(a.)有益的,有利可图的

Ⅱ. Fill in the blanks in the following sentences with the listed words or expressions.

as well	do business	go online	do one's research	first off
set up	free trial	look for	offer	tedious

1. You can ________ by mobile phone.
2. You can have a ________ for two weeks.
3. How can he give us such a ________ lecture?
4. ________, let's see where we agree and disagree.
5. I write my own songs and I play the guitar ________.
6. As a scientist, he has the capability of ________.
7. As commission agent we ________ on commission basis.
8. He thumbed through the directory to ________ her number.
9. The kind old lady ________ to take in the poor homeless boy.
10. A committee ________ to look into the workers' grievances.

Ⅲ. There are four choices marked A. B. C. and D. in the following questions. You should decide on the best choice and mark the corresponding letter with a circle.

1. What is an ecommerce solution?
   A. It is for anyone doing business on the web.
   B. It is a way to define electronic shopping carts.
   C. It is used for businesses that sell things on the web.
   D. It is a software used just for selling products or services on the web.
2. Many ecommerce solution stores offer some favors except ________.
   A. free trials　　B. free access
   C. guaranteed results　　D. customizable solutions

3. Which of the following statements is NOT true according to the passage?
   A. It is an easy job to find a good ecommerce solution.
   B. Most ecommerce solution stores offer a set yearly fee.
   C. You use credit cards and other forms of payment online.
   D. An ecommerce solution makes it possible to make any transactions.
4. Who may be the readers of this passage?
   A. Teachers.
   B. Students.
   C. Businesspersons.
   D. All the above.
5. What is the best title of this passage?
   A. Ecommerce Solution
   B. Ecommerce Solution Stores
   C. Ecommerce Solution for the Big and Small Business
   D. Different Options for People to Conduct Business

Passage 11

"If a man cuts himself with a razor, it's the razor's fault," quipped Bettina Whyte, a managing director at corporate turnaround advisory firm Alvarez & Marsal. "But if a woman cuts herself with a razor, she wonders, 'What did I do wrong?'"

That was just one of the, umm, razor-sharp comments at a panel discussion during private equity firm Solera Capital's annual meeting last week. Solera, which is run by founding chairman and CEO Molly Ashby, is often noted for its commitment to diversity — hence the discussion topic, "Women: Power and Success."

The conversation, which was led by my *Fortune* colleague Pattie Sellers, addressed women's abilities to argue for themselves. "Women are bad at negotiating," said Julie Daum, who is a go-to recruiter for companies interested in bringing on more women to their boards. Daum, who works for executive search firm Spencer Stuart, noted that women often start working at smaller base salaries because they typically accept opening financial offers as fair. To a man, that same offer is often "an opening gambit," Daum said.

In an email exchange following the discussion, Daum expanded on her point: "It is not just [women's] initial packages. It is throughout their career. When they make changes to another organization or get promoted, they tend to do less negotiating."

Bettina Whyte argued that women "do not use money to validate themselves."

Former WNBA chief Donna Orender noted, though, that while some women may find it difficult to negotiate for themselves, women can be very strong negotiators in other business deals.

Postcards is no stranger to this topic. Susan Wilson, CEO of the Judgment group, asked, "Are girls afraid of money?" on the site in April. And last week, Gerry Laybourne, who founded Oxygen Media, claimed that women "don't know how to toot [their] own horns."

Laybourne suggested, "If you don't toot your own horn, toot another woman's horn." Indeed, Whyte contended with her own reluctance to discuss pay with her bosses by hiring a female attorney to argue on her behalf.

Do you agree that women are bad at negotiating for themselves? What can women do to resolve the problem?

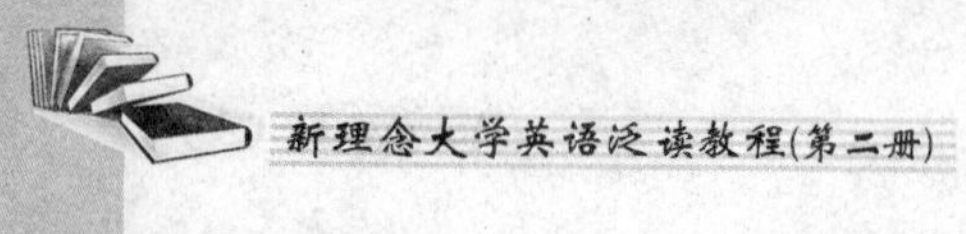

Ⅰ. New Words and Expressions

razor	[ˈreɪzə]	(*n.*) 剃刀
corporate	[ˈkɔːpərɪt]	(*a.*) 法人的,公司的
turnaround	[ˈtɜːnəˌraʊnd]	(*n.*) 周转时间,转身,转型
advisory	[ədˈvaɪzərɪ]	(*a.*) 顾问的,咨询的,劝告的
razor-sharp	[ˈreɪzəʃɑːp]	(*a.*) 锋利的,犀利的
comment	[ˈkɒment]	(*n.*) 注释,评论,闲话
panel	[ˈpænl]	(*n.*) 专门问题小组
equity	[ˈekwɪtɪ]	(*n.*) 权益,股权
annual	[ˈænjʊəl]	(*a.*) 每年的,年度的,一年生植物
CEO		(*abbr.*) 首席执行官,执行总裁(Chief Executive Officer)
commitment	[kəˈmɪtmənt]	(*n.*) 承诺,保证,信奉
diversity	[daɪˈvɜːsɪtɪ]	(*n.*) 多样性,差异,分集
Fortune	[ˈfɔːtʃən]	《财富》杂志
colleague	[ˈkɒliːg]	(*n.*) 同事
address	[əˈdres]	(*v.*) 称呼,发表演说,写地址
negotiate	[nɪˈgəʊʃɪeɪt]	(*v.*) 谈判,商议
recruiter	[rɪˈkruːtə]	(*n.*) 招募者,招聘人员
executive	[ɪgˈzekjʊtɪv]	(*n.*) 行政主管,决策者
base salary		底薪
expand	[ɪksˈpænd]	(*v.*) 使……膨胀,详述,扩张
initial	[ɪˈnɪʃəl]	(*a.*) 开始的,最初的,字首的
validate	[ˈvælɪdeɪt]	(*v.*) 使生效,证实,验证
Postcards	[ˈpəʊstˌkɑːdz]	《财富》杂志的专栏
toot	[tuːt]	(*v.*) 发嘟嘟声
contend	[kənˈtend]	(*v.*) 竞争,争斗,争辩
reluctance	[rɪˈlʌktəns]	(*n.*) 不愿,勉强
attorney	[əˈtɜːnɪ]	(*n.*) (辩护)律师
resolve	[rɪˈzɒlv]	(*v.*) 解决,决定

Ⅱ. Fill in the blanks in the following sentences with the listed words or expressions.

be interested in	be noted for	be bad at	toot one's own horn	argue
on one's behalf	expand on	tend to	bring on	resolve

1. The west lake ________ its scenery.

2. He _______ for a continuation of the search.
3. The locals _______ be suspicious of strangers.
4. Reading in a poor light may _______ a headache.
5. Ken is not present, so I shall accept the prize _______.
6. If the dispute is to _______ there must be some give and take.
7. Some of Hollywood's leading studios _______ signing her.
8. Janet is not a friendly person. She _______ communicating with others!
9. The boy wanted his mother to _______ what she had said about the haunted house.
10. A person who does things well does not have to _______; his abilities will be noticed by others.

Ⅲ. There are four choices marked A. B. C. and D. in the following questions. You should decide on the best choice and mark the corresponding letter with a circle.

1. Who argued that women can be very strong negotiators for other business deals?
   A. Gerry Laybourne.　　B. Susan Wilson.
   C. Donna Orender.　　D. Julie Daum.
2. Who argued that women are not good at negotiating for themselves?
   A. Bettina Whyte.　　B. Molly Ashby.
   C. Julie Daum.　　D. Pattie Sellers.
3. From the context, the sentence that women "don't know how to toot [their] own horns" means that _______.
   A. women don't know how to drive their cars
   B. women don't know how to sing their praises
   C. women don't know how to use the horns properly
   D. women don't know how to discuss pay with her bosses
4. From the context, we can infer that the author of this article works for _______.
   A. Alvarez & Marsal　　B. Solera Capital
   C. Spencer Stuart　　D. Fortune
5. What is the best title of this passage?
   A. Women: Power and Success.
   B. Are Women Lousy Negotiators?
   C. Negotiation Skills for Women.
   D. Different Abilities of Men and Women.

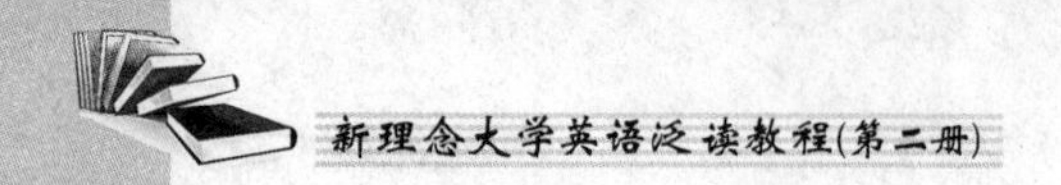

Passage 12

Gregory Lampson couldn't believe it. His 21-year-old son Joe, six months from graduation, had just announced that he was dropping out of Stanford University to launch his own software company. "Can't you wait a few months?" his father pleaded.

"No," Joe said quietly. "In software being first is everything."

The younger Lampson knew that software companies were already helping big business save millions by streamlining some office work, such as shipping and receiving. Yet buying and selling — the lifeblood of business — was still being done by instinct. For instance, the average hospital could choose among many bandage suppliers. But there was no easy way to calculate which supplier offered the best price while meeting all the customer's needs. Lampson was sure that he and his four partners could develop a computer program that would solve this problem.

In spite of Lampson's confidence, no one would finance his start-up company, called Trilogy Development Group. Banks told him to get lost. Venture capitalists explained that new enterprises needed experienced managers and technicians; Joe Lampson had neither.

So he turned to the great investment bank of his generation, plastic. Lampson used 35 credit cards to finance the business and living expenses for him and his partners. Two years later he was half a million dollars in debt.

Meanwhile he persuaded engineers at Hewlett-Packard — who had tried to develop a similar program — to test the Trilogy software. To Hewlett-Packard's surprise, it worked. The company offered Trilogy 53 million for the right to use the program. Since then, orders from other Fortune 500 companies have flooded in.

Today the Trilogy Development Group, based in Austin, Texas, has close to 499 employees. The company's 1996 incomes have been estimated at more than $ 120 million.

Lampson, who just celebrated his 29th birthday, is one of a huge number of under-35 entrepreneurs. According to a study, nearly ten percent of Americans between the ages of 25 and 34 are actively involved in trying to start their own businesses — at least three times the rate of any other age group.

Ⅰ. New Words and Expressions

announce	[əˈnaʊns]	(v.) 宣布
bandage	[ˈbændɪdʒ]	(n.) 绷带
plead	[pliːd]	(v.) 诉求,乞求
calculate	[ˈkælkjʊleɪt]	(v.) 计算
decade	[ˈdekeɪd]	(n.) 十年
employee	[ˌemplɔɪˈiː]	(n.) 雇员
enterprise	[ˈentəpraɪz]	(n.) 企业
explorer	[ɪksˈplɔːrə]	(n.) 探索者,探险者
finance	[faɪˈnæns]	(v.) 资助
flood	[flʌd]	(v.) 大量涌入
hack	[hæk]	(v.) 乱砍
instinct	[ˈɪnstɪŋkt]	(n.) 本能
involve	[ɪnˈvɒlv]	(v.) 投入
jungle	[ˈdʒʌŋgl]	(n.) 丛林
launch	[lɔːntʃ]	(v.) 开办
lifeblood	[ˈlaɪfblʌd]	(n.) 生命线
entrepreneurs	[ˌɒntrəprəˈnɜːs]	(n.) 企业家,主办人
choose among / between		在……当中/之间选择
mean business		言出必行
by instinct		本能地
turn to (sb. / sth.)		求助于
credit card		信用卡
age group		年龄组
drop out (of)		(中途)退学
get lost		走开
meet one's needs		满足……的需要
in spite of		尽管,不顾
venture capitalist		风险投资者
in debt		负债
to one's surprise		令人吃惊的是
close to		将近
Austin		奥斯丁(美国德克萨斯州首府)
Fortune		《财富》
Gregory Lampson		格雷戈里·兰普森

Hewlett-Packard 美国惠普公司
Joe Lampson 乔·兰普森
Texas 德克萨斯

Ⅱ. Fill in the blanks in the following sentences with the listed words or expressions.

announce	launch	by instinct	choose among	calculate
meet one's needs	finance	turn to	get lost	start

1. The leader ________ that the new regulations have been established now.
2. The big company ________ the purchase of new equipment.
3. Mr. Smith ________ with anger because of his being criticized by his leader.
4. He mentioned that he would like to ________ a school.
5. The designers again ________ the workers for advice.
6. We all try our best to ________ a new enterprise for making a profit of our collective.
7. The child makes a natural action ________.
8. The whole people try to expand production to ________ of life.
9. The representative will be ________ the broad masses.
10. I ________ that we would arrive at 6 p. m.

Ⅲ. There are four choices marked A. B. C. and D. in the following questions. You should decide on the best choice and mark the corresponding letter with a circle.

1. Why did Joe drop out of Stanford University?
   A. He wanted to look for a good job.
   B. He was eager to make money.
   C. He wanted to run a software company.
   D. He wanted to make a fortune.
2. What did Joe and his partners do was for calculating which supplier offered the best price of products while meeting all the customer's needs?
   A. They tried to help all the customers.
   B. They tried to develop a computer program.
   C. They tried to launch a computer company.
   D. They tried to help all the customers of choosing products.
3. "Joe Lampson had neither" in the passage means ________.
   A. Joe Lampson had no rich experience

B. Joe Lampson had no technologies

C. Joe Lampson was both not an experienced manger and not a technician at all

D. Joe Lampson was not something of it

4. Joe Lampson's software company was finally _______.

A. successful　　B. stopped

C. failing　　D. deserted

Passage 13

Diesel is a global clothing and lifestyle brand. With a history stretching back over 30 years, the company now employs some 2,200 people globally with a turnover of 1.3 billion and its products are available in more than 5,000 outlets. However, this list of numbers is far less interesting than the company, people and founder behind them. Diesel is a remarkable company with a unique mindset. A mindset which puts sales and profit second to building something special, something "cool" and something which can change the world through fashion.

The story begins with a young Renzo Rosso passionate about the clothes he wears but disappointed in the options available to him in his hometown Molvena, Italy. Acting on impulse, he decided to use his passion to make the clothes he wanted to wear. Renzo was drawn to the rebellious fabric of the 1960s and rock & roll: denim. It inspired him to create jeans which would allow him and others to express themselves in ways other clothing simply could not. Proving popular, Renzo made more and more of his hand-crafted creations, selling them around Italy from the back of his little van. The still-young Renzo is the proud owner and CEO of Diesel along with that impressive list of figures. That impulse and passion apparently paid off.

Product

Diesel sells nice jeans. Close, but no "A". Actually, it's not that close. The reason Diesel has grown is because it knows it is about a lot more than selling nice jeans. Diesel is a lifestyle: if that lifestyle appeals to you, you might like to buy the products. Renzo describes this as an end of the "violence" towards the customer forcing them to buy and rather an involvement in the lifestyle.

It might be useful to ask a question — what actually is a brand? The answer could take a variety of routes and go on for pages but a useful way to think of a brand is as a set of promises. Those promises form the basis of the customer's relationship with that company. In the case of Diesel those promises are very personal, very passionate.

The Diesel brand promises to entertain and to introduce customers to new, experimental experiences. Its product line now goes far beyond premium jeans and includes fragrances, sunglasses and even bike helmets. These products complement, convey and support the promises of passion and experience made

by the Diesel brand.

Being such a crucial element of its work you might imagine the product design team at Diesel to "plot" in something akin to a war room, pushing little squadrons of well-dressed soldiers around with long sticks. Actually, this is where that elemental passion which created Diesel sets them apart from many others. The whole team at Diesel lives the brand. They are all incredibly passionate about their creations. So when it comes to expressing that passion, ideas come naturally. Living and breathing the set of promises the Diesel brand communicates means employees can listen to their instincts, creating products straight from within.

Ⅰ. New Words and Expressions

stretch [stretʃ] (*v.*) 追溯,伸展
employ [ɪmˈplɔɪ] (*v.*) 雇佣,使用
turnover [ˈtəːnˌəuvə] (*n.*) 营业额
outlet [ˈautlet] (*n.*) 批发商店
mindset [ˈmaɪndset] (*n.*) 精神状态,意向
rebellious [rɪˈbelɪjəs] (*a.*) 叛逆的
fabric [ˈfæbrɪk] (*n.*) 织物
van [væn] (n.) 面包车,运货车
involvement [ɪnˈvɒlvmənt] (*n.*) 卷入,牵连,参与
convey [kənˈveɪ] (*v.*) 表达,传达
akin [əˈkɪn] (*a.*) 近似的
squadron [ˈskwɒdrən] (*n.*) 骑兵中队,装甲连;一群

Ⅱ. Fill in the blanks in the following sentences with the listed words or expressions.

stretch back	employ	draw to	inspire	pay off
convey	communicate	prove	imagine	in the case of

1. In olden times, ________ fevers, the physician always let blood from the patient.
2. The 20th century is ________ an end.
3. Sincere congratulations on your son wedding please ________ our best wish.
4. Male nurses are often ________ in hospitals for the mentally ill.
5. The audience was carried away by his ________ speech.
6. This information ________ via the Watchdog.
7. He has a criminal record ________ twenty years.
8. He ________ to be innocent of the charge.
9. ________ a rocket that can travel at the rate of light!

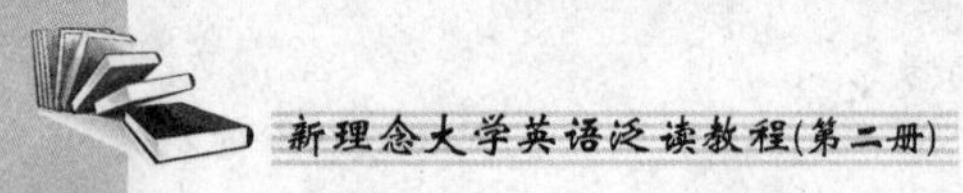

10. At worst we'll have to sell the house so as to ________ our debts.

Ⅲ. There are four choices marked A. B. C. and D. in the following questions. You should decide on the best choice and mark the corresponding letter with a circle.

1. From the passage we can see Diesel team is ________.
   A. efficient B. lazy C. inactive D. slack
2. ________ have been made though Diesel has a history of merely 30 years.
   A. Hand-crafted creations B. Great achievements
   C. Deep impression D. A variety of products
3. Diesel's success lies in ________ rather than products themselves.
   A. theory B. principle C. ideas D. emotion
4. The promises Diesel has formed on the basis of the customer's relationship are ________.
   A. desirous B. fervent C. excitable D. enthusiastic
5. In Diesel, employees' creation can be ________.
   A. allowed B. measured C. encouraged D. pressed

Passage 14

With the launch of the recent marketing campaign around the phrase "Be Stupid", Diesel took a look at what brought its current pipeline: it was Renzo Rosso, all those years ago, taking the "stupid" move to make jeans he wanted to wear. Then he took the even more stupid move of trying to sell those jeans to others, believing he might not be the only fool in Molvena! As it turned out, there were quite a few more to be found and Renzo's "stupid" move ended up creating something which millions of people around the world now enjoy.

Promotion and marketing at Diesel takes a very different route to many other companies. It is always about engaging with the customer as opposed to selling at them: creating an enjoyable two-way dialogue as opposed to a hollow one-way monologue.

All elements of Diesel's promotion aim to engage the customer with the lifestyle. If they like the lifestyle, they might like the products. For example, the Diesel team saw music as an inseparable part of that lifestyle and realised that exploring new music and new artists was all part of trying something different and experimenting with the unusual. 10 years later, Diesel:U:Music is a global music support collaborative, giving unsigned bands a place where they can be heard and an opportunity to have their talent recognised. It's not about selling, it's about giving people something they will enjoy and interact with.

Tied to Diesel:U:Music is an online radio station. It is another example of where Diesel unconventionality has created something which pushes conceptions and the usual ways of doing things. The radio station takes a rather unusual approach of not having a traditional play list but rather gives the choice to the resident DJ. This freedom is reflected in the eccentric mix of music which is played on the station.

In promotion and marketing, we often talk about "above-the-line" and "below-the-line" methods of reaching consumers. Above-the-line marketing is aimed at a mass audience through media such as television or radio. Below-the-line marketing takes a more individual, targeted approach using incentives to purchase via various promotions. In this case passion again acts to blur and gel the boundaries between the two approaches. If we had to define this approach in terms of theory, we would call it "through-the-line", i. e. a blend of the two. The passion and energy embodied by the Diesel lifestyle is communicated through a mix of above-the-line and below-the-line approaches. The balance and composition of that mix is what the Diesel team hands over to their passion and feel for the company and brand. That energy guides the way this abstract theory is realized in projects such as Diesel: U: Music and the "Be Stupid" campaign, which entertain and interact with their potential customers.

Ⅰ. New Words and Expressions

launch	[lɔːntʃ]	(*n*.) 产品推介
engage	[ɪnˈɡeɪdʒ]	(*v*.) 参加,从事
hollow	[ˈhɒləʊ]	(*a*.) 空的,空洞的
inseparable	[ɪnˈsepərəbl]	(*a*.) 不能分的
approach	[əˈprəʊtʃ]	(*n*.) 途径,方法,靠近
eccentric	[ɪkˈsentrɪk]	(*a*.) 古怪的,反常的
target	[ˈtɑːɡɪt]	(*v*.) 把……作为目标
embody	[ɪmˈbɒdɪ]	(*v*.) 使具体化,包含
incentive	[ɪnˈsentɪv]	(*n*.) 刺激,鼓励

Ⅱ. Fill in the blanks in the following sentences with the listed words or expressions.

turn out	end up	engage with	interact	approach
reflect	aim at	target	embody	one-way

1. If he carries on driving like that, he'll ________ dead.
2. The new car ________ many improvements.
3. How much is a ________ ticket to Boston?
4. A stationary target is easiest to ________.
5. Her sad looks ________ the thought passing through her mind.
6. The film ________ to be a great success.
7. Heavy footsteps signaled the teacher's ________.
8. He fired several shots at the ________.
9. The general ordered his soldiers to ________ the enemy.
10. Mother and baby ________ in a very complex way.

Ⅲ. There are four choices marked A. B. C. and D. in the following questions. You should decide on the best choice and mark the corresponding letter with a circle.

1. The campaigns such as "U: Music", "Be Stupid" and something akin are launched ________.

   A. to win over prestige from more consumers

   B. to get its consumers informed of what to do

C. to make the locals excited

D. to interact with its prospective customers

2. Diesel's marketing tactics is ________.

A. old-fashioned B. conventional

C. flexible D. traditional

3. ________ is always the central theme Diesel has followed over the past 30 years.

A. Innovation B. Hard work

C. Creation D. Renovation

4. Diesel story tells us that any enterprise eager to have a share in the international market must be aware that whatever it does should ________.

A. meet the needs of a small targeted people

B. stick to tradition

C. continue without a change

D. be people-oriented in a new style

5. We can infer from the passage that Diesel team ________.

A. is quite successful B. is still inexperienced

C. has a long way to go D. on the verge of dissolution

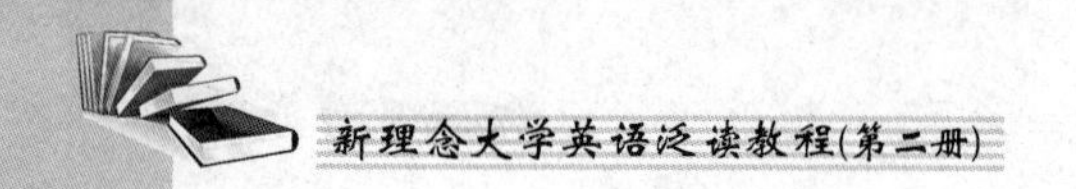

Mother Teresa and Lady Gaga are the latest icons of the leadership industry. Don't laugh.

Lady Gaga has the "ability to build emotional commitment" in those she leads, says Mr Reckhenrich. This ability is increasingly valuable in today's business world, he believes. In *The Fine Art of Success* , a book he and his co-authors released last year, they examine it at length. They are now working with Egon Zehnder, an executive-recruitment firm, to figure out how to identify whether candidates for top corporate jobs have the ability to "project leadership" the way Lady Gaga does.

One risk of this leadership style is that "telling a personal story opens you up to personal attack," admits Mr Reckhenrich. Lady Gaga has been accused of lacking authenticity, and a dull, literal judge would no doubt find her guilty. Her new album cover depicts her as half-woman and half-motorbike, and claims that she was "Born This Way" . This is obviously not true. However, to accuse an artist of artifice is a bit like accusing a banker of being interested in money: it may be true, but it is still trite.

Mother Teresa had her critics, too. Christopher Hitchens, a polemical atheist, called her "Hell's Angel" . In his book, *The Missionary Position* , he berated her for spreading an extreme form of Catholicism and for accepting money from dodgy people such as "Papa Doc" Duvalier, the late dictator of Haiti.

The mystery of charisma

Management tracts with famous names in the titles are mostly guff. There is only so much a manager can learn from Genghis Khan — it is no longer practical to impale competitors on spikes. Likewise, skeptics may doubt that the secrets of Lady Gaga's success, or Mother Teresa's, can usefully be applied to, say, a company that makes ball-bearings. A manager who calls her minions "little monsters" will probably not win their hearts. A boss who declares that God wants the sales team to meet its targets will be laughed at. Skeptics might also point out that Lady Gaga is not much of a manager. Her recent world tour attracted legions of fans but still lost money, because she kept changing the sets.

Yet charisma matters in business, and celebrities do tell us something about how it can be wielded. It is no longer enough for a corporate boss to be

clever and good at giving orders. Modern knowledge workers may not put up with a hard, old-fashioned boss like Jack Welch, who used to run General Electric. Many respond better to one who communicates warmly: Indra Nooyi of PepsiCo sometimes writes to the parents of her managers to thank them for bringing up such fine children. Employees crave a sense of purpose, and the boss who can supply it will get the best out of them. Personal stories help: Steve Jobs and Richard Branson, whose business empires depend on their charisma, both play up their pasts as educational dropouts. Charisma is tough to learn, but it is not gaga to seek guidance in the stars.

Ⅰ. New Words and Expressions

commitment	[kəˈmɪtmənt]	(*n.*) 承诺，保证
at length		(*adv.*) 终于(最后，详细地)
candidate	[ˈkændɪdeɪt]	(*n.*) 候选人，应试者
authenticity	[ˌɔːθenˈtɪsɪtɪ]	(*n.*) 真实性
dodgy	[ˈdɒdʒɪ]	(*a.*) 躲闪的，不可靠的，善于骗人的
old-fashioned	[ˈəʊldˈfæʃənd]	(*a.*) 老式的，老派的，守旧的
bring up		养育
monster	[ˈmɒnstə]	(*n.*) 怪物，恶人
celebrity	[sɪˈlebrɪtɪ]	(*n.*) 名人，名誉，社会名流
dropout	[ˈdrɒpaʊt]	(*n.*) 中途退出者，退学学生
gaga	[ˈgɑːgɑː]	(*a.*) 〈美俗〉天真的，愚蠢的，非常起劲的，狂热的

Ⅱ. Fill in the blanks in the following sentences with the listed words or expressions.

bring up	gaga	commitment	candidate	authenticity
celebrity	monster	dodgy	old-fashioned	at length

1. The opposing forces _______ met and at once joined battle.
2. The _______ of the manuscript is beyond doubt.
3. If you are serious about our relationship, you should make a _______.
4. There are three _______ for the vacancy.
5. He's a _______ bloke I wouldn't trust him an inch.
6. I'm frightened of the _______.
7. He has gone quite _______.
8. _______, money and possessions are too often the touchstones for teenagers.
9. That style of dressing is very _______ here.
10. Mary _______ her son on her own.

Ⅲ. There are four choices marked A. B. C. and D. in the following questions. You should decide on the best choice and mark the corresponding letter with a circle.

1. According to Mr Reckhenrich, what ability of Lady Gaga is seen as increasingly valuable in today's business world?
   A. To make herself look sexy.
   B. To have others accept her emotionally.
   C. To make others misjudge her.
   D. To sing an odd song.
2. The following are words best describing Lady Gaga except ________.
   A. lacking authenticity B. dull
   C. guilty D. beautiful
3. Why does the author mention "like accusing a banker of being interested in money" in paragraph 3?
   A. True but hackneyed. B. True but unconvincing.
   C. True but original. D. True but unreasonable.
4. What critics did Christopher Hitchens have for Mother Teresa ?
   A. She only helps those from poor countries.
   B. She doesn't like donate money to the Red Cross.
   C. She is not passionate about helping the old.
   D. She doesn't care who donates the money to her.
5. In business, what can celebrities tell us about in terms of charisma matters?
   A. To know how to increase the profits for the company.
   B. To know how to communicate warmly.
   C. To know how to love your employees.
   D. To know how to help your elders.

Passage 16

Travelers who signed up for a British Airways Visa card issued by JP Morgan Chase got a sweet deal in a recent promotion: 100,000 frequent flier miles after spending $2,000 with the card — theoretically, enough for two free round-trip tickets between New York and London.

But those "free" tickets actually cost about $530 each, in addition to the 50,000 miles per ticket, because the airline passed along taxes, fees and a $350 fuel surcharge.

Although many carriers charge passengers flying with award tickets some government taxes and fees, foreign airlines are increasingly adding fuel surcharges to the bill, a practice that has not caught on yet in the United States.

Delta Airlines did experiment with a fuel surcharge on award tickets in 2007, but dropped the fee in 2008 when competitors did not follow suit and oil prices declined.

Paul Skrbec, a Delta spokesman, said the airline continued to monitor this policy as oil prices hovered around $100 a barrel, but was not currently assessing a fuel surcharge on domestic or international awards.

That does not mean passengers traveling on frequent flier tickets with American airlines are exempt from other fees, particularly when traveling abroad.

One way travelers have found to dodge this fee is to use their frequent flier miles on a partner carrier that does not impose a fuel surcharge, since miles earned on one carrier can often be redeemed for flights on a partner within the same global alliance.

Besides fuel surcharges and government taxes, other fees associated with redeeming frequent flier tickets have been increasing in recent years, as airlines have relied on à la carte charges to offset higher oil prices.

American, Delta and US Airways charge $150 to change an award ticket, while other carriers typically charge about $75 to $100. It costs roughly the same amount to cancel an itinerary and redeposit the miles back in your account — although these and many other fees are often reduced or waived for elite members of an airline's frequent flier program.

The fee to book an award ticket by phone instead of online can run as high as $30 on US Airways ($15 to $25 is the norm). US Airways also charges an "award processing fee" of $25 to $50 per ticket, a fee most other carriers do not impose.

But given that Web booking tools for frequent flier tickets do not always display all the available options for award seats, particularly on partner carriers, Mr. Winship said the phone booking fee was sometimes worth challenging.

Another charge that surprises many frequent fliers is a fee to book an award ticket at the last minute, which airlines generally consider to be within three weeks before the start of a trip. That charge ranges from $ 50 to $ 100, but is more inconsistent among airlines. Delta dropped this fee last year, while United will begin charging a $ 75 fee on June 15 for award tickets booked less than 21 days before departure.

Many airlines have also imposed fees to use frequent flier miles to upgrade a paid ticket, which can be hundreds of dollars for an international flight.

Although there is no publicly available data on how much airlines collect in award fees, Mr. Winship pointed out that it was high enough to make the idea of a "free ticket" obsolete.

Ⅰ. New Words and Expressions

round-trip	[ˈraʊndˌtrɪp]	(*n.*) 来回旅行,双程旅行
surcharge	[ˈsɜːtʃɑːdʒ]	(*n.*) 额外费
practice	[ˈpræktɪs]	(*n.*) 练习,实行,习惯,业务
hover	[ˈhʌvə]	(*v.*) 盘旋,徘徊
exempt	[ɪgˈzempt]	(*a.*) 免除的
dodge	[dɒdʒ]	(*v.*) 避开,躲避
itinerary	[aɪˈtɪnərərɪ]	(*n.*) 旅行计划,旅程
impose	[ɪmˈpəʊz]	(*v.*) 强加,课征,强迫,征收(税款)
inconsistent	[ˌɪnkənˈsɪstənt]	(*a.*) 不一致的,反复无常的
obsolete	[ˈɒbsəliːt]	(*a.*) 已废弃的,过时的

Ⅱ. Fill in the blanks in the following sentences with the listed words or expressions.

exempt	round-trip	impose on	surcharge	hover
dodge	itinerary	inconsistent	obsolete	practice

1. The army plans to phase out the equipment as it becomes ________.
2. I don't want to ________ you by staying too long.
3. He is ________ from military service.
4. You'd better buy a ________ ticket beforehand if you don't want to stay there very long.
5. Daily ________ is the trick in learning a foreign language.

6. The hawk is ________ overhead.
7. I need to discuss our ________ with you.
8. His accounts of the event were ________.
9. They've ________ us 10% on the price of the holiday because of a rise in air fares.
10. She was sharp-witted enough to ________ her attacker.

Ⅲ. There are four choices marked A. B. C. and D. in the following questions. You should decide on the best choice and mark the corresponding letter with a circle.

1. According to the writer, why is the "free" ticket not free?
   A. Because the passengers will be charged more afterwards.
   B. Because the passengers will have to buy a lot more souvenirs on the plane.
   C. Because the passengers will have to spend a lot of money on buying redundant tickets.
   D. Because there are a lot of surcharges passengers will have to pay.
2. In paragraph 2, what does author mean by saying "a practice that has not caught on yet in the United States"?
   A. The U.S will charge passengers flying with award tickets.
   B. The U.S will not charge passengers flying with award tickets.
   C. The U.S will not charge passengers flying with award tickets until crisis take place.
   D. The U.S has not charged passengers flying with award tickets yet.
3. What' the author's attitude towards "a fee to book an award ticket at the last minute"?
   A. Reasonable. B. Unreasonable.
   C. Worth-praising. D. Unworthy-praising.
4. In the last paragraph, what does Mr. Winship think of "free ticket"?
   A. It's a great idea.
   B. It's a popular idea.
   C. It's an unpopular idea.
   D. It's an old but still popular idea.
5. What's the key tone of the whole passage?
   A. Objective. B. Subjective.
   C. Optimistic. D. Pessimistic.

Passage 17

Power, power, power-sales negotiations are all about who has the most power, right? Well, no — sometimes it's about who doesn't have the power. A case in point is when you find yourself in a situation where you have limited authority — your hands are tied. It turns out that there are four ways that you can both be limited in your authority while at the same time gaining more power in the negotiations. I'm going to tell you how to do this...

Organizational Limits

Organization limits are the most common type of limits that people encounter in a sales negotiation. How many times have you heard "I will have to talk to my boss" while working on a deal? This kind of limit can be a great way for you to get more time to consider the offer that is on the table before you.

Structural Limits

Structural limits have to do with restrictions on your negotiation power that have been placed on you by virtue of the job that you have, the company that you work for, or other type of limits that come with your job. The power of these types of limits is that the other side of the table rarely questions them. Once you say that your hands are tied due to a structural limit, the other side will almost immediately start to find other issues that can be worked without probing to find out why you have this limit.

Financial Limits

Financial limits rarely require much explanation — they just are. When you state that your ability to deal with the other side's offer is limited due to financial restrictions, then your statement is given instant credibility. If the other side of the table knows that you have a financial limit, then you'll be amazed at how often they are able to present you with a deal that comes in just under that limit in order to get you to approve it on the spot!

Legal Limits

One of the most powerful limits that you can bring to the table is a government restriction. Master negotiators often suggest that if it is possible that you bring a printed copy of the government regulations to the table just as a show of force. The other side will quickly accept that this is a limit that can't be moved and will shift to negotiating on other topics.

Ⅰ. New Words and Expressions

authority	[ɔːˈθɔːrɪtɪ]	(*n*.) 权力
encounter	[ɪnˈkaʊntə]	(*v*.) 遇到
restriction	[rɪsˈtrɪkʃən]	(*n*.) 限制,约束
probe	[prəʊb]	(*v*.) 详细调查
approve	[əˈpruːv]	(*v*.) 同意

Ⅱ. Fill in the blanks in the following sentences with the listed words or expressions.

gain	encounter	consider	on the table	by virtue of
due to	probe	find out	deal with	on the spot

1. The governor appointed a committee to ________ the causes of the strike.
2. We have to ________ the question of where to sleep.
3. They had red tapers ________ at Christmas time.
4. He is hit by a falling tree and killed ________.
5. Many movies ________ commonplace themes.
6. ________ what the conditions of the contract are.
7. The two countries were on the point of war ________ the diplomatic disputes.
8. ________ sense of responsibility the employees worked overtime.
9. No pain, no ________.
10. Our troops ________ only token resistance.

Ⅲ. There are four choices marked A. B. C. and D. in the following questions. You should decide on the best choice and mark the corresponding letter with a circle.

1. In sales negotiation, the one who has the most power does not ________ mean that he gains the upper hand.

   A. eventually　　B. firstly　　C. finally　　D. necessarily

2. When one side says, "I will have to talk to my boss," this means that the deal they are working on is ________ him.

   A. under　　B. beyond　　C. in　　D. of

3. Naturally, when a negotiator resorts to organizational limits, his real intension is to ________.

   A. avoid a different situation

   B. reach an agreement as soon as possible

   C. get more time to think about the offer on the table

   D. respect his boss

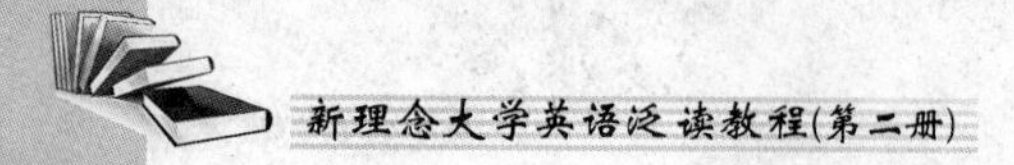

4. An experienced negotiator will take advantage of the four "limits" mentioned above to ________.
   A. show what he says does not work
   B. indicate that he has no final say
   C. suggest he is a green hand
   D. tell the other side that he can go no further on a certain issues
5. The writer appears to favor those who are ________ in negotiation.
   A. stubborn B. passive C. flexible D. naive

Passage 18

What are the qualities for a good negotiator? To this question, there can be a great variety of answers. Not everyone is cut out to be a negotiator. Generally speaking, he must possess a wide variety of technical, social, communication, and ethical skills or a good personality with the ability to make others understand his position, to approach the counterpart with great ease and confidence and to appreciate the other person's position. To achieve satisfactory results in negotiation, a negotiator must pay heed to the following points:

1. Shrewdness

A successful negotiator must be capable of allowing the other side to see only what deserves the strategy best, and this requires an ethical mixture of honesty and cunning. People who "wear their hearts on their sleeves" or insist on transparency in all dealings will make sorry negotiators in the marketplace. While there's no room for duplicity, a negotiator must know which cards to lay on the table and when. Because of this, shrewdness ranks as the first for desirable characteristics.

2. Resourcefulness

A good negotiator should be flexible enough and adeptly deals with a great amount of ever-emerging information and uncertainties. It is of actual significance to survive and acquire the ability for development in an environment where a negotiator does not know what will befall him.

3. Endurance

Negotiating is primarily a mental activity, but it can be physically demanding. A negotiator must be available for all sessions and eight-hour days will be rare. Add in travel fatigue, climatic change, jet lag, foreign food, late-night socializing, and work stress and you have the makings of burn-out. Many cultures use the tactic of physically and mentally wearing down their counterparts in order to achieve concessions.

4. Patience

This is chiefly because a negotiation will be limited if a negotiator starts it in too straightforward a way , which may yield some short-term results only; the use of some coercion to bring this opponent closer to the objectives of negotiation will certainly lead to more stubbornness on the other side. So to make both negotiator and his opponent nearer their common goals is but a time-

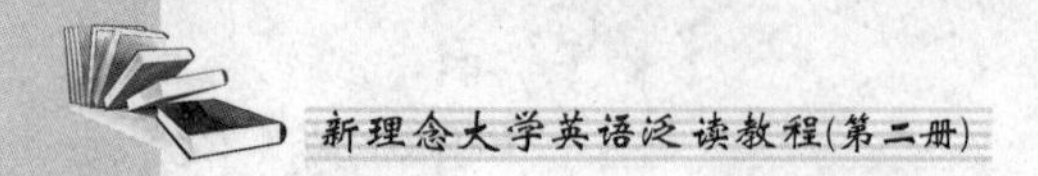

consuming job.

5. Adaptability

Having an inflexible strategy and limited tactics will almost instantly bring negotiations to an unproductive close. Negotiations seldom go completely according to plan, nor will they always change in preconceived patterns. Being able to "think on your feet" will go a long way toward success at the negotiation table.

6. Concentration

Counterparts will often attempt to put as many points as possible "on the table" in an effort to cloud the main issue. The negotiator must be able to maintain the team's (and his own) focus at all times.

7. The Ability to Articulate

People who cannot communicate their ideas or understand those put forth by counterparts are of little use around negotiation table. Good negotiators must be practical listeners as well as articulate speakers.

8. Sense of Humor

Negotiation can be a very stressful affair, and there will be moments when it hardly seems worth the effort. A good negotiator must be equipped with a highly developed sense of humor in order to weather persistent storms. Facing such problems with a humorous eye and avoiding the syndrome of taking yourself too seriously can make all the difference in keeping negotiations on track.

Ⅰ. New Words and Expressions

possess	[pəˈzes]	(*v.*) 拥有,持有
counterpart	[ˈkaʊntəpɑːt]	(*n.*) 对应方
heed	[hiːd]	(*n.*) 注意,留心
shrewdness	[ˈʃruːdnɪs]	(*n.*) 精明
transparency	[trænsˈpærənsɪ]	(*n.*) 透明度
adeptly	[əˈdeptlɪ]	(*adv.*) 熟练地,老练地
befall	[bɪˈfɔːl]	(*v.*) 发生,降临
endurance	[ɪnˈdjʊərəns]	(*n.*) 忍耐,忍耐力
concession	[kənˈseʃən]	(*n.*) 让步,特许权,租界,妥协
coercion	[kəʊˈɜːʃən]	(*n.*) 强迫,威压
adaptability	[əˌdæptəˈbɪlɪtɪ]	(*n.*) 适应性
unproductive	[ˈʌnprəˈdʌktɪv]	(*a.*) 无生产力的,没有收获的
preconceive	[priːkənˈsiːv]	(*v.*) 预见,预先形成
articulate	[ɑːˈtɪkjʊleɪt]	(*v.*) 清楚地讲话
syndrome	[ˈsɪndrəʊm]	(*n.*) 症候群,综合征

Ⅱ. Fill in the blanks in the following sentences with the listed words or expressions.

a variety of	be capable of	because of	befall	maintain
equip with	in order to	attempt to	worth	be able to

1. We started early ________ arrive before dark.
2. These discoveries are not ________ the candle.
3. At this rate we won't ________ afford a holiday.
4. The room ________ air conditioning.
5. Only human beings ________ speech.
6. ________ food is sold at a supermarket.
7. Her boss landed all over her ________ her carelessness.
8. The plan is merely designed to ________ their nuclear superiority.
9. Bad luck may ________ to anyone at any time.
10. Don't ________ do so much in such a short time.

Ⅲ. There are four choices marked A. B. C. and D. in the following questions. You should decide on the best choice and mark the corresponding letter with a circle.

1. Generally speaking, a good negotiator must possess a wide variety of skills expect ________.
   A. technical knowledge　　B. social contact
   C. communication　　D. rudeness
2. Regarded as one of the basic skills, resourcefulness requires a good negotiator ________.
   A. to be flexible enough in dealing with uncertainties
   B. to be casual in daily activities
   C. to do anything systematically
   D. to follow rules and regulations strictly
3. A negotiator with little patience won't be able to make both sides nearer the common goals, because negotiation is a(n) ________ job.
   A. ordinary　　B. part-time
   C. painstaking　　D. easy
4. In the sentence "Being able to 'think on your feet' will go a long way toward success at the negotiation table", the phrase "think on your feet" means "________".
   A. thinking under the influence
   B. thinking independently
   C. thinking while standing

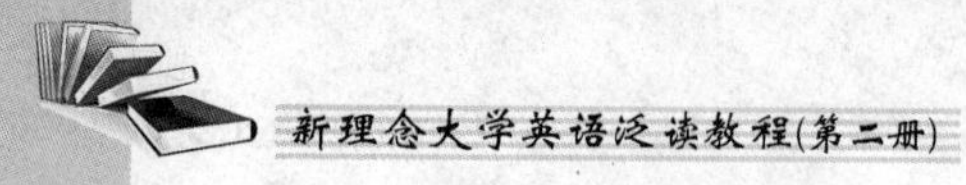

D. thinking hard

5. We can infer from the passage that ________.

A. a good negotiator must have patience, resourcefulness, sense of humor, etc

B. a good negotiator must be a practical listener as well as an articulate speaker

C. a good negotiator must be well informed

D. a good negotiator must have had long-term practice

Passage 19

There are many different ways to sell your product on the Web, but most techniques tend to fall into one of the following categories:

1. Gifts and Impulse Products

Sometimes you don't know what you want until you see it. Merchants who offer gift items are very familiar with this. If you're offering impulse buys, you may want to design a site that's easy and entertaining to explore; let them go window shopping. Red Envelope makes its site as fun to explore as it is to shop, creating impulses and ideas that drive sales.

2. Commodity Products

Everyone knows what a CD or a book looks like. They are pretty low-risk purchases since you don't have to worry about whether they're the right color or compatible with your system. What matters is that the seller has them in stock at a good price. Merchants who offer commodity-type products are differentiated by their products' price, selection, and availability.

3. Considered Purchase Products

Some products require a lot of deliberation before a purchase is made. Expensive items that come in various models, each with different options and different pricing, require customers to consider a number of factors before they buy. We're talking about consumer electronics, cars, cellular phone service programs, and something you should be thinking about in the near future: e-commerce software packages. There are now a number of middleman services popping up to help consumers make their buying decisions. Sites such as my Simon offer side-by-side comparisons of different products.

4. Configurable Products

Sometimes a product is all about the options it comes with. A case in point is computer workstations and servers. The basic components are the same, but you can choose how roomy or fast each of those parts will be. Computer manufacturers like Dell and Apple enable their customers to design their own products, blending one-on-one marketing with customizing mass-market products: Their motto is, "Tell us what you want and we'll build it for you." But these techniques are now showing up in other fields. Take a look at Smith + Noble, where you can design your own window treatments by selecting and combining different attributes and features.

Ⅰ. New Words and Expressions

tend	[tend]	(*v.*) 趋向,倾向
impulse	[ˈɪmpʌls]	(*n.*) 冲动,刺激
explore	[ɪksˈplɔː]	(*v.*) 探测,探索
compatible	[kəmˈpætəbl]	(*a.*) 兼容的,能共处的,可并立的
availability	[əˌveɪləˈbɪlɪtɪ]	(*n.*) 可用性,有效性,实用性
deliberation	[dɪˌlɪbəˈreɪʃən]	(*n.*) 熟思,考虑
middleman	[ˈmɪdlˌmæn]	(*n.*) 中间人,调解人,经纪人
pop	[pɒp]	(*v.*) 突然出现
configurable	[kənˈfɪgərəbl]	(*a.*) 可配置的,结构的
differentiate	[ˌdɪfəˈrenʃɪeɪt]	(*v.*) 区分,区别
option	[ˈɒpʃən]	(*n.*) 选择权,选项
workstation	[ˈwɜːkˌsteɪʃən]	(*n.*) 工作站
blend	[blend]	(*v.*) 混合
customize	[ˈkʌstəmaɪz]	(*v.*) 定做,按客户具体要求制造
treatment	[ˈtriːtmənt]	(*n.*) 处理,对待
attribute	[əˈtrɪbjuːt]	(*n.*) 属性,特质

Ⅱ. Fill in the blanks in the following sentences with the listed words or expressions.

be familiar with	take a look at	tend to	show up	entertaining
go window shopping	come with	in stock	pop up	combine

1. The organizer ________ the protocol of royal visits.
2. The policeman said to him, "You'd better ________ me and tell me all about the accident."
3. A little embroidery made the story quite ________.
4. Weeds ________ displace other plants.
5. Her main occupation seems to ________.
6. She was greatly tempted to ________ it.
7. As we walked along, we saw a rabbit ________ from its burrow and scurry across the field.
8. We can't always ________ work with pleasure.
9. The grocer's has varieties of goods ________.
10. Careful contrast of the two plans ________ some key difference.

Ⅲ. There are four choices marked A. B. C. and D. in the following questions. You should decide on the best choice and mark the corresponding letter with a circle.

1. For Red Envelope, which of the following statements is not true?
   A. It sells gifts and impulse products.
   B. One can go window shopping on its site.
   C. Its site is easy and entertaining to explore.
   D. Customers don't know what it sells until they visit its site.
2. The merchants who sell commodity products can compete in ________.
   A. price B. selection
   C. availability D. all of the above
3. My Simon is a site that ________.
   A. sells expensive items
   B. helps customers make their buying decisions
   C. sells e-commerce software packages
   D. sells cars and cell phones
4. Computer workstations and servers ________.
   A. belong to the category of configurable products
   B. are expensive because they come with many options
   C. are very difficult to choose
   D. are very difficult to build
5. Smith + Noble is doing e-business in the field of ________.
   A. customizing mass-market products
   B. computers
   C. window treatments
   D. one-to-one marketing

Passage 20

The year 2000 has been tough for online retailers. Changes in the market have driven many sites out of business, and many others are only barely surviving. The holidays, promising greatly increased sales, offer hope for many e-commerce sites. The good news for retailers is that the holiday market will grow; this year's holiday sales are predicted to be 66% higher than last year's.

In a year when over half the U.S. population has access to the Internet, e-commerce sites can expect dramatic increases in site traffic before the holidays. Forrester Research predicts $ 10 billion in holiday revenues, and Jupiter forecasts the U.S. holiday market as $ 12 billion. Gartner Group predicts $ 10.7 billion in North American holiday sales and worldwide sales of $ 19.5 billion.

While revenue estimates vary, it's clear that Holiday 2000 will be big for e-commerce. Customers will shop online this holiday season for convenience; by shopping online, customers avoid crowds, transportation hassles, and inconvenient store hours. One customer commented in our tests that she would shop online "to avoid the hassle of going to different stores."

Despite the eager shoppers and the predictions of a big holiday season, there is bad news for online retailers: the e-commerce industry is losing billions of dollars in potential sales. Shoppers want to purchase online, but many sites make it too hard to buy.

To gain the most from the holiday season, sites must pursue a simple strategy: improve the customer experience. Improving the customer experience can yield an additional $ 8 billion in North American sales, and $ 14 billion in worldwide online sales this holiday season.

According to Gartner Group projections, worldwide online revenues for the holiday season will be $ 19.5 billion.

In our consumer tests of major sites across key holiday categories, we found that 43% of buying attempts failed. These findings suggest that the $ 19.5 billion represent only 57% of potential sales this holiday season.

Lost sales due to poor customer experience thus total more than $ 14 billion: $ 34.2 billion - $ 19.5 billion= $ 14.7 billion.

It is worth noting that our $ 14 billion does not include future losses due to poor experience this holiday season. Millions of consumers will shop online for

the first time this holiday season. If they have a good experience, they are likely to continue shopping on their favorite sites in the future. If they have a bad experience, they will likely never return to the sites where they were unable to buy(if indeed they return to shop online at all). The actual losses due to poor customer experience may thus be significantly higher than our $ 14 billion estimate.

In our tests, problems with the checkout process were the greatest cause of failed purchase attempts. More than 40% of failures were due to difficulty with checkout. Customers had found a product they wanted, added it to their cart and decided to place an order. They were ready to buy and wanted to pay. Unfortunately, the checkout process was too difficult and made it impossible for them to buy.

There were several different types of problems that arose in the checkout process. The most important lesson is that poor checkout experience will cost the industry billions in holiday sales.

Ⅰ. New Words and Expressions

retailer	[rɪˈteɪlə]	(*n.*) 零售商
predict	[prɪˈdɪkt]	(*v.*) 预报,预言
revenue	[ˈrevɪnjuː]	(*n.*) 税收,国家的收入,收益
forecast	[ˈfɔːkɑːst]	(*v.*) 预报,预测;预示
estimate	[ˈestɪmeɪt]	(*v.*) 估计,估价
hassle	[ˈhæsl]	(*n.*) 困难,麻烦;激战
yield	[jiːld]	(*v.*) 生产,获利
attempt	[əˈtempt]	(*n.*) 企图,试图;攻击
potential	[pəˈtenʃəl]	(*adj.*) 可能的;潜在的
significantly	[sɪgˈnɪfɪkəntlɪ]	(*adv.*) 值得注目地;意味深长地
checkout	[ˈtʃekaʊt]	(*n.*) 付款,结账

Ⅱ. Fill in the blanks in the following sentences with the listed words or expressions.

out of business	have access to	forecast	represent	due to
be worth noting	place an order	return to	add... to	shop online

1. Exiles long to ________ their native land.
2. If you come down to the old price, we can ________ of a large quantity.
3. Students must ________ good books.
4. This essay ________ a considerable improvement on your recent work.
5. She uses tongs to ________ coals ________ the fire.

6. The company has made gigantic losses this year, and will probably be ________.
7. They tried to ________ the result of the football match.
8. Mr. Black bowed out of politics ________ poor health.
9. Internet users are finding a new way to ________.
10. A few details are ________.

Ⅲ. There are four choices marked A. B. C. and D. in the following questions. You should decide on the best choice and mark the corresponding letter with a circle.

1. By shopping online, people can avoid ________.
   A. traffic jams B. crowds
   C. getting up early D. both A and B
2. It is implied by the author that ________.
   A. it is difficult to buy things on some sites
   B. it is difficult to buy things on all sites
   C. it is easy to buy things on all sites
   D. it is easy to buy things on few sites
3. If sites made it easier to shop and buy, sites' actual income would ________.
   A. be the same B. decrease a lot
   C. increase a little D. increase a lot
4. The e-commerce industry is losing much money in potential sales because ________.
   A. people are not familiar with many sites
   B. about half of the buying attempts fail
   C. many people don't have the access to the Internet
   D. there is too much competition from traditional business
5. E-commerce sites can earn more money from the holiday season by ________.
   A. improving the customer experience
   B. forming valid identification
   C. advertising widely
   D. providing more content

As I've built TerraCycle, one of my priorities has been maintaining our unusual company culture. While I don't believe in overdoing it — we have no pool tables, yoga studios or climbing walls — I have found a few affordable yet surprisingly effective ways to build morale and have some fun.

1. LUNCH: About a year ago we adopted a lunch program whereby we order lunch from a nearby restaurant for participating employees, changing up the menu every day. We ask for a \$4 contribution per person, but the company picks up the rest. We bought plates and installed a dishwasher. The effect on productivity has been amazing. Instead of various teams taking long one- or two-hour lunch breaks (where people have to drive to a local restaurant, wait to order and then eat) everyone grabs lunch, eats and typically is back at their desks within 20 minutes or so. Funny how spending about \$6 per person (on top of the \$4 employee contribution) can make a difference.

2. THE GONG: Last year we installed a massive gong in our offices in Trenton. People who accomplish something awesome are encouraged to hit the gong as loudly as they can. Then they send out an e-mail to the entire company with the subject line "GONG HIT: Closed a major deal!" or "GONG HIT: New company logo available!" The effect is that whenever the gong tolls in the office or everyone receives a gong-hit e-mail (even from a distant office), positive energy is released. We all smile and feel great to be part of the team and send a congratulatory e-mail. While I prefer to reserve this kind of tool for positive events, there has long been a standing joke in the office that we should create a "Toilet Flush" for less-than-awesome news.

3. TRANSPARENCY: When I started TerraCycle more than eight years ago, I wasn't the most transparent leader. I would share good news but hold back on bad — especially with less senior employees. While this made me feel more in control, it had the opposite effect on everyone else. So a few years ago we started doing something different: the leaders of every team and every office must submit a report to the entire company every Friday that details everything positive and negative that has happened in their areas in the past week. I then take some time on the weekend and reply with comments, copying the entire company. So everyone, from a customer service rep in our Brazilian office to a team leader sees every department's report along with my comments. While this reporting structure requires an investment of time, it has

created an extremely transparent corporate culture.

4. NERF GUNS: When you join TerraCycle, you are issued a Nerf gun and ammo by our C.N.O. (chief Nerf-gun officer). They are totally safe and essentially self-cleaning because everyone picks up the bullets to shoot them again. Most important, the games are intense but short. Once or twice a day our office erupts in a massive 50- to 75-person war. Everyone blows off some steam but within a few minutes, everyone is back to work analyzing financial data or designing products made from waste.

5. GRAFFITI: Art and color have always been an integral part of our office vibe. Ever since our first office, which was in a basement, we have invited artists, especially graffiti artists, to paint our walls with cool, vibrant designs. The result is an office that is covered in art. The graffiti on the exterior changes weekly.

It seems obvious that a dynamic company culture can boost morale and build a sense of community among staffers, but I find it also helps with visiting clients. When we give tours through our offices, you can just see people smile, and you can tell they want to work with us — and in most cases, it costs us nothing. (Tom Szaky is the chief executive of TerraCycle, which is based in Trenton, N.J.)

Ⅰ. New Words and Expressions

priority	[praɪˈɒrɪtɪ]	(*n.*) 优先权,优先,优先顺序
morale	[mɒˈrɑːl]	(*n.*) 士气,斗志,道德准则
awesome	[ˈɔːsəm]	(*a.*) 了不起的,精彩的,绝妙的
toll	[təʊl]	(*v.*) 敲钟
transparency	[trænsˈpærənsɪ]	(*n.*) 透明度
graffiti	[grəˈfiːtɪ]	(*n.*) 涂鸦
vibe	[vaɪb]	(*n.*) 气氛,环境
vibrant	[ˈvaɪbrənt]	(*a.*) (颜色)鲜明的,醒目的
staffer	[ˈstɑːfə]	(*n.*) 职员

Ⅱ. Fill in the blanks in the following sentences with the listed words or expressions.

maintain	adopt	pick up	grab	reserve
hold back	intense	blow off	erupt	check out

1. At least 3,000 people were killed in a week of ________ fighting.
2. Britain wants to ________ its position as a world power.
3. Why should the taxpayer ________ the tab for mistakes made by a private company?

4. Hey, man, ________ my new look! Do you like it?
5. The store recently ________ a drug testing policy for all new employees.
6. After the big quarrel with my mum, I went running to ________ my anger.
7. A separate room ________ for smokers.
8. Violence ________ after police shot a student during the demonstration.
9. Tell me all about it — don't ________ anything ________!
10. Let's ________ a bite to eat before we go.

Ⅲ. There are four choices marked A. B. C. and D. in the following questions. You should decide on the best choice and mark the corresponding letter with a circle.

1. How much does TerraCycle actually spend per person on lunch?
   A. \$6 B. \$4 C. \$10 D. \$2
2. What is "Gong"?
   A. Kong Fu show. B. Mirror.
   C. A musical instrument. D. Bowl.
3. The author started news sharing system for the purpose of ________.
   A. making himself feel more in control
   B. sharing good news with all employees
   C. killing some time on the weekend
   D. creating an extremely transparent corporate culture
4. "Everyone blows off some steam but within a few minutes, everyone is back to work." The correct understanding of "blow off some steam" is ________.
   A. to cook something in steam
   B. to get rid of your anger, excitement, or energy
   C. to start doing something very quickly
   D. to produce power by exercises
5. Who paints the graffiti on company office walls?
   A. Artists. B. Managers. C. Boss. D. Workers.

Passage 22

A colleague of mine at Kotter International shared the following story with me. I've seen similar episodes many times.

On a client engagement, during a meeting of division managers discussing what was important to weave into the fabric of the firm's desired corporate culture, the CEO stepped out of the session early. When catching up with my colleague later, the CEO asked him to "handle the culture thing" on his own and to not include her in more meetings on the subject. The CEO reasoned, "I have too many other things going on, and that's not really my job."

But whose job is it? Who raises red flags if the culture is impeding performance? Who figures out how to change it if it is a problem, or maintain it if it is an asset? If you ask the employees and managers of most companies, the most common answer is "the folks in HR." And that's not a very good answer. The truth is that top leadership, including the CEO, has to take responsibility if the culture is to be strong.

When Jack Ma, CEO of Alibaba, the Chinese e-trading company, was asked by CNN about his corporate culture, he had this to say:

All the business people say, "Jack, what are you busy with, now?" And I say "Building the vision and the values and the culture." And they say, "Jack, you are so stupid. 99% of [the] business doesn't care about that. What they care about is making money!" And I don't believe that. I want to be the 1% of the company [who is] thinking that making money is the result — not the goal.

Jack Ma believes that Alibaba's culture is his job. And he is not alone. Great business leaders throughout history — such as Tom Watson, Sam Walton, and Herb Kelleher — have argued that the cultural buck stops with them.

The reason that the Watsons, Waltons, Kellehers, and Mas of the world are the exceptions and not the rule is that we have too many managers and not enough leaders in today's business world. Managers focus on timelines, budgets, organizational structures, metrics, controls, and numbers. Leaders focus on vision, buy-in, motivation, culture, and people. Of course management is important. But while you may get the top job by excelling at management, you thrive in the top job by excelling at leadership. Culture is always in a leader's job description.

Ⅰ. New Words and Expressions

episode	[ˈepɪsəʊd]	(*n.*)(人生的)一段经历;(小说的)片段,插曲,
client engagement		客户联系和互动
weave	[wiːv]	(*v.*)编织,组合,编排
fabric	[ˈfæbrɪk]	(*n.*)组织,构造
session	[ˈseʃən]	(*n.*)会议
impede	[ɪmˈpiːd]	(*v.*)阻碍,妨碍,阻止
buck	[bʌk]	(*n.*)责任,过失
timeline	[ˈtaɪmˈlaɪn]	(*n.*)时间表
metric	[ˈmetrɪk]	(*n.*)标准,度量
buy-in	[ˈbaɪɪn]	(*n.*)买进,补进(为了接管某公司买进其控制股权),补仓
excel	[ɪkˈsel]	(*v.*)胜出
thrive	[θraɪv]	(*v.*)大获成功,兴旺发达
job description		职业描述,工作说明书

Ⅱ. Fill in the blanks in the following sentences with the listed words or expressions.

argue	thrive	focus	excel	episode
division	weave	impede	figure out	folk

1. She decided she would try to forget the ________ by the lake.
2. The Computer Services ________ has just been founded in that company.
3. Only a few of the women still ________ nowadays.
4. Storms at sea ________ our progress.
5. Can you ________ how to do it?
6. Thanks to the ________ at CCTV.
7. It could ________ that a dam might actually increase the risk of flooding.
8. She tried to ________ her mind on her work.
9. Rick has always ________ at foreign languages.
10. Southwest Airlines is a business which managed to ________ during a recession.

Ⅲ. There are four choices marked A. B. C. and D. in the following questions. You should decide on the best choice and mark the corresponding letter with a circle.

1. In the second paragraph, the CEO's real reason for stepping out of the sessions is ________.

   A. he doesn't understand the importance of corporate culture

   B. he is busy with more important things

C. he has good helpers to assist him with corporate culture

D. he is catching up with his colleague

2. Who should take responsibility of strengthening corporate culture?

A. H.R Manager. B. Top leadership.

C. Department managers. D. Training experts.

3. In the sentence "such as Tom Watson, Sam Walton, and Herb Kelleher — have argued that the cultural buck stops with them", the phrase "the buck stops with them" means ________.

A. corporate culture is so important that it often stops company's progress

B. the money making process has been slowed because of corporate culture

C. they have been too busy to deal with corporate culture and they learned a lesson

D. they are responsible for improving corporate culture

4. We can infer from the last paragraph that ________.

A. today's managers are too busy

B. management is more important than leadership

C. we are in great need of leaders in today's business world

D. leaders should pay great attention to corporate culture all the time

Passage 23

Advertisers tend to think big and perhaps this is why they're always coming in for criticism. Their critics seem to resent them because they have a flair for self-promotion and because they have so much money to throw around. "It's iniquitous," they say, "that this entirely unproductive industry (if we can call it that) should absorb millions of pounds each year. It only goes to show how much profit the big companies are making. Why don't they stop advertising and reduce the price of their goods? After all, it's the consumer who pays..."

The poor old consumer! He'd have to pay a great deal more if advertising didn't create mass markets for products. It is precisely because of the heavy advertising that consumer goods are so cheap. But we get the wrong idea if we think the only purpose of advertising is to sell goods. Another equally important function is to inform. A great deal of the knowledge we have about household goods derives largely from the advertisements we read. Advertisements introduce us to new products or remind us of the existence of ones we already know about. Supposing you wanted to buy a washing machine, it is more than likely you would obtain details regarding performance, price, etc., from an advertisement.

Lots of people pretend that they never read advertisements, but this claim may be seriously doubted. It is hardly possible not to read advertisements these days. And what fun they often are, too! Just think what a railway station or a newspaper would be like without advertisements. Would you enjoy gazing at a blank wall or reading railway bylaws while waiting for a train? Would you like to read only closely printed columns of news in your daily paper? A cheerful, witty advertisement makes such a difference to a drab wall or a newspaper full of the daily ration of calamities.

We must not forget, either, that advertising makes a positive contribution to our pockets. Newspapers, commercial radio and television companies could not subsist without this source of revenue. The fact that we pay so little for our daily paper, or can enjoy so many broadcast programs is due entirely to the money spent by advertisers. Just think what a newspaper would cost if we had to pay its full price!

Another thing we mustn't forget is the "small ads" which are in virtually every newspaper and magazine. What a tremendously useful service they per-

form for the community! Just think about anything can be accomplished through these columns. For instance, you can find a job, buy or sell a house, announce a birth, marriage or death in what used to be called the "hatch, match and dispatch" column but by far the most fascinating section is the personal or "agony" column. No other item in a newspaper provides such entertaining reading or offers such a deep insight into human nature. It's the best advertisement for advertising there is!

Ⅰ. New Words and Expressions

flair	[fleə]	(*n.*) 天资;(特别的)才能
iniquitous	[ɪˈnɪkwɪtəs]	(*a.*) 极不公正的;邪恶的
claim	[kleɪm]	(*n.*) 主张,断言,声称
bylaw	[ˈbaɪˌlɔː]	(*n.*) 内部章程
drab	[dræb]	(*a.*) 单调的;无趣的;无生气的
calamity	[kəˈlæmɪtɪ]	(*n.*) 灾难;大祸;大灾害
subsist	[səbˈsɪst]	(*v.*) 存在;继续存在
agony column		(报刊中关于个人疑难问题征询意见的)读者来信专栏

Ⅱ. Fill in the blanks in the following sentences with the listed words or expressions.

make a contribution to	come in for	derive... from	tend to
accomplish	make a difference to	consumer goods	mass market
perform	gaze at		

1. I approach every new job with a long-term view. I would like to think that I can ________ your corporation for the foreseeable future.
2. As it ventures out of niches into the ________, Haier is starting to do consumer advertising.
3. We should not try to ________ two tasks at once.
4. Shoppers crowded into downtown stores, snapping up once-rationed ________.
5. The Government's economic policies have ________ much criticism in the newspapers
6. Imperialist powers always ________ gobble up their weaker neighbors.
7. We shall ________ much benefit ________ reading good novels.
8. The sea air has ________ (ie improved) her health.
9. Members of certain tribes ________ special ceremonies when they reach manhood.
10. Charter flights no longer bring tourists to ________ the dunes.

Ⅲ. There are four choices marked A. B. C. and D. in the following questions. You should decide on the best choice and mark the corresponding letter with a circle.

1. What is main idea of this passage?
   A. Advertisement.
   B. The benefits of advertisement.
   C. Advertisers perform a useful service to communities.
   D. The costs of advertisement.
2. The attitude of the author toward advertisers is ________.
   A. appreciative　　B. trustworthy
   C. critical　　D. dissatisfactory
3. Why do the critics criticize advertisers?
   A. Because advertisers often brag.
   B. Because critics think advertisement is a "waste of money".
   C. Because customers are encouraged to buy more than necessary.
   D. Because customers pay more.
4. Which of the following is Not true?
   A. Advertisement makes contribution to our pockets and we may know everything.
   B. We can buy what we want.
   C. Good quality products don't need to be advertised.
   D. Advertisement makes our life colorful.
5. The passage is ________.
   A. narrative　　B. descriptive
   C. critical　　D. argumentative

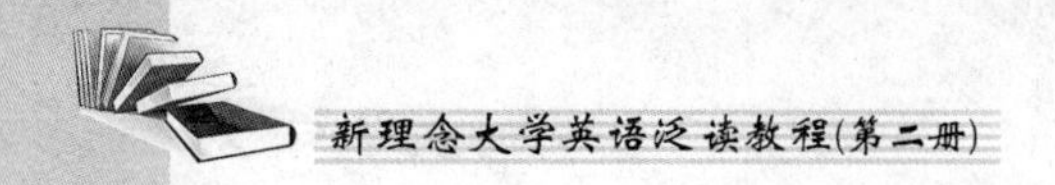

Will Facebook, MySpace and other social-networking sites transform advertising?

Depending on your age and memory, it was a week of radically new or reassuringly old developments in the advertising industry. To Mark Zuckerberg, the boss of Facebook, a popular social-networking website, it was the former. Standing in front of about 250 mostly middle-aged advertising executives on November 6th, he announced that Facebook was offering them a new deal. "For the last hundred years media has been pushed out to people," he said, "but now marketers are going to be a part of the conversation." Using his firm's new approach, he claimed, advertisers will be able to piggyback on the "social actions" of Facebook users, since "people influence people."

Mr Zuckerberg's underlying idea is hardly new. But, says Randall Rothenberg, the boss of the Interactive Advertising Bureau, a trade association, the announcements this week by Facebook and its larger rival, MySpace, which has a similar ad system, could amount to a big step forward in conversational marketing. If new technologies that are explicitly based on social interactions prove effective, he thinks, they might advance web advertising to its fourth phase.

From the point of view of marketers, the existing types of online ads already represent breakthroughs. In search, they can now target consumers who express interest in a particular product or service by typing a keyword; they pay only when a consumer responds, by clicking on their ads. In display, they can track and measure how their ads are viewed and whether a consumer is paying attention better than they ever could with television ads. Yet now the holy grail of observing and even participating in consumers' conversations appears within reach.

The first step for brands to socialize with consumers is to start profile pages on social networks and then accept "friend requests" from individuals. On MySpace, brands have been doing this for a while. For instance, Warner Bros, a Hollywood studio, had a MySpace page for "300", its film about Spartan warriors. It signed up some 200,000 friends, who watched trailers, talked the film up before its release, and counted down toward its DVD release.

Facebook, from this week, also lets brands create their own pages. Coca-Cola, for instance, has a Sprite page and a "Sprite Sips" game that lets us-

ers play with a little animated character on their own pages. Facebook makes this a social act by automatically informing the player's friends, via tiny "news feed" alerts, of the fun in progress. Thus, at least in theory, a Sprite "experience" can travel through an entire group, just as Messrs Lazarsfeld and Katz once described in the offline world.

In many cases, Facebook users can also treat brands' pages like those of other friends, by adding reviews, photos or comments, say. Each of these actions might again be communicated instantly to the news feeds of their clique. Obviously this is a double-edged sword, since they can just as easily criticise a brand as praise it. Facebook even plans to monitor and use actions beyond its own site to place them in a social context. If, for instance, a Facebook user makes a purchase at Fandango, a website that sells cinema tickets, this information again shows up on the news feeds of his friends on Facebook, who might decide to come along. If he buys a book or shirt on another site, then this implicit recommendation pops up too.

Ⅰ. New Words and Expressions

radically	[ˈrædɪkəlɪ]	(*adv*.) 根本地;彻底地;完全地
piggyback	[ˈpɪgɪbæk]	(*v*.) 广告连播
underlying	[ˌʌndəˈlaɪɪŋ]	(*a*.) 潜在的,根本的
explicitly	[ɪkˈsplɪsɪtlɪ]	(*adv*.) 明白地;明确地
grail	[greɪl]	(*n*.) 传说中耶稣最后晚餐所用之杯(或盘)
trailer	[ˈtreɪlə]	(*n*.) 电影预告片;预告节目
news feed		新闻供应(一种能主动把用户主页上的变动向所有好友广播的内置功能)

Ⅱ. Fill in the blanks in the following sentences with the listed words or expressions.

transform	amount to	base on	socialize with	make a purchase
show up	within reach	pop up	release	a double-edged sword

1. His debts ________ 5,000 pounds.
2. Flourishing market economy is ________.
3. He seems to ________ in the most unlikely places.
4. The new ________ is at our local cinema.
5. Customers actually vote for products and companies when they ________.
6. His show-off only serves to ________ his ignorance.
7. He was happy to sense that his dream was ________.
8. Under certain conditions we can ________ the bad into the good.

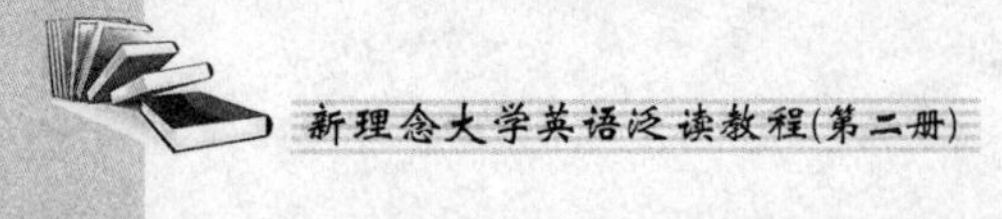

9. Compensation trade is a form of international trade ________ credit.
10. A good seller should needs to learn how to ________ his or her customer.

Ⅲ. There are four choices marked A. B. C. and D. in the following questions. You should decide on the best choice and mark the corresponding letter with a circle.

1. The fourth phase of web advertising is ________.
   A. creating brands' own pages on social-networking websites
   B. the strategy of conversational marketing
   C. on-line advertising through various means
   D. interactive advertising
2. The new advertising model makes breakthrough in ________.
   A. allowing marketers to find consumers with a keyword
   B. providing marketers access to measure their ads' effectiveness
   C. encouraging consumers to have more communication and interaction
   D. endow marketers with the right of creating their own pages
3. The case of Warner Bros implies that ________.
   A. MySpace is having a step further than Facebook
   B. the "friend request" approach is effective
   C. some initial steps of the new advertising model have been taken
   D. this kind of advertising model fits the film industry
4. About Facebook, which one of the following statements is TRUE?
   A. It has reached a consensus with MySpace in pushing forward the new advertising model.
   B. It is marching into a new phase of the advertising industry based on its expertise in advertisement.
   C. It will make full use of the social actions of its users in the new advertising model.
   D. It provides customized service to commercial organizations to facilitate their success.
5. Facebook's principle of "people influence people" is best reflected in its ________.
   A. special pages for famous brands like Coca-cola
   B. "Sprit Sips" game on the Sprite page
   C. tiny alerts of news feeds
   D. profile pages and "friends request" to socialize people

Gracious Manner Makes You Charming

No matter how nicely we dress, how beautifully we decorate our homes, or how lovely our dinner parties are, we can't be truly stylish without good manners. It's impossible.

In fact, I think of good manners as a sort of hidden beauty secret. Haven't you noticed that the kindest, most generous people seem to keep getting prettier? It's funny how that happens, but it does.

Take the long-lost art of saying "thank you" for example. Like wearing a little lipstick or making sure your hair is neat, getting into the habit of saying "thank you" can make you feel better about yourself, and then you look better to everyone around you. A gracious manner not only sets an excellent example for your children and grandchildren but it adds priceless panache to your image. A grumpy, angry face makes even the most stylishly dressed person look ugly.

Of course, saying "thank you" does wonders for the person on the receiving end too. I recently got a thank-you note from a guest who attended a 40th birthday party that Frank and I hosted for Frank's daughter-in-law. The note was lovely enough, but even lovelier was the fact that the guest had also included a recipe for a dish I'd complimented her on at an earlier gathering. It was a sweet gesture that makes me feel terrific and put me in a great mood. What a gift! Many of us know we should write thank-you notes, but we think we don't have the time or energy. Now, I know we all have busy lives, but I bet the note my guest sent me didn't take long to write.

Just as powerful as a thank-you note is the simple phrase "excuse me". Don't you just hate it when someone knocks an enormous carry-on bag into your head when he's barreling down the aisle to board an airplane — and then doesn't bother to say he's sorry? But when someone does stop and turn around and genuinely apologizes, doesn't it melt away most — if not all — of the irritation you felt?

Same for holding the door open for others when you see their hands are full. I think we can all remember a time when we were juggling packages while people passed by and let the door slam in our faces as if they didn't even see us. It's awful!

And punctuality is not a thing of the past, either. Being on time for lunch dates, for example, shows the person we're meeting that we value his or her precious time as much as we do our own.

Moreover, we shouldn't forget to use good manners with our own families. That's where it counts the most because those are the people we love the most. Find ways to show your care every day. Bringing home the most insignificant little presents for people you cherish will go a long way. It shows they're in your thoughts and you want to make them happy.

Good manners are infectious. Now, if only we could just get everyone to catch them.

Ⅰ. New Words and Expressions

stylish	[ˈstaɪlɪʃ]	(*a*.) 时髦的,流行的,潇洒的
panache	[pəˈnæʃ]	(*n*.) 羽饰,炫耀,假威风
grumpy	[ˈɡrʌmpɪ]	(*a*.) 性情乖戾的,脾气暴躁的
terrific	[təˈrɪfɪk]	(*a*.) 可怕的,极好的,非常的
barrel	[ˈbærəl]	(*v*.) 快速移动
aisle	[aɪl]	(*n*.) 侧廊,(席位间的)通道
juggle	[ˈdʒʌɡl]	(*v*.) 玩杂耍,篡改,欺骗
slam	[slæm]	(*v*.) 砰地关上,猛放,猛烈攻击
infectious	[ɪnˈfekʃəs]	(*a*.) 传染的,有感染力的

Ⅱ. Fill in the blanks in the following sentences with the listed words or expressions.

think of... as	no matter how	get into	pass by	bet
turn around	go a long way	knock into	melt away	bother

1. I'm really _______ jazz these days.
2. A cork, bobbing on water as waves _______, is not swept along with the water.
3. The problem _______ me for weeks.
4. A little formatting _______.
5. I _______ an old friend of mine in the park.
6. _______ hard he works, he can not get a promotion.
7. I _______ they are making a pile out of.
8. He speaks English so well that he _______ a native speaker.
9. The crowd _______ when the storm broke.
10. The reporters kept following her and asking personal questions. Finally she _______ and laid them out.

Ⅲ. There are four choices marked A. B. C. and D. in the following questions. You should decide on the best choice and mark the corresponding letter with a circle.

1. According to the author, we can not be truly stylish without ________.
   A. money
   B. beauty
   C. decoration
   D. good manners
2. In the author's opinion, which of the following is NOT true?
   A. Most generous people seem to become prettier.
   B. We should still keep saying thank you as before.
   C. A gracious manner sets a good example for your parents.
   D. The habit of saying thank you can make one feel better.
3. The example of Frank's letter to the author indicates that ________.
   A. the author was glad to be a guest of Frank's daughter-in-law's birthday party
   B. saying "thank you" can give terrific feeling to the person on the receiving end
   C. a thank-you note is not necessary
   D. people who are busy do not need to write thank-you notes
4. How should we treat our own families according to the author?
   A. We should treat our family members with good manners.
   B. Make them happy by buying expensive presents to them.
   C. We don't need to respect family members.
   D. Love our families but there is no need to show this.
5. What is the main idea of the passage?
   A. We shouldn't forget to use good manners with family members.
   B. We should often say thank you.
   C. Punctuality is not a thing of the past.
   D. Genuine fashion and good manners go hand in hand.

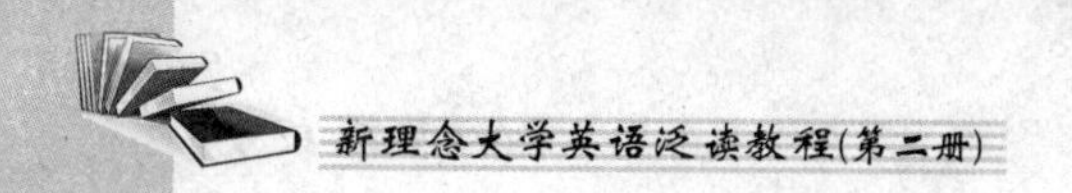

Has it ever occurred to you how much you are saying to people even when you are not speaking? Unless you are a master of disguise, you are constantly sending messages about your true thoughts and feelings whether you are using words or not.

In the business setting, people can see what you are not saying. Studies show that your words account for only 7% of the messages you convey. The remaining 93% is non-verbal. 55% of communication is based on what people see and the other 38% is transmitted through tone of voice. If your body language doesn't match your words, you are wasting your time.

Eye contact is the most obvious way you communicate. When you are looking at the other person, you show interest. When you fail to make eye contact, you give the impression that the other person is of no importance. Maintain eye contact about 60% of the time in order to look interested, but not aggressive.

Facial expression is another form of non-verbal communication. A smile sends a positive message and is appropriate in all but a life and death situation. Smiling adds warmth and an aura of confidence. Others will be more receptive if you remember to check your expression.

The position of your head speaks to people. Keeping your head straight will make you appear self-assured and authoritative. People will take you seriously. Tilt your head to one side if you want to come across as friendly and open.

How you use your arms can help or hurt your image as well. Waving them about may show enthusiasm to some, but others see this gesture as one of uncertainty and immaturity. The best place for your arms is by your side. You will look confident and relaxed. If this is hard for you, do what you always do when you want to get better at something — practice. After a while, it will feel natural.

Control your hands by paying attention to where they are. In the business world, particularly when you deal with people from other cultures, your hands need to be seen. That would mean you should keep them out of your pockets and you should resist the urge to put them under the table or behind your back. Having your hands anywhere above the neck, fidgeting with your hair or rubbing your face, is unprofessional.

Legs talk, too. A lot of movement indicates nervousness. How and where you cross them tells others how you feel. The preferred positions for the polished professional are feet flat on the floor or legs crossed at the ankles. The least professional and most offensive position is resting one leg or ankle on top of your other knee. Some people call this the "Figure Four". It can make you look arrogant.

You may not be aware of what you are saying with your body, but others will get the message. Make sure it's the one you want to send.

ByLydia Ramsey

Ⅰ. New Words and Expressions

disguise	[dɪsˈgaɪz]	(n.) 伪装,伪装物
remaining	[rɪˈmeɪnɪŋ]	(a.) 剩余的
transmit	[trænzˈmɪt]	(v.) 传达,传染,传送,代代相传
aggressive	[əˈgresɪv]	(a.) 侵略的,进攻性的,好斗的,有进取心的
aura	[ˈɔːrə]	(n.) 气氛,氛围,气味,光环,[医]先兆
authoritative	[ɔːˈθɔːrɪˌteɪtɪv]	(a.) 权威性的,命令式的
immaturity	[ɪməˈtjʊərɪtɪ]	(n.) 不成熟
fidget	[ˈfɪdʒɪt]	(v.) 坐立不安;玩弄
offensive	[əˈfensɪv]	(a.) 令人不快的,冒犯的,侮辱的,与进攻有关的
arrogant	[ˈærəgənt]	(a.) 傲慢的,自大的

Ⅱ. Fill in the blanks in the following sentences with the listed words or expressions.

account for	base on	be of no importance	come across	receptive
deal with	rest on	pay attention to	be aware of	indicate

1. We ________ our friends when we are in trouble.
2. Modesty: the gentle art of enhancing your charm by pretending not ________ it.
3. He spoke for a long time but his meaning did not really ________.
4. This survey results seem to ________ a connection between poor housing conditions and bad health.
5. Evidence is ________ the reports of others rather than the personal knowledge of a witness and therefore generally not admissible as testimony.
6. We have no space to ________ such details.
7. He's not very ________ to my suggestions.
8. Petrochemicals today ________ one fourth of all the chemicals made, and in ten years this amount is expected to double.

9. But I don't understand your joke! Oh, skip it, it ________.
10. Please ________ this clause in the sentence.

Ⅲ. There are four choices marked A. B. C. and D. in the following questions. You should decide on the best choice and mark the corresponding letter with a circle.

1. According to the author, which of the following is true?
   A. We can't send messages about or true thoughts when we don't speak.
   B. We can let others know our feelings when we don't speak.
   C. Everyone can become a master of disguise.
   D. We can't communicate with each other without verbal language.
2. According to the passage, which of the following is NOT mentioned?
   A. Eye contacting.
   B. Facial expression.
   C. The position of your hand.
   D. Head shaking.
3. According to Paragraph 4, which of the following is NOT the intended effect of a smile?
   A. To disagree with others.
   B. To send a positive message.
   C. To welcome others.
   D. To show one's confidence.
4. The word "polished" in Paragraph 8 means ________.
   A. shiny as a result of polishing
   B. elegant, confident and highly skilled
   C. being killed
   D. sth. is changed in order to be improved
5. What's the best title for the passage?
   A. The Importance of Communication
   B. Spoken Language Is Important than Written Language
   C. Body Language Speaks Louder than Words
   D. Non-verbal Language Is More Important than Verbal Language

Imagine you're a manager in the IT department and you're chatting one day in the corridor with a few software engineers who work for you. One of them turns to you and asks a technical question. After a moment's hesitation, with all eyes on you, you say, "I don't know," and immediately one of the other people provides the answer.

Afterward, you realize that brief episode left you feeling off-balance, as though you'd failed a test in front of the people who look to you for help.

Did you know the answer? Not really. It concerned some recent technical development, one of dozens in your field. You try to keep up, but it's just impossible. Still, it didn't feel good.

Can you see yourself reacting that way in those circumstances? Is it difficult for you to say, "I don't know" or "I'm not sure," or to ask for information and answers in the areas you manage — the areas you're supposed to know a lot about?

As the boss, are you supposed to be the one who knows the most, the smartest one, the most able? Is that what people expect of you because you're in charge?

Probably not, according to internal research conducted by Google. A short while ago, the *New York Times* reported on the results of the tech giant's Project Oxygen, during which Google analyzed employee performance reviews and feedback to identify common phrases and keywords that were used to describe highly effective managers.

Google's research yielded a list of eight managerial directives or "good behaviors," ranked in order of importance. What was least important on that list to being a good boss? — Technical expertise.

If you still think you need to be the best and brightest in your area, you probably need to rethink what makes you an effective boss. You were probably promoted because you were truly good at what you did. Perhaps you were the best in the group. Your ability to write better code, or sell more, or come up with better ideas than anyone else didn't just make you stand out — it defined you. Perhaps that's how you've always defined yourself, first at home with your brothers and sisters, then in school, in sports, and now at work.

No wonder, as the boss, it's hard to give up that way of thinking. You can tell yourself it's not your job anymore to know more than anyone else, but you probably find that need still shapes what you do and how you think. It's so ingrained that that's just how your mind works.

If so, that's a problem. As a manager and leader, such thinking can limit and even hurt you.

Ask yourself: Do you hire people who know more than you, or are better than you technically? Or do you find some fault with them in order to avoid hiring them?

Do you compete with those who work for you? Do you find yourself comparing yourself to them in terms of knowledge, skill, and proficiency? Do you find yourself arguing with them, seeking to prove that they're wrong?

Are you determined to remain as technically knowledgeable and proficient as you used to be? Most managers we know find it impossible to do their work as managers and keep abreast of every development. What if you relied on your people to help you stay on top of things?

Believing you must be the best and brightest in your group will make you a less able boss and limit your team's performance. It will also hold you back. As you advance, you'll soon reach a level where you must manage people involved in areas you know little about. What will you do then?

How much do you need to know? Enough. Enough to understand the work, enough to be able to make good judgments about it, enough to understand the common hurdles, and enough to coach or find help for those you manage when they struggle with problems.

You must be knowledgeable and bright, but those areas are not where you are most needed. Instead of being the best yourself, it's your job to make others the best, to make them productive as individuals and as part of a group. You stand on their shoulders and will rise or fall based on their work. Your group's success does not depend on your individual knowledge and intelligence; it now rests on your ability to bring out the best in others.

An executive once told us how he learned to deal with his need to be better than everyone else. He imagined himself in the shoes of J. Robert Oppenheimer, who led the Manhattan project that produced the atomic bomb in the late stages of World War II.

Without doubt, Oppenheimer was supremely bright and had made important contributions in the fields of atomic structure and astrophysics. But he gathered and managed a group of world-class geniuses. Would this group have succeeded if he had spent his time trying to prove he was the sharpest tool in that shed? Did he think they all expected him to have the answers to their problems? No, they expected him to create the conditions in which they could find the answers and all succeed together.

Ⅰ. New Words and Expressions

feedback	[ˈfiːdbæk]	(*n.*) 反馈,反馈意见
yield	[jiːld]	(*v.*) 生产,屈服
managerial	[ˌmænəˈdʒɪərɪəl]	(*a.*) 管理的
directive	[dɪˈrektɪv]	(*n.*) 指令
expertise	[ˌekspɜːˈtiːz]	(*n.*) 专门知识/技术
ingrain	[ˈɪnˈgreɪn]	(*v.*) 使根深蒂固
proficiency	[prəˈfɪʃənsɪ]	(*n.*) 熟练,精通
hurdle	[ˈhɜːdl]	(*n.*) 栏架,难关,障碍
supremely	[sʊˈpriːmlɪ]	(*adv.*) 崇高地,极度地
astrophysics	[ˌæstrəʊˈfɪzɪks]	(*n.*) 天体物理学
look to		指望,依赖,照看
expect... of		希望,期待
come up with		赶上,提出,想出
stand out		突出,脱颖而出
performance review		绩效评价
keep abreast of		了解……的最新情况
rest on		依靠
in the shoes of		处在某人的位置

Ⅱ. Fill in the blanks in the following sentences with the listed words or expressions..

expect... of	look to	come up with	stand out	yield
keep abreast of	rest on	in the shoes of	be involved in	off-balance

1. The research _______ a rich harvest.
2. Our policy should _______ our own strength.
3. The young woman _______ at the party.
4. People _______ the day when world peace will be reality.
5. We will never fail to live up to what our parents _______ us.
6. The programmer _______ a solution to the system problem.
7. You should read the newspapers to _______ current affairs.
8. The reporter is curious to know whether the official _______ the case.
9. The news that someone else had been given the job threw him momentarily _______.
10. Empathy, the ability to put oneself _______ another, is the foundation of the moral sense.

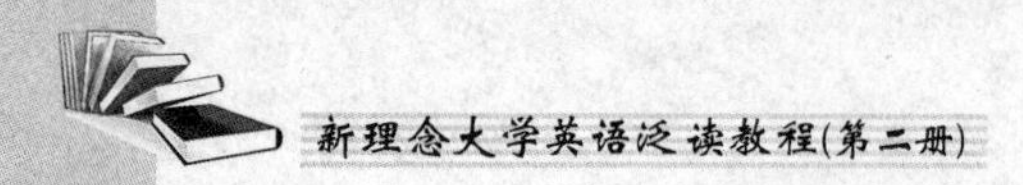

Ⅲ. There are four choices marked A. B. C. and D. in the following questions. You should decide on the best choice and mark the corresponding letter with a circle.

1. At the beginning of the article, the authors assume the case for the purpose of telling us ________.
   A. that a manager in the IT department must know everything in his field
   B. that a manager must get along well with the employees
   C. that a manager felt very embarrassed because he couldn't answer the questions
   D. that a manager doesn't have to know more about his field than the employees
2. Google carried out the research named Project Oxygen in order to ________.
   A. know what kind of managers people like
   B. know who is the smartest manager in the company
   C. analyze employee performance reviews feedback in Google
   D. find out common expressions and keywords to describe the highly effective managers
3. From the Project Oxygen, the conclusion was made that ________ is least important among the eight principals of effective managers.
   A. technical expertise
   B. managerial competence
   C. communication skills
   D. team cooperation
4. From the authors' view, it can be inferred that ________ before you are promoted.
   A. you need to know the most in your field
   B. you acquire help and support from your colleagues
   C. you have the ability to communicate well with others
   D. you need to be the best with the quality of an effective manager
5. From the authors' view, it can be inferred that ________ after you are promoted.
   A. you need to know the most in your field
   B. you acquire help and support from your colleagues
   C. you have the ability to communicate well with others
   D. you need to be the best with the quality of an effective manager
6. In the sentence "it's hard to give up <u>that way of thinking</u>", the underlined part refers to ________.
   A. you need to be the best and brightest in your area
   B. you need to keep up with the recent technical development
   C. it's not your job any more to know more than anyone else
   D. you need to be the best with the quality of an effective manager

7. It can be inferred that as a manager and leader, you ________.
   A. compete with those who work for you
   B. try to do your managerial work and keep up with every development
   C. hire people who know more than you
   D. try to remain as technically knowledgeable and proficient as you used to be
8. Which of the following is NOT the job of an effective manager?
   A. To make others the best.
   B. To try to bring out the best in others.
   C. To find all the answers to the technical problems.
   D. To make them productive as individuals and as part of a group.
9. The case of J. Robert Oppenheimer tells us that an effective manager ________.
   A. must have the most technical expertise
   B. must be the sharpest tool in that shed
   C. must have the answers to the problems
   D. must create the conditions in which others could find the answers
10. What is the main idea of the article?
    A. How to know all the answers
    B. How to be an effective manager
    C. How to be the best in your group
    D. How to be more knowledgeable than others

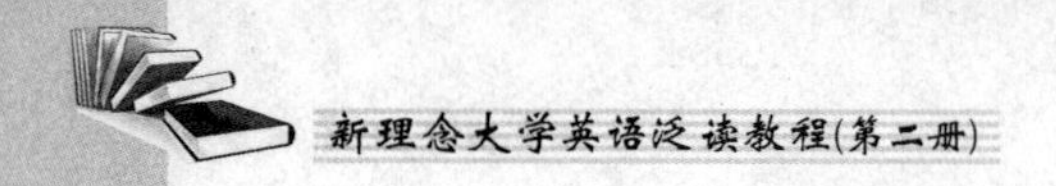

FORTUNE — A CEO who accepts an annual salary of ＄1 sends a powerful message — namely, that he or she is a team player who wants to make a sacrifice for the good of the company. True, the executive is probably receiving generous stock options on the side, but those payments depend on the corporation's success. The buck-a-year salary is a grand gesture, intended to broadcast the CEO's confidence in the future of the business.

It may also be a smokescreen. A recent study by Professors Gilberto Loureiro, Anil K. Makhija, and Dan Zhang says that, in many cases, ＄1 paydays are nothing more than public relations ploys: "We find evidence consistent with the view that ＄1 CEO salaries are a ruse hiding the rent-seeking pursuits of CEOs adopting these pay schemes," they wrote. "Thus, rather than being the sacrificial acts they are projected to be, our findings suggest that adoptions of ＄1 CEO salaries are opportunistic behavior of the wealthier, more overconfident, influential CEOs."

The ＄1 salary was pioneered by former Chrysler head Lee Iacocca, who slashed his pay in the late 1970s while the struggling car company lobbied the government for help. Other CEOs followed suit: Nelson Peltz of Wendy's/Arby's Group, Sumner Redstone of CBS, and a flurry of tech executives including Apple's Steve Jobs, Oracle's Larry Ellison, and Cisco's John Chambers.

The idea has gained even more traction in recent years, with corporate leaders like Google's Eric Schmidt and Whole Foods' John Mackey embracing it. During the financial crisis, the CEOs of automakers GM, Chrysler, and Ford all pledged to pay themselves a dollar. So did Citigroup chief Vikram Pandit, who received a single greenback in 2009 and 2010 (his asceticism was short-lived: the bank recently awarded Pandit with a multi-year pay package worth more than ＄20 million).

It's no secret that these self-abnegating chieftains often make up what they lose in salary by loading up on stock options. Loureiro and his co-authors looked at the total compensation for the fifty CEOs of publicly listed companies who made ＄1 or less between 1992 and 2005 and found that, when equity-based pay was included, they made just as much as their peers did. The ＄1 CEOs gave up a median of ＄610,000 in annual wages, but they gained more than ＄2 million in incremental options awards.

Stock compensation can be a good thing. When CEOs forgo a large salary or bonus in exchange for equity, they align their wealth with the company's success, which should motivate them to pursue growth. According to the study, this "alignment hypothesis" is the most frequently cited rationale for the $1 salary. But it isn't supported by the facts. The authors found that the companies that cut CEO pay didn't have a demonstrable need to align executive performance with results. They also didn't have significant growth opportunities or a history of rewarding leaders with options.

The alignment hypothesis is further undermined by the high rate of turnover amongst $1 CEOs. Once the salary plan was discontinued, only 48% of the CEOs who accepted the cut stayed in their positions. Between 1993 and 2001, total turnover amongst the CEOs of publicly traded companies was just 9%.

The study's authors argue that the stunt salary is better explained by the "managerial power hypothesis," which posits that $1 CEOs are pursuing their own interests. The businesses that instituted $1 salaries, they wrote, had weaker corporate governance. Only 34% had independent compensation committees, compared to an average of 67%. Power at the $1 companies was concentrated at the top; their CEOs had an average ownership stake of 10% (vs. their peers' 3.2%). Outside institutions owned just 53% of the companies (vs. 61%).

One dollar CEOs are wealthy and confident, even more so than the average executive. This further corroborates the managerial power hypothesis, the study says, because rich and brash leaders are more likely to pursue their own agendas. A whopping 30% of $1 CEOs were on the Forbes 400 list of the richest Americans, compared to an average of less than 5% among CEOs in general. They were twice as likely to be described in news reports as "optimistic" or "confident."

Confidence alone isn't cause for concern. But the study also found that $1 CEOs frequently had issues that made them vulnerable to public outrage, like pending government inquiries, corporate underperformance, and personal dilemmas. Of the 50 CEOs who accepted a $1 salary, 25 had explicit public relations risks. That could be a coincidence — but the authors doubt it: "It is not surprising that this group has chosen to adopt $1 salaries as camouflage for their benefits."

If that seems cynical, consider this: In the first year after companies announced $1 CEO salaries, they achieved returns on assets that were comparable to their peers; after that, their returns deteriorated. One-dollar companies significantly underperformed their peers in the stock market after three years.

The authors' findings are damning — but they may not be completely con-

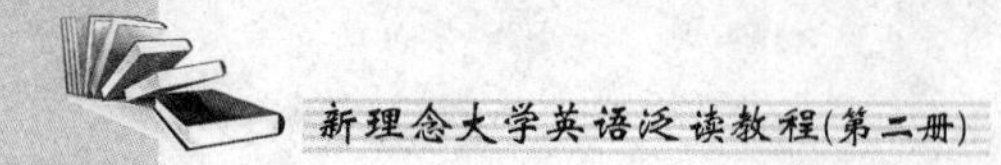

clusive, according to another recent study. This one, authored by Sophia J.W. Hamm, Michael J. Jung, and Clare Wang, looked at the different CEOs taking $ 1 salaries and found vast disparities within the group.

While the executives who received higher total paydays were likely to underperform going forward, they wrote, those who actually did receive lower pay packages were likely to achieve improved stock returns and performance. In the end, the $ 1 salary was irrelevant; what mattered was the bottom line.

Ⅰ. New Words and Expressions

buck	[bʌk]	(*n*.)(俚)美元
option	[ˈɒpʃən]	(*n*.)选择权
smokescreen	[ˈsməʊkskriːn]	(*n*.)烟幕弹,掩护
ploy	[plɔɪ]	(*n*.)计谋;计划
ruse	[ruːz]	(*n*.)策略;花招;诈术
pioneer	[ˌpaɪəˈnɪə]	(*v*.)开辟,倡导
slash	[slæʃ]	(*v*.)大幅度削减
lobby	[ˈlɒbɪ]	(*v*.)对……进行游说
traction	[ˈtrækʃən]	(*n*.)牵引,牵引力;追捧
embrace	[ɪmˈbreɪs]	(*v*.)接受,赞同
greenback	[ˈgriːnbæk]	(*n*.)美元纸币;美钞
asceticism	[əˈsetɪsɪzəm]	(*n*.)苦行,禁欲主义
abnegate	[ˈæbnɪgeɪt]	(*v*.)放弃,舍弃,克制
chieftain	[ˈtʃiːftən]	(*n*.)酋长,首领
equity	[ˈekwɪtɪ]	(*n*.)股份
peer	[pɪə]	(*n*.)同等的人,同行,同僚
median	[ˈmiːdjən]	(*n*.)中位数,中值,公路隔离带
incremental	[ɪnkrɪˈməntl]	(*a*.)增加的,增量的
forgo	[fɔːˈgəʊ]	(*v*.)放弃,对……断念
align	[əˈlaɪn]	(*v*.)使一致,使成一行
rationale	[ˌræʃəˈnɑːl]	(*n*.)基本原理,基础理论
demonstrable	[ˈdemənstrəbl]	(*a*.)可论证的,明显的
undermine	[ˌʌndəˈmaɪn]	(*v*.)削弱
stunt	[stʌnt]	(*n*.)特技,噱头
posit	[ˈpɒzɪt]	(*v*.)假定
institute	[ˈɪnstɪtjuːt]	(*v*.)开始,制定,创立
stake	[steɪk]	(*n*.)赌注,利害关系,股票
corroborate	[kəˈrɒbəreɪt]	(*v*.)确证,证实
brash	[bræʃ]	(*a*.)盛气凌人的,傲慢无礼的

whopping	[ˈwɒpɪŋ]	(*a*.)巨大的,天大的
vulnerable	[ˈvʌlnərəbl]	(*a*.)易受伤害的,脆弱的
outrage	[ˈaʊtreɪdʒ]	(*n*.)暴行,愤怒,义愤
pending	[ˈpendɪŋ]	(*a*.)待定的,即将来临的
explicit	[ɪksˈplɪsɪt]	(*a*.)明确的,清晰的
camouflage	[ˈkæməˌflɑːʒ]	(*n*.)伪装,掩饰
cynical	[ˈsɪnɪkəl]	(*a*.)愤世嫉俗的,悲观的
deteriorate	[dɪˈtɪərɪəreɪt]	(*v*.)恶化,变质,衰退
disparity	[dɪsˈpærɪtɪ]	(*n*.)不一致
a grand gesture		故作豪爽的举动
on the side		暗地里
follow suit		纷纷效仿
a flurry of		一阵,大批
make up for		补偿
load up on		大量摄入,买进,囤积
alignment hypothesis		相关联假说

Ⅱ. Fill in the blanks in the following sentences with the listed words or expressions.

a grand gesture	on the side	follow suit	make up for	vulnerable
load up on	be likely to	a flurry of	deteriorate	slash

1. I was ________ Tom in the discussion.
2. He tried hard to ________ the lose time.
3. The potato is ________ to several pests.
4. The government ________ back its spending.
5. He goes to bed and she ________ after a few minutes.
6. Some criminals ________ offend again when they are released.
7. ________ excitement went round the crowd as the film star arrived.
8. People ________ bottled water because of water pollution.
9. Make ________, ie a generous act intended to make a great impression.
10. Relations between the two countries ________ sharply in recent week.

Ⅲ. There are four choices marked A. B. C. and D. in the following questions. You should decide on the best choice and mark the corresponding letter with a circle.

1. The intension of adopting $ 1 salaries is to ________.

   A. make sacrifice for the benefit of the company

   B. spread the CEO's confidence to the public

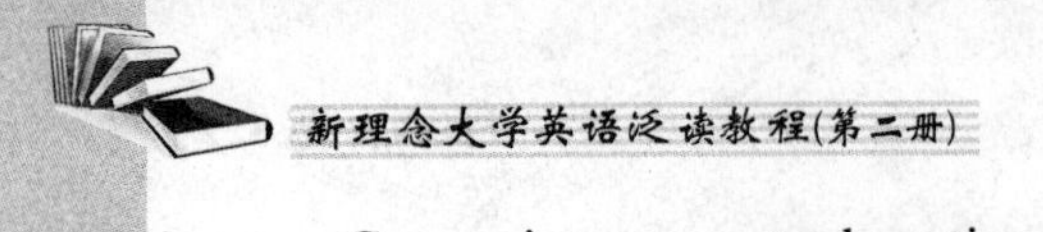

C. receive more stock options on the side

D. get less salary because of the poor performance

2. The $1 salary for CEO was first started by ________.

A. Steve Jobs B. John Chambers

C. Sumner Redstone D. Lee Iacocca

3. What attitude does the author take to the $1 CEO?

A. Negative. B. Supportive.

C. Sarcastic. D. Skeptical.

4. What can we infer from the last sentence in the last paragraph "In the end, the $1 salary was irrelevant; what mattered was the bottom line."?

A. It was considerably unfair to pay CEOs only $1.

B. No CEOs receive their salaries below one dollar.

C. The most importance for the CEOs is loyalty.

D. The salaries for the CEOs should be greatly improved.

5. "Alignment hypothesis" implies that ________.

A. the CEOs' returns is supposed to be in proportion to the corporate performance

B. the CEOs' salaries should have a little to do with the company's success

C. the company's success should encourage the CEOs to pursue more returns

D. the CEOs should connect their wealth with the company's success

6. Here "It" in the first sentence of the second paragraph refers to ________.

A. $1 salary B. A $1 CEO

C. CEO's confidence D. the recent study

7. Which of the following statements is NOT true based on the study?

A. The $1 CEOs make up their loss in salary by receiving stock options.

B. All the $1 CEOs connected their salaries with actual performance.

C. The $1 CEOs gain more interests because of weaker corporate governance.

D. The $1 CEO has had much influence on other executives in recent years.

8. The $1 CEOs often had the following problems according to the study except ________.

A. pending government inquiries

B. personal dilemmas

C. overconfidence

D. corporate underperformance

9. Which of the following statements is true based on the study?

A. 52% of CEOs didn't accept the pay cut and left their positions.

B. Businesses adopting $1 salaries had independent compensation committees.

C. The $1 CEOs had fewer stock options than their peers.

D. About 35% of CEOs were on the Forbes 400 list of the richest Americans.

10. The $1 CEOs are more confident and wealthy than the average executives because ________.

A. they have even stronger managerial power

B. they are frequently pursuing their own interests

C. they are more likely to pursue their own agendas

D. they are receiving more salaries and awards

Passage 29

Engaging in foreign direct investment as a multinational enterprise has advantages as well as disadvantages in the areas of employing host country locals for employees, the location that the firm decides on, exchange rate fluctuations, and convertibility of currency.

First, the main advantage of using a host country local is that they are familiar with the local environment, language, culture, and customs. This may be good because they would require less training. Because they are locals, they may be able to be productive right away; they do not need time to adapt to the local environment, where someone coming from the home country would need this adaptation period. If you hire a host country local into an upper level management position, it may enhance your company's image in the host country. This person may be vital to establishing important relationships with customers, clients, employees, and the public. Host country locals are usually cheaper to employ than an expatriate due to cheaper labor costs overseas.

Along with the advantages of using host country locals, there are also some disadvantages. It is important when hiring a host country local, that they are loyal to the company. Sometimes, their loyalty may be with their country, not with the company. Due to lack of education, and differing levels of the economy, it may be quite difficult to find someone from the host country who is qualified to perform the duties that the position may require. This may also make it more difficult to assess their abilities. Although they may be quite capable of performing certain tasks in their country, they may not be able to perform adequately the differing levels of technologies and education. Host country locals may not understand the typical corporate culture of US or other home country companies; they may do things very differently in their companies. They may not be able to communicate effectively with the home office in the domestic market, they may not know the other language, or there may be certain parts of the language that do not translate into the other language the way that it was meant. A host country local may not be mobile because of family in or around the area. Some cultures that have strong family values ensure that the family's needs come before the needs of the corporation. A firm must also be careful when hiring a host country local to ensure that they do not have ulterior motives. A local may be hired that is currently employed with the competition, and they are serving as a spy and selling the

secrets of the foreign firm, keeping their loyalty with their country. A firm may have to spend more money on training them to get them acquainted with the customary corporate culture of the firm, language training, and so on.

The advantages of the location that the firm chooses in other countries could be to lower the basic costs of the goods and services provided to customers. There may be access to critical supplies, natural resources, and lower labor costs. The firm must be managed effectively in order to gain the full benefits of the advantages of the location chosen.

Some factors that affect multinational enterprises are exchange rate fluctuations and the convertibility of the currency. When exporting to or importing from another country, the export terms must be established. These may include which country's currency will be used, when the payment is made, and the shipping terms. A firm should be sure to make the export and receive payment relatively quickly. If the exchange rate happens to fluctuate during that period, they may lose money. Money may also be gained from exchange rate fluctuations. A firm can protect itself by stating a certain payment amount no matter what the current exchange rate is at that time. With the convertibility of currency concern, when trading with a country with soft currency that is hard to exchange, barter, or counter trade may be considered for terms of payment instead. This could also prevent loss from exchange rate fluctuations if a certain amount of goods is agreed upon for the trade or payment.

Multinational enterprises may help the economy of the host country. They may employ locals for positions in the firm or in production plants if they also manufacture the products in the same country. It may also help because it will create more taxes for the foreign government. The firm may have to pay extra taxes or duties for certain products, but will have to pay taxes to the government of the host country. However, the presence of another firm will cause more competition for the local businesses. It could also put local firms out of business.

Ⅰ. New Words and Expressions

multinational	[ˈmʌltɪˈnæʃənl]	(*a.*) 多国的,多种国籍的
enterprise	[ˈentəpraɪz]	(*n.*) 企业
fluctuation	[ˌflʌktjʊˈeɪʃən]	(*n.*) 波动
convertibility	[kənˌvɜːtəˈbɪlɪtɪ]	(*n.*) 可兑换性
currency	[ˈkʌrənsɪ]	(*n.*) 货币,流通
enhance	[ɪnˈhɑːns]	(*v.*) 提高,增加,加强
expatriate	[eksˈpætrɪeɪt]	(*n.*) 侨民,移居外国者
customary	[ˈkʌstəmərɪ]	(*a.*) 习惯的,惯例的
assess	[əˈses]	(*v.*) 评定,评估,估算

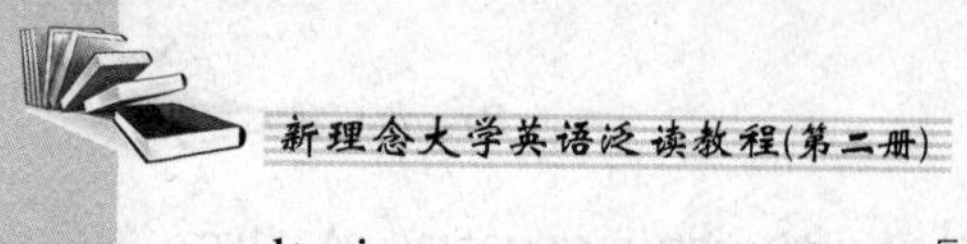

ulterior	[ʌlˈtɪərɪə]	(*a.*)不可告人的,隐蔽的
access	[ˈækses]	(*n.*)入口,通道
engage in		从事……活动
host country		东道国
home country		本国
exchange rate		汇率
home office		公司本部
put... out of business		使……退出市场

Ⅱ. Fill in the blanks in the following sentences with the listed words or expressions.

engage in	put... out of business	enhance	assess	fluctuation
as well as	be familiar with	adapt to	along with	no matter what

1. She came to dinner ______ her boyfriend.
2. Is it wise to ______ active sports at your age?
3. He shared in my sorrows ______ in my joys.
4. ______ happened, I will not say a word.
5. She looked at the house and ______ its market value.
6. These styles can ______ suit individual tastes.
7. The decision was affected by his ______ of mood.
8. The intimacy of the room ______ by its warm colors.
9. Most people ______ the idea that all matter consist of atoms.
10. If the money was not paid promptly, the gangsters would quickly ______ a man ______ by destroying his shop.

Ⅲ. There are four choices marked A. B. C. and D. in the following questions. You should decide on the best choice and mark the corresponding letter with a circle.

1. The main idea of the article is ______.
   A. the comparisons between host country and home country
   B. advantages and disadvantages of multinational enterprises
   C. how to establish the multinational enterprises
   D. introduction to foreign exchange and currency
2. The factors on the foreign direct investment of the multinational enterprises are as follows except ______.
   A. host country's support　　B. choice of location
   C. exchange rate fluctuations　　D. convertibility of currency
3. The reasons for the multinational enterprise using host country locals are as fol-

lows except ________.

A. they are familiar with the local environment, language, culture, and customs

B. they may enhance your company's image in the host country

C. they can spend a little time to adapt to the local environment

D. they are usually cheaper to employ due to cheaper labor costs overseas

4. From the author's view, ________ is very important when the multinational enterprises employ locals.

A. the family values
B. the education background
C. the labor cost
D. the loyalty

5. It may be quite difficult to find someone from the host country qualified for some positions provided by a multinational enterprise because of ________.

A. the typical corporate culture of US

B. the degree of loyalty

C. lack of education and differing levels of the economy

D. the poor ability

6. Host country locals may not be mobile because ________.

A. they love the jobs provided

B. they have strong family values

C. they have no opportunity for job-hopping

D. their family is far away

7. Which of the following statements is NOT true based on the third paragraph?

A. Some host country locals may have loyalty only with their country.

B. A firm needn't spend any money on training the host country locals.

C. Some host country locals place the family's needs before those of the corporation.

D. Some host country locals may not be able to communicate effectively with the home office.

8. A multinational enterprise chooses a location for its firm because of the following except ________.

A. critical supplies
B. natural resources
C. lower labor costs
D. better services

9. In order to prevent loss, a firm should set up the following terms except ________.

A. the terms of shipment
B. the terms of payment
C. the rate of exchange
D. the choice of currency

10. The last paragraph tells us that multinational enterprises ________.

A. may help the economy of the host country

B. may cause more competition for the local businesses

C. may put local firms out of business

D. all the above

Passage 30

There are some unique problems in international trade and companies doing business overseas must be aware of them. In particular, there include (a) cultural problems, (b) monetary conversion, and (c) trade barriers.

When companies do business overseas, they come in contact with people from different cultures. These individuals often speak a different language and have their own particular custom and manners. These differences can create problems.

For example, in France, business meetings begin promptly at the designated time and everyone is expected to be there. Foreign business people who are late are often left outside to cool their heels as a means of letting them know the importance of promptness. Unless one is aware of such expected behaviors he may end up insulting the people with whom he hopes to establish trade relations.

A second traditional problem is that of monetary conversion. For example, if a transaction is conducted with Russia, payment may be made in rubles. Of course, this currency is of little value to the American firm. It is, therefore, necessary to convert the foreign currency to American dollars. How much are these Russian rubles worth in terms of dollars? This conversion rate is determined by every market, where the currencies of countries are bought and sold. Thus there is an established rate, although it will often fluctuate from day to day. For example, the ruble may be worth \$0.75 on Monday and \$0.72 on Tuesday because of an announced wheat shortage in Russia. In addition, there is the dilemma associated with converting at \$0.72. Some financial institutions may be unwilling to pay this price, feeling that the ruble will sink much lower over the next week. As a result, conversion may finally come at \$0.69. These "losses" must be accepted by the company as one of the costs of doing business overseas.

A third unique problem is trade barriers. For one reason or another, all countries impose trade barriers on certain goods crossing their borders. Some trade barriers are directly related to exports. For example, the United States permits strategic military material to be shipped abroad only after government permission has been obtained. Most trade barriers, however, are designed to restrict imports. Two of the most common import barriers are quotas and tariffs.

A quota is a quantitative restriction that is expressed in terms of either physical quantity or value. For example, a quota that states that no more than 50,000 Class A widgets may be imported from Europe each year is a restriction stated in terms of physical quantity. Meanwhile, a quota that restricts the importation of a certain type of Japanese glassware to no more than $1 million worth a year is stated in terms of value.

A tariff is a duty or fee levied on goods being imported into the country. These tariffs can be of two types: revenue or protective. A revenue tariff is designed to raise money for the government. These tariffs are usually low, often amounting to less than twenty-five cents per item or pound. A protective tariff is designed to discourage foreign businesses from shipping certain goods into the country. The basic reason for a protective tariff is to keep out goods that will undersell products made in the home country. For this reason, protective tariffs are often very high, thus forcing the foreign business to raise its prices to cover the tariff.

Tariff duties are of three types: specific, ad valorem, and compound. Specific duties are levied at the rate of so much per unit or pound. For example, the specific duty on one product might be $10 per unit, while on another it might be 25c per pound.

Ad valorem duties are levied on the basis of the product's value. For example, an ad valorem duty of 7 percent on a particular product valued at $100 would result in a $7 tariff.

Compound duties are a combination of specific and ad valorem duties. One example is suits. In the past the duty on them has been $37\frac{1}{2}$c per pound and 21 percent ad valorem.

Ⅰ. New Words and Expressions

conversion	[kənˈvɜːʃən]	(*n.*) 兑换,转变
promptness	[prɒmptnɪs]	(*n.*) 迅速及时
insult	[ˈɪnsʌlt]	(*v.*) 侮辱,辱骂,凌辱
designate	[ˈdezɪgneɪt]	(*v.*) 指定,标出
ruble	[ˈruːbl]	(*n.*) 卢布(俄罗斯货币单位)
dilemma	[dɪˈlemə]	(*n.*) (进退两难的)窘境,困境
quota	[ˈkwəʊtə]	(*n.*) 限额,定量
quantitative	[ˈkwɒntɪtətɪv]	(*a.*) 数量的
widget	[ˈwɪdʒɪt]	(*n.*) 典型小产品
revenue	[ˈrevɪnjuː]	(*n.*) (国家的)税收,收入
undersell	[ˌʌndəˈsel]	(*v.*) 以低于……价格出售
ad valorem	[ˈædvəˈlɔːrem]	(*a.*) 按照价格的

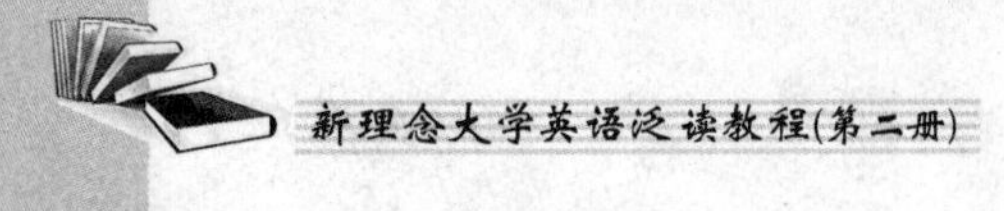

cool one's heels	久等，空等
designated time	约定时间
impose... on	把……强加于
amount to	总计，等于
discourage... from	阻拦
revenue tariff	财政关税
protective tariff	保护性关税

Ⅱ. Fill in the blanks in the following sentences with the listed words or expressions.

discourage... from	cool one's heels	impose... on	amount to	dilemma
come in contact with	be aware of	in terms of	end up	undersell

1. I ________ her by telephone.
2. We ________ the problem beforehand.
3. It is difficult to express it ________ science.
4. New taxes ________ wines and spirits.
5. His parents ________ him ________ joining the air force.
6. Did you know that Stone ________ marrying his secretary?
7. This store can ________ other stores because it sells by cash.
8. She was in a ________ as to whether to stay at school or get a job.
9. Let him ________ for a while: that'll teach him to be impolite.
10. The business done this month ________ ten thousand dollars as against eight thousand dollars last month.

Ⅲ. There are four choices marked A. B. C. and D. in the following questions. You should decide on the best choice and mark the corresponding letter with a circle.

1. This article mainly discusses the following problems except ________.
   A. trade barriers　　B. cultural problems
   C. monetary conversion　　D. importance of promptness
2. Cultural problems refer to the following except ________.
   A. different languages　　B. different customs
   C. different manners　　D. different hobbies
3. In France, tardy business people ________.
   A. are often insulted
   B. often suffer from coldness
   C. are often left outdoors waiting
   D. are often asked to polish their shoes

4. According to the passage, conversion rates ________.
   A. are always changing
   B. are determined by financial institutions
   C. are agreed upon by two trading countries
   D. vary from day to day
5. From the example in paragraph 4, it can be inferred that ________.
   A. American business persons don't like Russian rubles
   B. one may run into some risks while doing international trade
   C. Russian rubles are becoming more and more worthless
   D. one should conduct transactions in dollars
6. Which of the following doesn't belong to the tariff duties?
   A. Specific duties. B. Ad valorem duties.
   C. Compound duties. D. Importing quotas.
7. A country keeps foreign businesses from shipping certain goods in not by ________.
   A. levying revenue tariff B. levying protective tariff
   C. restricting quotas D. imposing high duties
8. Who may be interested in this article?
   A. Professors of economics. B. Business officers.
   C. Beginners of business. D. Business people.
9. Which of the following statements is true according to the passage?
   A. If you are doing business in France, you must wait outside until someone calls you in.
   B. Monetary conversion rates are established by America.
   C. Trade barriers are imposed on certain goods transported in and out of a country.
   D. A protective tariff is levied to raise money for the government.
10. The main idea of the passage would be ________.
    A. How to Succeed in International Trade
    B. Monetary Conversion
    C. Trade Barriers
    D. Unique Problems in International Trade

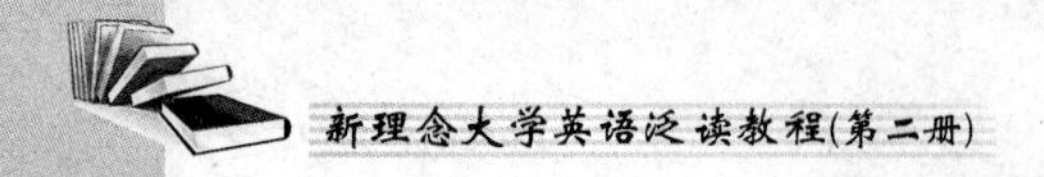

Passage 31

Financial crisis is a situation where the capital chain of financial system breaks. Superficially, there is not enough currency in an economic system. Actually, the reason is that the circulation of currency is not good. Superficially, companies or merchants do not have funds or lack funds and cannot get loans from banks. Money can not flow freely. These have led to the fact that companies go bankrupt, or reduce their size of production, or even slow down their trade expansion. The shrinkage in production and manufacturing industry can be seen directly from less orders and substantially reduced procurement volume of importers. On the side of retailers, they sell their inventory as soon as possible, sell at discounted prices to recover cash, and control inventory or even keep zero inventory.

As the financial turbulence hit normal trade circulation, it results in big fluctuations of the exchange rate and depreciation of currency. As a result, the procurement cost will be higher. Trade is hit severely by both increase of purchasing cost and decrease of purchasing power. At this time, merchants need inexpensive goods more than ever before to compensate the loss caused by the financial shock. If the sales volume of low-price goods soars in one country or region, trade friction between trading countries will come forth, without exception during the time of financial crisis. If there are too many imported goods in a country, this will directly lead to the rise of trade protectionism and more trade barriers that violate the principle of free and fair trade. In the previous crises, countries set trade barriers to hold back low-price goods from exporters, with the purpose to protect its local industries from being hit, to lower unemployment rate, and to avoid spread of crisis to a larger scope. Such measures based on individualism will conversely further the depression of global economy. The measures, aimed at protecting domestic or local companies, are not good for recovery from a crisis. It will take longer for the economy to recover when it falls to the bottom.

In this financial crisis, headlines of newspaper report that governments have invested a huge amount of money to rescue the market and central banks have greatly lowered interest rate consecutively to stimulate economy, drive consumption, avoid long-time economic depression, abate financial fluctuation and reduce the huge damage brought about by the crisis. At this very moment, it is both a risk and an opportunity for international trade. Risk means that

companies and banks may go bankrupt at any time while opportunity means that consumers of the world need more low-price goods. The bull commodity market of the world has ended. It seems to tell us that people need to have more inexpensive goods with good quality when facing lack of money. Under such an economic environment, how do companies on the trade chain face the situation? After each crisis, there are cheap shares and assets everywhere. It is perfect time for companies to reconstruct, merge and acquire. Those companies with abundant cash flow will expand and develop themselves at this time. Exporters shall seize opportunities to cooperate with international brand companies. Strength of low cost will play a more important role in future trade.

Ⅰ. New Words and Expressions

circulation	[ˌsɜːkjʊˈleɪʃən]	(*n*.) 流通,发行量
bankrupt	[ˈbæŋkrʌpt]	(*a*.) 破产的
shrinkage	[ˈʃrɪŋkɪdʒ]	(*n*.) 收缩
inventory	[ˈɪnvəntərɪ]	(*n*.) 库存,存货
turbulence	[ˈtɜːbjʊləns]	(*n*.) 动荡,骚乱
depreciation	[dɪˌpriːʃɪˈeɪʃən]	(*n*.) 贬值
compensate	[ˈkɒmpenseɪt]	(*v*.) 补偿
violate	[ˈvaɪəleɪt]	(*v*.) 违反
depression	[dɪˈpreʃən]	(*n*.) 萧条,不景气
consecutively	[kənˈsekjʊtɪvlɪ]	(*adv*.) 连续地
abate	[əˈbeɪt]	(*v*.) 减轻,缓和
discounted price		折扣价
purchasing power		购买力
trade friction		贸易摩擦
bull market		牛市

Ⅱ. Fill in the blanks in the following sentences with the listed words or expressions.

play a role in	superficially	bankrupt	compensate	abate
as a result	result in	come forth	hold back	soar

1. He was late ________ of the snow.
2. She smiled and could not ________ tears of joy.
3. Internet ________ very important ________ modern life.
4. The ship waited in the harbour until the storm ________.
5. I've heard whispers that the firm is likely to go ________.
6. ________, such uses look a lot like playing a video game.

7. The reform ________ tremendous change in our country.
8. She ________ by the insurance company for her injuries.
9. Certainly, more and more new plastics will ________ before long.
10. The merchants there made a ring on the sugar market and prices ________ tremendously.

Ⅲ. There are four choices marked A. B. C. and D. in the following questions. You should decide on the best choice and mark the corresponding letter with a circle.

1. In fact during the time of financial crisis, ________.
   A. there is not enough currency in an economic system
   B. companies or merchants do not have funds or lack funds
   C. companies go bankrupt, or reduce their size of production
   D. companies have to get loans from banks in order to survive
2. When the financial turbulence hits normal trade circulation, which of the following is NOT one of the possible consequences?
   A. Big fluctuation of exchange rate.
   B. Inexpensive goods.
   C. Higher procurement cost.
   D. Depreciation of currency.
3. If the sales volume of low-price goods soars in one country or region in the financial crisis, ________.
   A. trade friction between trading countries will sometimes come forth
   B. it will lead to the rise of trade protectionism and more trade barriers
   C. merchants can seize opportunities to buy the low-price goods to compensate the loss caused by the crisis
   D. it will go against the principle of free and fair trade
4. What can we learn from the previous crises?
   A. Local industries can be protected from being hit by holding back low-price goods from exporters.
   B. Less low-price goods from exporters, lower unemployment rate.
   C. We should not take any measures during crisis since they would further the depression of global economy anyway.
   D. The measures used to protect domestic or local companies usually do little to help the situation and in fact exacerbated problems.
5. What can be inferred from the passage?
   A. The lessons learned from protectionism during the Depression mean that it will be very foolish to implement such measures again.
   B. International trade has proven immune to the pressures of the global econom-

ic slowdown.

C. Imports and exports should start to see recovery and even growth by the end of the year.

D. Governments have invested a huge amount of money to rescue the market in this crisis, instead of resorting to protectionism to help their ailing economy.

6. Which is NOT true for the retailers to sell their inventory?

A. To sell at discounted prices to recover cash.

B. To control inventory.

C. To keep zero inventory.

D. To get more profits.

7. What will the financial turbulence lead to when it hit normal trade circulation?

A. It results in big fluctuations of the exchange rate and depreciation of currency.

B. The procurement cost will be higher.

C. Trade is hit severely by both increase of purchasing cost and decrease of purchasing power.

D. All of above.

8. What will the phenomenon lead to if there are too many imported goods in a country?

A. It results the rise of trade protectionism and more trade barriers that violate the principle of free and fair trade.

B. It leads to the free and fair trade.

C. It is convenient for the customers to buy more imported goods.

D. All of above.

9. Why does the writer say that it is the perfect time for the companies to reconstruct, merge and acquire?

A. Because those companies with abundant cash flow will expand and develop themselves at this time.

B. Exporters shall seize opportunities to cooperate with international brand companies.

C. Strength of low cost will play a more important role in future trade.

D. All of above.

10. Which of the following is true?

A. Financial crisis is a situation where the capital chain of financial system cuts off.

B. The reason of the financial crisis is the circulation of the currency is good.

C. The measures, aimed at protecting domestic or local companies, are good for recovery from a crisis.

D. It will not take longer for the economy to recover when it falls to the bottom.

Passage 32

Mergers and acquisitions continue apace in spite of an alarming failure rate and evidence that they often fail to benefit shareholders, writes Michael Skapinker.

The collapse of the planned Deutsche-Dresdner Bank merger tarnished the reputation of both parties. Deutsche Bank's management was exposed as dividend and confused. But even if the takeover had gone ahead, it would probably still have claimed its victims. Most completed takeovers damage one party — the company making the acquisition.

A long list of studies have all reached the same conclusion: the majority of takeovers damage the interests of the shareholders of the acquiring company. They do, however, often reward the shareholders of the acquired company, who receive more for their shares than they were worth before the takeover was announced. Mark Sirower, visiting professor at New York University, says surveys have repeatedly shown that about 65 percent of mergers fail to benefit acquiring companies, whose shares subsequently underperform their sector.

Why do so many mergers and acquisitions fail to benefit shareholders? Colin Price, a partner at McKinsey, the management consultants, who specializes in mergers and acquisitions, says the majority of failed mergers suffer from poor implementation. And in about half of those, senior management failed to take account of the different cultures of the companies involved.

Melding corporate cultures takes time, which senior management does not have after a merger, Mr. Price says. "Most mergers are based on the idea of 'let's increase revenues', but you have to have a functioning management team to manage that process. The nature of the problem is not so much that there's open warfare between the two sides. It's that the cultures don't meld quickly enough to take advantage of the opportunities. In the meantime the marketplace has moved on."

Many consultants refer to how little time companies spend before a merger thinking about whether their organizations are compatible. The benefits of mergers are usually couched in financial or commercial terms: cost-savings can be made or the two sides have complementary businesses that will allow them to increase revenues.

Mergers are about compatibility, which means agreeing whose values will

prevail and who will be the dominant partner. So it is no accident that managers as well as journalists reach for marriage metaphors in describing them. Merging companies are said to "tie the knot". When mergers are called off, the two companies fail to "make it up the aisle" or their relationship remains "unconsummated". Yet the metaphor fails to convey the scale of risk companies run when they launch acquisitions or mergers. Even in countries with high divorce rates, marriages have a better success rate than mergers.

Mark Sirower asks why managers should pay a premium to make an acquisition when their shareholders could invest in the target company themselves. Mr. Sirower denies he is saying companies should never make acquisitions. If 65 percent of mergers fail to benefit shareholders, 35 percent are successful.

How can acquirers try to ensure they are among the successful minority? Ken Favaro, managing partner of Marakon, a consultancy which has worked for Coca-Cola, Lloyds TSB and Boeing, suggests, two conditions for success. The first is to define what success means. "The combined entities have to deliver better returns to the shareholders than they would separately. It's amazing how often that's not the pre-agreed measure of success," Mr. Favaro says.

Second, merging companies need to decide in advance which partner's way of doing things will prevail. "Mergers of equals can be so dangerous because it is not clear who is in charge," Mr. Favaro says. Mr. Sirower adds that managers need to ask what advantages they will bring to the acquired company that competitors will find difficult to replicate.

Managers need to remember that competitors are not going to hang around waiting for them to improve the performance of their new acquisition. Announcing a takeover will have alerted competitors to the acquiring company's strategy. Given how heavily the odds are stacked against successful mergers, managers should consider whether their time and the shareholders' money would not be better employed elsewhere.

Ⅰ. New Words and Expressions

merger	[ˈmɜːdʒə]	(*n.*) 兼并
acquisition	[ˌækwɪˈzɪʃən]	(*n.*) 收购
apace	[əˈpeɪs]	(*adv.*) 急速地；飞快地
shareholder	[ˈʃeəˌhəuldə]	(*n.*) 股东；股票持有人
collapse	[kəˈlæps]	(*n.*) 失败
tarnish	[ˈtɑːnɪʃ]	(*v.*) 使……失去光泽
takeover	[ˈteɪkˌəuvə]	(*n.*) 收购；接管
underperform	[ˌʌndəpəˈfɔːm]	(*v.*) 表现不佳
consultant	[kənˈsʌltənt]	(*n.*) 顾问，咨询者
meld	[meld]	(*v.*) 结合；融合

organisation	[ˌɔːgənaɪˈzeɪʃən]	(*n.*) 组织,团体
couch	[kaʊtʃ]	(*v.*) 表达,表述
compatibility	[kəmˌpætəˈbɪlətɪ]	(*n.*) 相容性
prevail	[prɪˈveɪl]	(*v.*) 盛行,流行
unconsummated	[ˌʌnˈkɒnsəmeɪtɪd]	(*a.*) 未实现的;未完成的
aisle	[aɪl]	(*n.*) 通道,走道;侧廊
entity	[ˈentətɪ]	(*n.*) 实体;存在;本质
the odds		可能性;机会

Ⅱ. Fill in the blanks in the following sentences with the listed words or expressions.

take account of	in spite of	call off	the odds	prevail
take one's time	suffer from	refer to	hang around	apace

1. ________ are that it will rain.
2. We should also ________ difficulties.
3. Misty weather ________ in this part of the country.
4. He does not wear a coat ________ the cool weather.
5. The business has been growing ________ for the last year.
6. The president's visit ________ at the eleventh hour.
7. Most of the important cities of the world ________ traffic jam.
8. Usually the discovery of the new continent ________ Columbus.
9. It is better to ________ at this job than to hurry and make mistakes.
10. The principal warned the students not to ________ the corner drugstore after school.

Ⅲ. There are four choices marked A. B. C. and D. in the following questions. You should decide on the best choice and mark the corresponding letter with a circle.

1. What is the main idea of the passage?
   A. Mergers and acquisitions continue apace in spite of an alarming failure rate and evidence that they often fail to benefit shareholders.
   B. The benefits of the mergers are usually couched in financial or commercial terms.
   C. Acquirers can try to ensure they are among the successful minority.
   D. Show the reasons why mergers and acquisitions fail to benefit shareholders.
2. If a merger suffers from poor implementation, what can be inferred?
   A. It is badly planned.
   B. It is badly put into practice.

C. It is tightly budgeted.

D. It is badly managed.

3. If two organizations are compatible, what can be inferred?

A. They are able to have a good relationship with each other.

B. They are able to be divided into smaller groups.

C. They are able to keep stable in the competitive market.

D. They are able to be closely linked with each other.

4. If you have complementary businesses, what can be inferred?

A. They are business that offer different products in the same range.

B. They are business that offer free products.

C. They are business that offer duplicate products.

D. They are business that offer various products.

5. Which of the following is NOT true?

A. Most mergers are based on the idea of "let's increase revenues".

B. Many consultants refer to how little time companies spend before a merger thinking about whether their organizations are compatible.

C. Managers need to remember that competitors are going to hang around waiting for them to improve the performance of their new acquisition.

D. Managers should consider whether their time and the shareholders' money would not be better employed elsewhere.

6. What is the author's attitude towards mergers and acquisitions?

A. Approving. B. Confused.

C. Negative. D. Biased.

7. Which of the following is true?

A. The majority of takeovers damage the interests of the shareholder of the acquired company.

B. Senior management has taken account of the different cultures of the companies involved.

C. Mergers are about compatibility, which means agreeing whose values will prevail and who will be the dominant partner.

D. None is right.

8. According to the article, whose shareholders benefit most in a takeover?

A. Those of the acquiring company.

B. Those of the one that is being acquired.

C. Those of the company which is concerned.

D. Those of the company which is not concerned.

9. Why do so many mergers fail, according to the article?

A. The majority of failed mergers suffer from poor implementation.

B. Senior management failed to take account of the different cultures of the

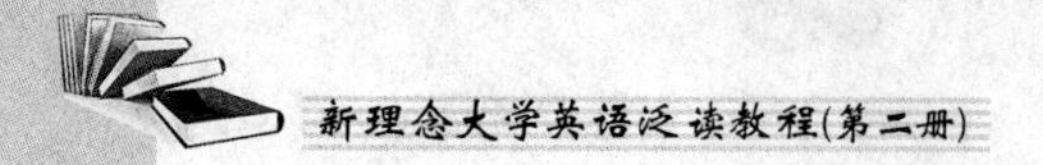

companies involved.

C. It's that the cultures don't meld quickly enough to take advantage of the opportunities.

D. All of above.

10. What do acquiring companies need to do to ensure success?

A. They should define what success is.

B. Merging companies need to decide in advance which partner's way of doing things will prevail.

C. Both A and B.

D. Melding corporate cultures takes time.

Modern US History of International Marketing

Marketing abroad is not a recent phenomenon. In fact, well-established trade routes existed three or four thousand years before the birth of Christ. Modern international marketing, however, can arguably be traced to the 1920s, when liberal international trading was halted by worldwide isolationism and increased barriers to trade. The United States furthered this trend by passing the Smoot-Hawley Tariff Act of 1930, raising the average U.S. tariff on imported goods from 33 to 53 cents. Other countries throughout the world imposed similar tariffs in response to the United States' actions, and by 1932 the volume of world trade fell by more than 40 percent. These protectionist activities continued throughout the 1930s, and the Great Depression, to which many say protectionism substantially contributed, was deeper and more widespread than any other depression in modern history. Furthermore, according to the United Nations, this protectionism undermined the standard of living of people all over the world and set the stage for the extreme military buildup that led to World War II.

One result of the Great Depression and World War II was strengthened political will to end protectionist policies and to limit government interference in international trade. Thus, by 1944 representative countries attending the Bretton Woods Conference established the basic organizational setting for the post-war economy, designed to further macroeconomic stability. Specifically, the framework that arose created three organizations: the International Trade Organization (ITO), the World Bank, and the International Monetary Fund (IMF).

Although negotiations undertaken for the ITO proved unsuccessful, the United States proposed that the commercial policy provisions that were originally included in the ITO agreements should be temporarily incorporated into the General Agreement on Tariffs and Trade (GATT). In 1947, 23 countries agreed to a set of tariff reductions codified in GATT. Although GATT was at first intended as a temporary measure, because ITO was never ratified, it became the main instrument for international trade regulation. GATT was succeeded by the World Trade Organization (WTO), which was established in January 1995 after GATT officially ended in April 1994. The WTO's main function has been to resolve trade disputes, and it developed procedures for handling

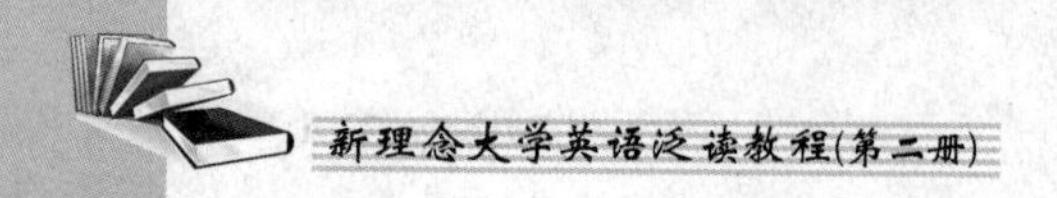

trade disputes that were much improved over the GATT procedures. In its first 18 months the WTO settled more than 50 trade disputes.

In the 1960s and 1970s, world trading patterns began to change. While the United States remained a dominant player in international trade, other less developed countries began to manufacture their own products. Furthermore, the United States became more reliant than ever on imported goods. For example, by 1982 one in four cars sold in the United States was foreign-made and more than 40 percent of electronic products were produced or assembled abroad. To make matters worse, the United States consistently imported a sizable portion of its fuel needs from other countries. All of these elements created a U.S. dependency on world trade.

As free market policies continued to be the dominant political force concerning trade around the world, a host of new markets opened. Specifically, in the late 1980s, Central and Eastern European markets opened with the dissolution of the Soviet Union. By the 1990s, world trade began with China, as well as with countries in South America and the Middle East — new markets that looked quite promising. In spite of the changes in the world trade arena, the United States, Japan, and Europe continued to play a dominant role, accounting for 85 percent of the world's trade.

Interestingly, while the trend of opening new world markets continued, there was another trend toward regional trade agreements. These agreements typically gave preferential trade status to nations that assented to the terms of a pact over those nations that did not participate. Two examples are the creation of a unified European Market and the ratification of the North American Free Trade Agreement (NAFTA). Created in 1958, and renamed most recently in 1993, the European Union (EU) is a regional organization designed to gradually eliminate customs duties and other types of trade barriers between members. Imposing a common external tariff against nonmember countries, EU countries slowly adopted measures that would unify and, theoretically, strengthen member economies. Member nations include Belgium, France, Germany, Great Britain, Italy, Luxembourg, the Netherlands, Denmark, Ireland, Greece, Spain, and Portugal.

Comprised of Canada, the United States, and Mexico, NAFTA was passed by the U.S. House and Senate in November 1994. In total, 360 million consumers are subject to the agreement, with spending power of about $6 trillion. Therefore, NAFTA is 20 percent larger than the EU.

With non-European multinational corporations facing tariff barriers put up by the EU, the most attractive international markets were those emerging in the developing countries of Asia, Russia, and Latin America. According to Christopher Miller, professor of international marketing at the Thunderbird Graduate School of International Management, "There's nowhere else to go. With the advent of the EU, it's harder and harder for non-European companies

to get into Europe. Anyone within the boundaries has no tariffs, and those outside it have more barriers." In emerging markets, companies could expect to achieve 30 to 40 percent growth rates, according to Miller.

Ⅰ. New Words and Expressions

arguably	[ˈɑːgjʊəblɪ]	(*adv.*) 雄辩地;可以认为
isolationism	[ˌaɪsəˈleɪʃənɪzəm]	(*n.*)(一国在政治上或经济上的)孤立主义
protectionist	[prəˈtekʃənɪst]	(*n.*) 贸易保护主义者
protectionism	[prəˈtekʃənɪzəm]	(*n.*) 保护贸易主义;保护贸易制
buildup	[ˈbɪldˌʌp]	(*n.*) 发展,增长
incorporate	[ɪnˈkɔːpəreɪt]	(*v.*) 包含;加上;吸收(in/into)
ratify	[ˈrætɪfaɪ]	(*v.*)(正式)批准;认可
dissolution	[ˌdɪsəˈluːʃən]	(*n.*) 分解;溶解;融化;崩溃;消失
preferential	[ˌprefəˈrenʃl]	(*a.*) 优先的;(关税)优惠的
assent	[əˈsent]	(*v.*) 同意,赞成(to)
advent	[ˈædvənt]	(*n.*) 出现;到来
be traced to		追溯到

Ⅱ. Fill in the blanks in the following sentences with the listed words or expressions.

be traced to	in response to	furthermore	undermine	put up
be comprised of	be subject to	eliminate	account for	adopt

1. We should ________ the consumers' suggestion.
2. A cricket team ________ eleven players.
3. He has been asked to ________ his conduct.
4. A new skyscraper ________ downtown.
5. At last the noise ________ a fault in the pipes.
6. ________ their hospitality, we wrote a thank-you note.
7. The house is unsafe since the foundations ________ by floods.
8. She went through the transcript carefully, to ________ all errors from it.
9. Quantity and price stated in the Invoice ________ our final confirmation.
10. The house isn't big enough for me, and ________, it's too far from the town.

Ⅲ. There are four choices marked A. B. C. and D. in the following questions. You should decide on the best choice and mark the corresponding letter with a circle.

1. The United States imposed heavy duties on imported goods so as to ________.

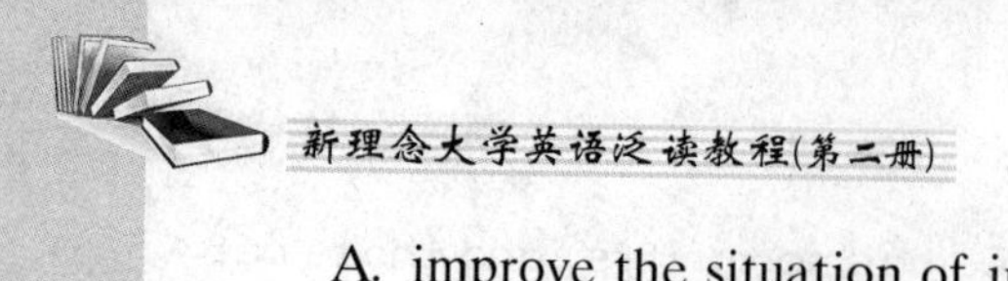

A. improve the situation of international trade
B. carry out isolationism and increase barriers to trade
C. protect its domestic economy
D. take revenge on its political enemies

2. Soon other countries throughout the world took similar actions in return for USA ________.
A. import B. export C. imposition D. imposing

3. It can be arguably said that protectionism substantially caused the following except ________.
A. the Great Depression B. arm expansion
C. low standard of living of people D. employment

4. What's the result of the Great Depression and WWII? There was ________.
A. an appeal for an effective international organization to ensure international trade
B. a worldwide armed uprising against the government
C. a short-term period of world peace
D. occurrence of protectionism

5. The three organizations: the International Trade Organization (ITO), the World Bank, and the International Monetary Fund (IMF) were set up shortly after ________.
A. World Health Organization
B. International Labor Organization
C. World Food Council
D. the Bretton Woods Conference

6. GATT came before WTO, so we can say WTO is the ________ to GATT
A. heir B. successor C. follower D. pacemaker

7. A large demand for a certain product or natural resources will create a country's ________ on world trade.
A. independence B. reliability C. unreliability D. dependence

8. With the prevalence of international trade, more and more countries will ________ advantages of selling their own products and importing foreign ones.
A. share B. cut C. resist D. refuse

9. According to the article China's role in world's trade is ________, though it is increasing its amount with each passing day.
A. still great B. dominant
C. far from satisfaction D. out of expectation

10. It can be expected that more world's trade will come from ________.
A. emerging markets B. old markets
C. traditional trade arena D. developed countries

Passage 34

A company's fans won't buy every product or service it offers. To keep followers engaged, Chris Guillebeau weaves stories into his marketing.

Last month, I traveled by train from Chicago to Portland, Ore. No offense to anyone who loves Amtrak, but 44 hours is a long time on a train. It was more expensive than flying, I had just come back from a long overseas trip followed by a speaking gig on the East Coast, and I was ready to get home.

Despite the fatigue, I took the train for the purpose of telling a good story. See, around the same time I was getting ready to launch a big project, the Empire Building Kit. Its goal is to help people build a sustainable small business in a year by doing one thing every day. In it, I use the case study method of interviewing "emperors" who successfully built a one-man or one-woman shop oriented toward something they were passionate about.

Sounds good, right? Well, I knew I had great material and I knew my blog followers would like it, but with a bunch of other projects on the pile, I kept procrastinating about setting a launch date. Around the same time, I was trying to book my ticket back from Chicago, and the best flight options were sold out. On a whim, I decided to check Amtrak, expecting it to be a last-ditch search before I bought a different plane ticket. Then I saw the train's name: It was called the Empire Builder.

"Now there's an interesting story," I thought to myself. "Why not launch the Empire Building Kit while riding the Empire Building train?"

After I heard that the train was called Empire Builder — on top of which a fun travel company in Seattle sent me an Empire Builder laptop bag — I was committed to the idea of doing a live product launch from the train. Sign me up.

Keep even non-buyers happy and engaged

Three weeks later, I met up with J. D. Roth, fellow blogger and author of *Your Money: The Missing Manual*, for the trek back from Chicago. We ended up doing the live product launch from what I called the "bloggers' lounge" on the train. (Apparently other people use it for sightseeing, but all those towns in North Dakota looked the same to me.) Amtrak isn't exactly wired for geeks, so we brought our own setup that made the train car look like a mini Apple Store, complete with multiple laptops, MiFis for Internet access, and a one-day-old iPad.

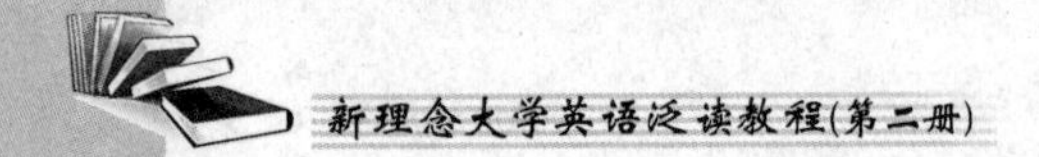

After we worked out the logistics, I still faced a problem: how to keep the rest of my community of blog readers happy and engaged. Whenever you sell something, not all of your prospects are interested. I think that's O.K. The key is not necessarily persuading them to join the group of buyers, but retaining their interest in your broader mission. They might buy something later — or in my case, keep reading my free blog, which is what I'm most interested in anyway.

I hoped that my story of roaming from place to place — complete with video updates, a contest, and a community survey — would keep things going so I wouldn't lose too many people. Normally my unsubscribing goes up during a product launch. I also hear complaints from people who think everything should be free. (I don't agree with that.)

The unsubscribe rate declined, instead of increasing. Twitter went haywire with people talking about it. Even though the price point was higher than the previous, I encountered virtually no objections or complaints.

I even got some unusual fan mail: "Chris, I'm probably not the best fit for the EBK, but I love the story. Every day we log in and wonder where you're at and what's happening."

I thought it was pretty good to get fan mail from someone who wasn't even interested in the product. Think about how you can use the power of story in your own business.

Relationship selling is all about building a friendship or relationship with your prospects and listening to their needs. Once you've built that relationship, shown you care, and earned their trust, you are on the road to making them a customer. Knowing their needs and finding out their secret fears (for example... your client may confide to you, "If I can't make this project work within budget, my boss will probably replace me!") can help you find solutions for them that are exactly on-target with their needs and build an even stronger relationship. With a relationship in place, working out details is a breeze. Those details become obstacles if you don't have the existing relationship.

Ⅰ. New Words and Expressions

engage	[ɪnˈgeɪdʒ]	(*v*.) 参与
offence	[əˈfens]	(*n*.) 冒犯
gig	[gɪg]	(*n*.) 演出
fatigue	[fəˈtiːg]	(*n*.) 疲劳
empire	[ˈempaɪə]	(*n*.) 帝国
sustainable	[səˈsteɪnəbl]	(*a*.) 可持续的
emperor	[ˈempərə]	(*n*.) 帝王
orient	[ˈɔːrɪənt]	(*v*.) 适应
passionate	[ˈpæʃənɪt]	(*a*.) 热情的

last-ditch	[ˈlæstˈdɪtʃ]	(*a.*)坚持到最后的
procrastinate	[prəʊˈkræstɪneɪt]	(*v.*)拖延,耽搁
commit	[kəˈmɪt]	(*v.*)致力于
launch	[lɔːntʃ]	(*v.*)发起
lounge	[laʊndʒ]	(*n.*)休息室
logistics	[ləʊˈdʒɪstɪks]	(*n.*)物流
roam	[rəʊm]	(*v.*)漫游
unsubscribe	[ˌʌnsəbˈskraɪb]	(*n.*)订购取消
decline	[dɪˈklaɪn]	(*v.*)下降
geek	[giːk]	(*n.*)电脑怪才
haywire	[ˈheɪˌwaɪə]	(*n.*)错乱

Ⅱ. Fill in the blanks in the following sentences with the listed words or expressions.

be committed to	despite	get ready to	a bunch of	sell out
meet up with	work out	earn one's trust	on the road to	in place

1. Spaghetti ________.
2. He cut off ________ grapes to entertain us.
3. ________ his cries no one came to his assistance.
4. The revolution set the country ________ democracy.
5. I believe that you can ________ this problem by yourself.
6. I think an expression of thanks to our host would be ________.
7. The family would have arrived on time, but they ________ a flat tire.
8. As Joe ________ kick a field goal, the result of the game hung by a hair.
9. I ________ attending the farewell dinner for a long time now.
10. The small arches of lower eyelids indicate that he is a loyal friend, but you must ________ and admiration.

Ⅲ. There are four choices marked A. B. C. and D. in the following questions. You should decide on the best choice and mark the corresponding letter with a circle.

1. According to paragraph 2, which of the following is true about author's attitudes towards Amtrak?
   A. Time-consuming.　　B. Pleasant.
   C. Comfortable and easy.　　D. Expensive and boring.
2. The author mentions "emperor" in paragraph 3 in order to ________.
   A. to tell people the history of dynasties
   B. to give the example of someone who succeeded in building a business
   C. to lecture people how to make their CEO the emperor of the company

D. to tell people how to manage a company

3. According to paragraph 4, which of the following is true about "blog followers"?
   A. Some people who have their own blogs.
   B. Some people who help the others write blogs.
   C. Some people who are interested in reading one's blogs.
   D. Some people who are interested in having his blogs read.
4. Why did the author have the idea of doing a live product launch from the train?
   A. The name of the train and the gift from a fun company is the same.
   B. The author thought about it for a long time.
   C. The author was very creative.
   D. He got the inspiration from the train.
5. How did the author manage to keep even non-buyers happy and engaged?
   A. To give non-buyers as many freebies as possible.
   B. To give more discounts to the non-buyers.
   C. To make the train access to the internet.
   D. To have a party on the train.
6. In author's opinion, what's the key to successfully selling something?
   A. To persuade them to join the group of buyers.
   B. To keep their interest in your broader mission.
   C. To launch various advertisement campaigns.
   D. To give them more coupons.
7. Adopting the new idea, what happened to the author's unsubscribing rate?
   A. Nothing changed. B. Kept increasing.
   C. Kept skyrocketing. D. Reduced dramatically.
8. What is the author's reaction towards that unusual fan mail?
   A. Neither happy nor down. B. Feels good.
   C. Feels so-so. D. Feels sorry.
9. What is true about relationship selling except?
   A. Building a friendship or relationship with your prospects.
   B. Listening to their needs.
   C. Trying to earn their trust.
   D. Trying to accept all their requests.
10. Where would the sentence, "This time, the opposite happened." best fit?
    A. The unsubscribe rate declined, instead of increasing.
    B. Twitter went haywire with people talking about it.
    C. Even though the price point was higher than the previous, I encountered virtually no objections or complaints.
    D. The opposite thing happened on time.

Passage 35

You've heard of the Five W's: who, what, when, where, and why. They're the elements of information needed to get the full story, whether it's a journalist uncovering a scandal, a detective investigating a crime, or a customer service representative trying to resolve a complaint. There's even an old PR formula that uses the Five W's as a template for how to write a news release.

Most of the time it doesn't matter in what order the information is gathered, as long as all five W's are ultimately addressed. The detective may start with where a crime was committed while details of who and what are still sketchy.

The Five W's are helpful in marketing planning as well. But unlike in other professions, the development of an effective marketing program requires that they be answered in a specific order: why, who, what, where, and when. The reasons may not be obvious, but by following this pathway you can avoid a great deal of confusion, trial and error, and blind alleys, preserving your company's precious time and resources.

Many marketers instinctively begin with questions about what and where, as in "what" their advertising should say or "where" it should appear. That's what gets them into trouble. They may have some success putting their plans together by relying on intuition and experience, but both can be misleading in a rapidly changing marketing world. These days it's easy for anyone to become confused by (or fall prey to) the latest and greatest trends and tactics.

First, Why Marketing?

Smart companies begin by asking "why" —why are we expending our limited resources in marketing? Why do we believe they're better invested here than in other aspects of our business? These questions, properly considered, force company leaders to clearly define their business and marketing objectives and confront their (often unrealized) assumptions before they get too far down the road.

In some cases they may have unrealistic expectations of their marketing efforts. In others, they may be looking to advertising to solve a non-advertising problem. In still others they may be reflexively reacting to a competitor's moves, or to any one of a number of other marketplaces or internal dynamics. Beginning with the "why" can be challenging, but starting here is critical to ensuring that your subsequent efforts are on target.

The second question is "who" — who is essential to our achieving our goals? To whom should we be directing our message? Whose hearts and minds must we win in order to succeed? The answers to these questions should be derived from the business objectives identified above so that the target audiences for your effort are clearly related to them.

For example, a marketing plan meant to generate significant new top-line revenue would likely focus on new customer attraction. An effort that's meant to enhance margins may concentrate on improving your brand's value equation among existing customers. And a plan to enhance your company's price/earnings ratio would focus on prospective investors and industry analysts as its primary target. The better any company defines its "who" — and the more it can know about their lifestyles, behaviors, attitudes, opinions, wants, and needs — the more effectively it can address the remaining three W's.

Next comes "what," as in what it is you need to offer your target audiences in order to accomplish your objectives. This, of course, encompasses a host of business decisions, from product to pricing, policy to packaging, and everything in between. But it is also where key branding issues are addressed, including positioning, differentiation, and a determination of the personality dimensions that are appropriate for both the brand and the task.

To be sure, as market conditions and customer needs change, the "what" of your offering will be a continually evolving proposition. But by having a solid understanding of the "who" and "why" of your efforts, you'll be more likely to get, and keep, the "what" right.

Finally, the last two W's can be addressed as you dive into the specifics of campaign planning. The questions now revolve around where and when the best places and times are to communicate your "what" to your "who" in service of your "why." At this stage you'll be required to make many tactical decisions, but if you've effectively addressed the first three W's you'll have the context and perspective you need to make the final two work as hard as possible on your behalf.

In some ways the principles of marketing are simple, but their simplicity can be deceptive. Beneath them often lie hidden complexities that you ignore at your peril. The common way of citing the Five W's — who, what, when, where, and why — rolls off the tongue and is a great mnemonic device. But if you want to optimize your marketing efforts, think why, who, what, where, and when. The order makes all the difference.

Ⅰ. New Words and Expressions

uncover	[ʌnˈkʌvə]	(*v.*) 发现
scandal	[ˈskændl]	(*n.*) 丑闻

investigate	[ɪnˈvestɪgeɪt]	(*v*.) 调查
resolve	[rɪˈzɒlv]	(*v*.) 解决
formula	[ˈfɔːmjʊlə]	(*n*.) 配方
template	[ˈtemplɪt]	(*n*.) 模板
sketchy	[ˈsketʃɪ]	(*a*.) 概略的
instinctively	[ɪnˈstɪŋktɪvlɪ]	(*adv*.) 直觉的
intuition	[ˌɪntjuːˈɪʃən]	(*n*.) 直觉
assumption	[əˈsʌmpʃən]	(*n*.) 猜测
dynamic	[daɪˈnæmɪk]	(*a*.) 活力的
subsequent	[ˈsʌbsɪkwənt]	(*a*.) 接下的
derive	[dɪˈraɪv]	(*v*.) 衍生
encompass	[ɪnˈkʌmpəs]	(*v*.) 包围
positioning	[pəˈzɪʃənɪŋ]	(*n*.) 定位
differentiation	[ˌdɪfərenʃɪˈeɪʃən]	(*n*.) 差别
proposition	[ˌprɒpəˈzɪʃən]	(*n*.) 提议
tactical	[ˈtæktɪkəl]	(*a*.) 战术的
address	[əˈdres]	(*v*.) 解决
deceptive	[dɪˈseptɪv]	(*a*.) 欺骗的
peril	[ˈperɪl]	(*n*.) 危险
mnemonic	[niːˈmɒnɪk]	(*a*.) 助记的
optimize	[ˈɒptɪmaɪz]	(*v*.) 优化

Ⅱ. Fill in the blanks in the following sentences with the listed words or expressions.

as long as	begin with	react to	be critical to	be derived from
focus on	a host of	in between	at one's peril	optimize

1. How did he ________ your suggestion?
2. Your decision ________ our future.
3. This fruit ________ the tropical islands.
4. ________ you drive carefully, you will be very safe.
5. You had better not invest so much money ________.
6. The proceedings will ________ a speech to welcome the guests.
7. We allocate our resources effectively to ________ business potential.
8. I'm sure the audience has ________ questions for our team of experts.
9. She had a habit of shrinking up whenever attention ________ her.
10. We have two lessons this morning, but there's some free time ________.

Ⅲ. There are four choices marked A. B. C. and D. in the following questions. You should decide on the best choice and mark the corresponding letter with a circle.

1. According to the first paragraph, why does the author mention the journalist?
   A. To illustrate the importance of information gathering.
   B. To explain the importance of information spreading.
   C. To tell people how to find a scandal.
   D. To inform people of big news.
2. Most of the time, why doesn't it matter in what order the information is gathered?
   A. The information itself is not important at all.
   B. Different situation has different requirements.
   C. They all look the same to them in whatever order the information is.
   D. They are too lazy to put the information in order.
3. Why effective marketing program requires that Five W's be answered in a specific order?
   A. Because it can better preserve your company's precious time and resources.
   B. Because it can help your company grow faster and stronger.
   C. Because it can help your company take more market shares.
   D. Because it can help your company go public more easily.
4. In author's opinion, what makes many marketers get into trouble?
   A. They don't know how to manage their business.
   B. They are not clear what will go on in the future market.
   C. The world financial crisis.
   D. They are not putting the Five W's in the right order.
5. In illustrating "Why Marketing", what does the author want to emphasize?
   A. The importance of defining their business and marketing objectives before too late.
   B. The importance of working out the future strategy for the company.
   C. The importance of going through the financial crisis.
   D. The importance of contributing more to the welfare of the society.
6. According to the author, why it is important for a company to define its "who"?
   A. It can help the company better understand their employees.
   B. It can help the company better understand their customers.
   C. It can effectively address the remaining three W's — what, when and where.
   D. It can be used as an important reference to appointing their future CEO.
7. Why does the author mention the "'what' of your offering will be a continually evolving proposition"?

A. Because of the change of the company leaders.

B. Because of the change of the world market.

C. Because of the change of the current market.

D. Because of the change of market conditions and customer.

8. According to the author, why can simplicity be deceptive?

A. The hidden complexities are easy to be neglected.

B. The simple thing is not important.

C. The market is full of deceptions.

D. The market is in short of watchdogs.

9. What is the meaning of the last sentence "The order makes all the difference"?

A. The order of the Five W's is always different.

B. The order of the Five W's can make things look different.

C. The order of the Five W's can make the market different.

D. The order of the Five W's is very important.

10. According to this passage, what should be the right order of Five W's?

A. who, what, when, where, and why

B. who, when, what, where, and why

C. why, who, what, where, and when

D. why, what, who, where, and when

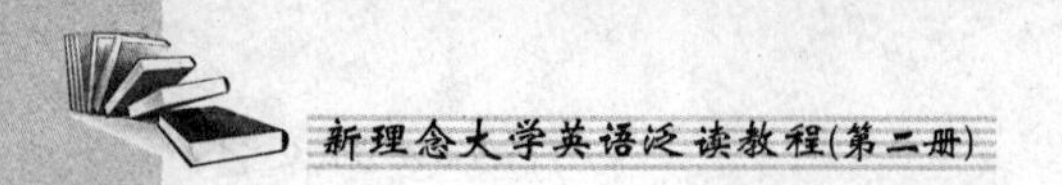

Does your business go through feast or famine when it comes to sales? If the answer is yes, you're not alone. Many businesses are vulnerable to dramatic swings in sales. Yet often simple changes to the way they manage their sales can reduce or even solve the problem. "From the time you generate a lead to the moment you close your sale, you have to be rigorous about your sales processes," says Nigel Robertson, BDC's regional training coordinator, Ontario. He shares some pointers here on how entrepreneurs can drive more consistent sales.

1. Be systematic about generating leads

The first step is to ensure that your company systematically generates sufficient leads to keep enough business in the pipeline. "You need to have specific targets for how many prospects should be in the funnel at any given time," Robertson explains. "Too many entrepreneurs get caught up in daily firefighting and ignore the fact that they have to think about where business is coming from down the road."

Much of this is a question of efficient time management, according to Robertson. "Before you start your week, it's a good idea to plan the number of appointments you intend to secure. If you're not always scheduling sales meetings with your clients, then you risk finding yourself in a state of famine. Generating leads is not necessarily the easiest part of your job, but it's a necessity if you want to drive consistent sales."

2. Know your sales cycle

The type of business you're in will determine your sales cycle, which is the amount of time that elapses between an initial meeting with a client and the closing of a deal. "This can vary greatly from one company to the next. But you need to understand exactly how much time it takes you on average, measured in weeks or months," Robertson advises.

To calculate the length of your sales cycle, Robertson recommends making a list of your 20 most recent closed sales, jotting down how long each took, and then computing the average. Using Customer Relationship Management (CRM) technology can also give business owners a better picture of their sales pipeline, help identify top clients and target specific groups.

But even if CRM technology is not within your budget, you can still apply its underlying principles to this problem. "What's important is that you can

see exactly what's speeding up or slowing down the transaction. That allows you to make adjustments and train employees to improve on specific steps of the sales process."

3. Know your numbers

Every company needs a minimum number of prospects at any given time just to maintain sales. Robertson advises looking at the number of closed transactions you want every month as well as the average sales cycle. Also helpful is to know what proportion of prospects contacted end up buying. "These figures don't lie," Robertson says. "They will help you set targets for your company."

Take, for example, a business that aims to sell three items per month. One out of every four prospects reached by sales staff in this business eventually buys, meaning it has a close ratio of 25%. It takes an average of four months from first contact with a client to close a sale. Therefore this business should have at least 48 active sales leads in the pipeline at any given time just to maintain current sales levels (3 desired closes multiplied by 4 months per average sell cycle, divided by a close rate of 25%, yielding a total of 48).

A new sales technique that has recently surfaced involves spending significant sales time only with those prospects who offer the highest probability of a sale. Arriving at that determination involves asking pointed questions and letting the prospect do the majority of the talking. The approach is to focus only on prospects who need your product, want you product, and can afford your product. Rather than using the effort trying to turn a low probability prospect into a high probability prospect, you focus your efforts entirely on the high probability group.

In this scenario, notes Robertson, "As long as you maintain 48 active leads at any one point in time, you can be confident you will close 3 transactions per month. It's that simple. If you decide one day to increase your monthly output to 4 closed transactions, then it follows that you will need to maintain a list of 64 active prospects, and so on."

Armed with this knowledge, entrepreneurs can set specific targets for team members. "It's a fair and productive way of clearly setting your expectations and customizing goals for each employee. Rather than telling people in your company that they simply have to do 'more', you're able to set real targets based on their performance history," Robertson says.

Ⅰ. New Words and Expressions

feast	[fiːst]	(*n.*) 宴会
famine	[ˈfæmɪn]	(*n.*) 饥荒
generate	[ˈdʒenəreɪt]	(*v.*) 产生
rigorous	[ˈrɪgərəs]	(*a.*) 严格的，严厉的

systematic	[ˌsɪstɪˈmætɪk]	(*a.*) 系统的
entrepreneur	[ˌɒntrəprəˈnɜː]	(*n.*) 企业家
coordinator	[kəʊˈɔːdɪneɪtə]	(*n.*) 协调人
initial	[ɪˈnɪʃəl]	(*a.*) 最初的
calculate	[ˈkælkjʊleɪt]	(*v.*) 计算
recommend	[ˌrekəˈmend]	(*v.*) 推荐
budget	[ˈbʌdʒɪt]	(*n.*) 预算
minimum	[ˈmɪnɪməm]	(*a.*) 最少的
scenario	[sɪˈnɑːrɪəʊ]	(*n.*) 情景
transaction	[trænˈzækʃən]	(*n.*) 交易
customize	[ˈkʌstəmaɪz]	(*v.*) 定制

Ⅱ. Fill in the blanks in the following sentences with the listed words or expressions.

get caught up	go through	jot down	entrepreneur	apply
be armed with	be based on	slow down	speed up	vary

1. In the recession, our firm _______ a bad time.
2. This film _______ a novel by D. H. Lawrence.
3. Many citizens do not _______ in local events.
4. We'd better _______ if we want to get there in time.
5. Social customs _______ greatly from country to country.
6. As they _______ for the turn, a grey car shot ahead of them.
7. Let me _______ your telephone number so that I can call you later.
8. The results of this research can _______ to new developments in technology.
9. _______ the new machine, a search party went into the cave hoping to find buried treasure.
10. He would not have succeeded in such a risky business if he had not been such a clever _______.

Ⅲ. There are four choices marked A. B. C. and D. in the following questions. You should decide on the best choice and mark the corresponding letter with a circle.

1. In paragraph 1, why does the author mention feast and famine?

A. Because one's business is always in stable situation.

B. Because there are always some ups and downs for one's business.

C. Because it is always good for a company to grow fast.

D. Because it is bad for a company to suffer from famine.

2. According to the writer, how to solve the problem in dramatic swings in sales?

   A. To stick to the way they manage their business.

   B. To turn to another kind of business.

   C. To merge or acquire a company.

   D. To change the way they manage their business.

3. What's the author's attitude to generating leads?

   A. It's a necessity to drive consistent sales.

   B. It's a necessity to win more customers.

   C. It doesn't serve any purpose.

   D. It's an obstacle for a company to promote sales.

4. According to the passage, what is the sales cycle?

   A. It is the amount of time that takes between promoting a product and the closing of a deal.

   B. It is the amount of time that takes between starting a business and the closing of a deal.

   C. It is the amount of time that takes between meeting with a client and the drafting a contract.

   D. It is the amount of time that takes between meeting with a client and the closing of a business.

5. Why does the author mention using Customer Relationship Management (CRM) technology?

   A. Because it can help business owners identify top clients and target specific groups.

   B. Because it can help business owners promote the image of their company.

   C. Because it can help business owners achieve their strategic objectives.

   D. Because it can bring business owners more profits.

6. What does "your number mean" in "knowing your numbers"?

   A. The numbers of your target customers.

   B. The figures of prospects contacted and closed transactions.

   C. The numbers of your future rivals.

   D. The figures of the future marketing prospect.

7. In the new sales technique, on what effort should the focus be put?

   A. On turning a low probability prospect into a high one.

   B. On the high probability group.

   C. On the clients you've already have.

   D. On the clients you would never have.

8. All the following sales techniques are involved in the passage except ________ .

   A. to be systematic about generating leads

   B. to know your sales cycle

C. to know your numbers

D. to have a global strategy

9. A business that aims to sell four items per month. One out of every four prospects reached by sales staff in this business eventually buys, meaning it has a close ratio of 25%. It takes an average of five months from first contact with a client to close a sale.

How many active sales leads in the pipeline should this business have to maintain current sales levels?

A. 64 B. 80 C. 90 D. 70

10. What's the key tone of the whole passage?

A. Informative. B. Humorous.

C. Truth-digging. D. Thrilling.

Passage 37

Fuzzy wording is multifunctional in business negotiation and can often be used as a kind of politeness strategy, which usually plays some unexpected positive part in business negotiation. By using fuzzy wording, speakers satisfy the opponent's negative face without interference in other's freedom of action. Fuzzy wording can, undoubtedly, not only improve the negotiating climate, thereby helping the negotiation go on smoothly, but also sound the opponent out about the question, in an effort to know the other's real intention.

This strategy has multi-faced functions, but the most striking is that it is persuasive and convincing without any force upon others. Look at the following dialogue, which may be of some help.

Mr Smith: Mr Wang, I am anxious to know your offer.

Mr Wang: Well, we've been holding it for you, Mr. Smith; here it is 80 dozens of Woolen Sweaters, at $ 160 per doz, CIF New York. Shipment will be in May.

Mr Smith: That's too high! It will be difficult for us to make any sales.

Mr Wang: I'm rather surprised to hear you say that, Mr. Smith. You know the price of woolen sweater has gone up since last year. Ours compares favorably with what you might get elsewhere.

Mr Smith: I'm afraid I can't agree with you here. Japan has just come into the market with lower price.

Mr Wang: Ah, but everybody in the woolen sweater trade knows that China's is of top quality. Considering the quality, I should say the price is reasonable.

Mr Smith: No doubt, yours is of high quality, but still there has been competition in the market. I understand some countries are actually lowering their price.

Mr Wang: So far our commodities have stood the competition well. The very fact that other clients keep on buying speaks for it. Few other woolen sweaters can compete with ours either for quality or price.

Mr Smith: But I believe we'll have a hard time convincing our clients at your price.

Mr Wang: To be frank with you, if it weren't for our good relation, we wouldn't consider making you a firm offer at this price.

Mr Smith: All right. It seems that I have no other choice but to accept it.

Mr Wang: I'm glad that we've settled the price.

There are a lot of fuzzy words in the above dialogue. We pick up some sentences for the convenience of illustration.

1. That's too high! It will be difficult for us to make any sales.

2. But I believe we'll have a hard time convincing our clients at your price.

3. No doubt, yours is of high quality.

4. Few other woolen sweaters can compete with ours either for quality or price.

In business negotiations, it is difficult for negotiators to force others to reach an agreement. Therefore, they must leave some leeway (room) to each other so as to change their position or standpoint without loss of their face. When Mr. Smith says sentence 1, he not only attempts to persuade Mr. Wang to lower his price, but also leaves some room for himself in case of the occurrence of the unforeseen circumstances. If Mr. Smith uses the word "impossible" instead of "difficult", the agreement is hard to reach, and he sinks into a dilemma. Sentence 2 is the same. In sentence 3, Mr. Smith has intention when he changes the words "of top quality" into "of high quality". He admits that at the time when the opponent's woolen sweater is good, there is still other competitors' good woolen sweaters and the opponent's is not the first rate product. In sentence 4, Mr. Wang preferably uses "few" instead of "none". These two words mean different in semantics. But they mean the same here in pragmatics. In this sense, Mr. Wang skillfully achieves communicative goal of "none" effect by means of "few", making Mr. Smith sure that Chinese Woolen Sweaters are the best. What's more, such diction is by far easier to be accepted by Mr. Smith.

Ⅰ. New Words and Expressions

fuzzy	[ˈfʌzɪ]	(*a.*) 模糊的，含糊不清的
unexpected	[ˈʌnɪkˈspektɪd]	(*a.*) 想不到的，意外的
opponent	[əˈpəʊnənt]	(*n.*) 对手，反对者，敌手
interference	[ˌɪntəˈfɪərəns]	(*n.*) 干扰，妨碍
undoubtedly	[ʌnˈdaʊtɪdlɪ]	(*adv.*) 无疑地
intention	[ɪnˈtenʃən]	(*n.*) 意图，目的，意向，打算
multi-faced	[mʌltɪ-feɪst]	(*a.*) 多方位的
striking	[ˈskraɪkɪŋ]	(*a.*) 显著的，吸引人的
persuasive	[pəˈsweɪsɪv]	(*a.*) 有说服力的，令人信服的
favorably	[ˈfeɪvərəblɪ]	(*adv.*) 赞同地，亲切地，好意地
leeway	[ˈliːweɪ]	(*n.*) 余地
standpoint	[ˈstændpɒɪnt]	(*n.*) 立场，观点

unforeseen	[ˈʌnfɔːˈsiːn]	(*a*.)无法预料的
preferably	[ˈprefərəblɪ]	(*adv*.)更好地，宁可，宁愿
semantics	[sɪˈmæntɪks]	(*n*.)语义学，符号学
pragmatics	[prægˈmætɪks]	(*n*.)语用学，语用论
diction	[ˈdɪkʃən]	(*n*.)措辞，发音
negative face		消极面子
sink into		沉到……里

Ⅱ. Fill in the blanks in the following sentences with the listed words or expressions.

undoubtedly	in case of	dozens of	sink into	go up
by means of	compete with	favorably	pick up	so far

1. When he left, she ________ melancholy.
2. The driver stopped to ________ a hitchhiker.
3. We express our thought ________ words.
4. The boys ________ each other for the prize.
5. The words ________ give the air of positiveness.
6. ________ the search for the missing boy has been fruitless.
7. In recent times the price of just about everything ________.
8. Many people are at a loss as to what to do ________ a real fire.
9. In fact, our end-users are ________ impressed with your exhibits.
10. The train pulled in, and ________ schoolchildren spilled out onto the platform.

Ⅲ. There are four choices marked A. B. C. and D. in the following questions. You should decide on the best choice and mark the corresponding letter with a circle.

1. Fuzzy wording is usually used in ________.
   A. classroom activity　　B. press conference
   C. scholar's lecture　　D. business negotiation
2. Which one of the following statements is NOT true?
   A. Fuzzy wording can improve the negotiating climate.
   B. Fuzzy wording can do everything.
   C. Fuzzy wording can help the negotiation go on smoothly.
   D. Fuzzy wording can help negotiators know the other's real intention.
3. What is the real purpose for businessmen to use fuzzy wording in business negotiations?
   A. To make friends.
   B. To get the smallest profit.

C. To get the maximum profit.

D. To show their language skills.

4. According to the text, what is the most striking function of using fuzzy wording?

A. It can save time.

B. It helps the business negotiators feel comfortable.

C. It is persuasive and convincing without any force upon others.

D. It is very useful.

5. From the sentence "Mr Wang, I am anxious to know your offer." We can infer that ________.

A. Mr. Smith is not worried to do business with Mr Wang

B. Mr. Smith is eager to do business with Mr Wang

C. Mr. Smith is happy to do business with Mr Wang

D. Mr. Smith is angry to do business with Mr Wang

6. From the above dialogue, we can infer that Mr Wang is a ________, and Mr Smith is a ________.

A. seller... buyer　　B. buyer... seller

C. buyer... buyer　　D. seller... seller

7. In the sentence "That's too high! It will be difficult for us to make any sales." If Mr. Smith uses "impossible" instead of "difficult", which result may happen in the end?

A. The agreement between them will be reached.

B. Mr. Wang will be happy to lower the price.

C. Mr. Wang will be happy to increase the price.

D. The agreement between them may be hard to reach.

8. According to the dialogue, we can infer that Mr. Wang is ________.

A. a skilled negotiator　　B. a green dog

C. a poor negotiator　　D. a bad negotiator

9. By using fuzzy wording, Mr. Smith skillfully make Mr. Smith believe that the quality of Chinese Woolen Sweaters are ________.

A. the poorest　　B. the best

C. just so so　　D. poor

10. According to the text, we can infer that using the fuzzy wording in business negotiation is ________.

A. a bad idea　　B. devastating

C. helpful　　D. doubtful

Passage 38

Based in Geneva, the WTO was set up in 1995, replacing another international organization known as the General Agreement on Tariffs and Trade (GATT). GATT was formed in 1948 when 23 countries signed an agreement to reduce customs tariffs.

The WTO has a much broader scope than GATT. Whereas GATT regulated trade in merchandise goods, the WTO also covers trade in services, such as telecommunications and banking, and other issues such as intellectual property rights.

Membership of the WTO now stands at 153 countries (as at July 2008). China formally joined the body in December 2001 after a 15-year battle. Russia wants admission, but must first convince the EU and US that it has reformed business practices.

The highest body of the WTO is the Ministerial Conference. This meets every two years and, among other things, elects the organization's chief executive — the director-general — and oversees the work of the General Council.

The Ministerial Conference is also the setting for negotiating global trade deals, known as "trade rounds" which are aimed at reducing barriers to free trade.

The General Council is in charge of the day-to-day running of the WTO and is made up of ambassadors from member states who also serve on various subsidiary and specialist committees.

Among these are the Dispute Settlement Panels which rule on individual country-against-country trade disputes.

WTO decisions are absolute and every member must abide by its rulings. So, when the US and the European Union are in dispute over bananas or beef, it is the WTO which acts as judge and jury. WTO members are empowered by the organization to enforce its decisions by imposing trade sanctions against countries that have breached the rules.

There are a number of ways of looking at the WTO. It's an organization for liberalizing trade. It's a forum for governments to negotiate trade agreements. It's a place for them to settle trade disputes. It operates a system of trade rules. (But it's not Superman, just in case anyone thought it could solve — or cause — all the world's problems!)

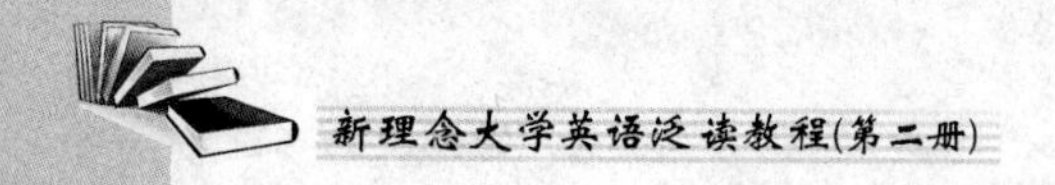

Above all, it's a negotiating forum. Essentially, the WTO is a place where member governments go, to try to sort out the trade problems they face with each other. The first step is to talk. The WTO was born out of negotiations, and everything the WTO does is the result of negotiations. The bulk of the WTO's current work comes from the 1986—1994 negotiations called the Uruguay Round and earlier negotiations under the General Agreement on Tariffs and Trade (GATT). The WTO is currently the host to new negotiations, under the "Doha Development Agenda" launched in 2001.

Where countries have faced trade barriers and wanted them lowered, the negotiations have helped to liberalize trade. But the WTO is not just about liberalizing trade, and in some circumstances its rules support maintaining trade barriers — for example to protect consumers or prevent the spread of disease.

It's a set of rules. At its heart are the WTO agreements, negotiated and signed by the bulk of the world's trading nations. These documents provide the legal ground-rules for international commerce. They are essentially contracts, binding governments to keep their trade policies within agreed limits. Although negotiated and signed by governments, the goal is to help producers of goods and services, exporters, and importers conduct their business, while allowing governments to meet social and environmental objectives.

The system's overriding purpose is to help trade flow as freely as possible — so long as there are no undesirable side-effects — because this is important for economic development and well-being. That partly means removing obstacles. It also means ensuring that individuals, companies and governments know what the trade rules are around the world, and giving them the confidence that there will be no sudden changes of policy. In other words, the rules have to be "transparent" and predictable.

And it helps to settle disputes. This is a third important side to the WTO's work. Trade relations often involve conflicting interests. Agreements, including those painstakingly negotiated in the WTO system, often need interpreting. The most harmonious way to settle these differences is through some neutral procedure based on an agreed legal foundation. That is the purpose behind the dispute settlement process written into the WTO agreements.

Pascal Lamy, a Frenchman and a former EU trade commissioner, became WTO head in September 2005. His campaign for the leadership focused on the developing world.

Mr Lamy said his priority would be to break an impasse over a long-awaited global trade deal, intended to cut subsidies, reduce tariffs and give a fairer deal to developing countries.

Discussions on this — the so-called Doha round of talks — began in 2001. But a breakthrough has proved elusive, with rows emerging among the WTO's key players over agricultural tariffs and subsidies.

G20 leaders called for an agreement before the end of 2008, but Mr Lamy called off a proposed ministerial meeting, citing the "unacceptably high" risk of failure. He said the worsening global economic crisis could mean there would be a better opportunity for a deal in 2009.

Mr Lamy's predecessor, Thailand's Supachai Panitchpakdi, was the first WTO director-general to come from a developing country.

Ⅰ. New Words and Expressions

regulate	[ˈregjʊˌleɪt]	(v.) 管理,控制
ambassador	[æmˈbæsədə]	(n.) 大使,代表
subsidiary	[səbˈsɪdɪərɪ]	(n.) 子公司,附属机构
jury	[ˈdʒʊərɪ]	(n.) 陪审团,评委会
empower	[ɪmˈpaʊə]	(v.) 授权,使能够
sanction	[ˈsæŋkʃən]	(n.) 批准,约束力
breach	[briːtʃ]	(v.) 违反,突破
liberalize	[ˈlɪbərəlaɪz]	(v.) 自由主义化
forum	[ˈfɔːrəm]	(n.) 讨论会,论坛
negotiate	[nɪˈgəʊʃɪeɪt]	(v.) 谈判,协商
dispute	[dɪˈspjuːt]	(v.) 争论,争议
bulk	[bʌlk]	(n.) 大块,大批
bind	[baɪnd]	(v.) 约束,强迫
override	[ˌəʊvəˈraɪd]	(v.) 推翻,凌驾,过度负重
transparent	[trænsˈperənt]	(a.) 透明的,易懂的
painstakingly	[ˈpeɪnsˌteɪkɪŋlɪ]	(adv.) 费力地,苦心地
harmonious	[hɑːˈməʊnɪəs]	(a.) 和谐的,和睦的
neutral	[ˈnjuːtrəl]	(a.) 中立的,中性的
priority	[praɪˈɒrɪtɪ]	(n.) 优先权,优先顺序
impasse	[ˈɪmpæs]	(n.) 僵局,死路
breakthrough	[ˈbreɪkˌθruː]	(n.) 突破
elusive	[ɪˈluːsɪv]	(a.) 难捉摸的,逃避的
predecessor	[ˈpriːdɪsesə]	(n.) 前辈,前任
customs tariffs		关税
intellectual property		知识产权
business practice		商业惯例
trade round		一轮贸易谈判
abide by		遵守,服从
sort out		整理,选出,分类
trade barriers		贸易壁垒

Ⅱ. Fill in the blanks in the following sentences with the listed words or expressions.

conduct one's business	in charge of	abide by	empower	call for
be made up of	intend to	sort out	oversee	call off

1. The appeal jury _______ 12 people.
2. You must employ someone to _______ the project.
3. If you join the club, you should _______ the rules.
4. These regulations _______ prevent accidents.
5. Congress _______ by the Constitution to make laws.
6. They _______ the peaceful dispersal of the demonstrators.
7. We urged them to _______ the problem sooner rather than later.
8. Since you cannot reduce the price, we may _______ the deal(business) as well.
9. The Chancellor of the Exchequer is the minister _______ finance in Britain.
10. They disliked each other too much to meet, so they _______ through an intermediary.

Ⅲ. There are four choices marked A. B. C. and D. in the following questions. You should decide on the best choice and mark the corresponding letter with a circle.

1. The WTO agreements cover the following trades except _______.
   A. trade in goods B. trade in money
   C. trade in services D. trade in intellectual property
2. From Paragraph 3, it can be inferred that _______.
   A. altogether there are 153 countries all over the world
   B. China joined GATT 15 years ago and WTO 10 years ago
   C. without permission from the EU, a country can't join WTO
   D. Russia wanted to join the WTO, but her people resisted it
3. When did China become one of the members of WTO?
   A. 1948. B. 1995. C. 2001. D. 2005.
4. The highest authority of WTO is _______.
   A. General Council
   B. Director-general
   C. Ministerial Conference
   D. Ambassadors from member states
5. The Ministerial Conferences are held at least once _______.
   A. every year B. every two years
   C. every three years D. every four years

6. Between the two Ministerial Conferences, the day-to-day operations of WTO is handled by ________.
   A. General Council
   B. Director-general
   C. Dispute Settlement Panels
   D. Ambassadors from member states
7. If a member state has some disputes against other members, it will ask ________ for solution.
   A. General Council　　B. Secretariat
   C. Ministerial Conference　　D. Dispute Settlement Panels
8. Which of the following functions of WTO is topmost?
   A. It's an organization for liberalizing trade.
   B. It's a forum for governments to negotiate trade agreements.
   C. It's a place for them to settle trade disputes.
   D. It operates a system of trade rules.
9. Who is the present Director-general of WTO?
   A. Ban Ki-moon.　　B. Pascal Lamy.
   C. Supachai.　　D. Panitchpakdi.
10. Which of the following statements is NOT true based on the passage?
    A. Doha rounds started from 2001.
    B. WTO is the continuity and development of GATT.
    C. Mr Lamy was elected WTO Director-general for his focus on developing countries.
    D. Mr Lamy was the first WTO director-general to come from a developing country.

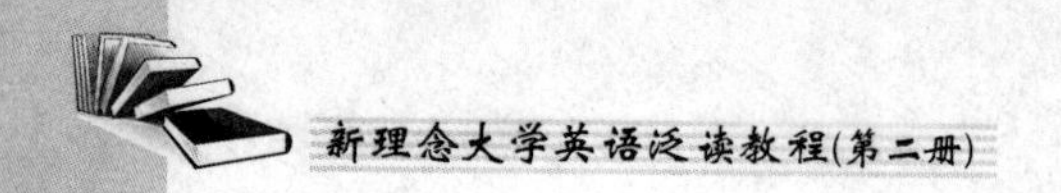

Passage 39

E-commerce is an important evolution for many organizations. However, the ultimate goal for organizations wishing to maximize the potential of the Web is E-business. IBM, the first major computer vendor to coin the term, defines E-business as "the transformation of key business process through the use of Internet technologies." Using this definition, it is clear that E-commerce is a subset of E-business, because the sales function is just one of the key business processes a commercial enterprise supports. Stated another way, E-commerce is a necessary but not sufficient criteria for achieving E-business.

The term "key business processes" in the definition has another strong implication for E-business. Unless an enterprise is very young to the extent that all its infrastructure is based on Web and Internet technologies (e.g., Amazon.com), the key business processes of an enterprise may rely on a variety of mission-critical legacy systems. Therefore, the achievement of E-business implies that an enterprise may have to integrate its Web systems with its legacy hierarchical and client/server systems. By definition, the enterprise that has achieved E-business is in the third stage of Web presence.

A primary example of a B2C E-business site is the Charles Schwab site. It was previously cited as the leading online brokerages, and Charles Schwab consistently ranks at or near the top. One of the reasons for the consistent ranking is the richness of the Web site. Customers can perform a wide range of functions and services through the singly, secure customer portal. The services currently offered to customers via its Web site include:

1. open new accounts.

2. receive delayed and real-time securities quotes.

3. view detailed account information, including overview, balances, positions, and history.

4. compare holdings against market indices.

5. move money into or out of one's account, or between various Schwab accounts.

6. place orders for stocks, mutual funds, options, corporate bonds, U.S. treasuries, futures, and after-hour trades.

7. view status of orders.

8. access company news, information, and charts.

9. access a rich set of research material.

10. receive customized alerts.

11. analyze current asset allocation and compare it to a model allocation

12. gain access to independent financial advisers

13. access various online planners to assist in setting goals and plans for retirement, college funding, etc.

14. modify account password, E-mail address, mailing address, and phone number.

15. request checks, deposit slips, deposit envelopes, W-8 form, and W-9 form.

16. fill our forms to transfer accounts to Schwab, set up electronic or wired funds transfer, receive IRA distribution, apply for options trading, and many other customer service functions.

This incredibly diverse list of services differentiates the Charles Schwab Web site from many of its competitors. It is clear by examining the list that Charles Schwab has crossed the line from E-commerce to E-business. Its core commerce function, securities trading, is available on the Web, but it augments that E-commerce offering with a rich set of customer service and account management features, external news feeds, external research services, and proactive alert services. Essentially, virtually every transaction or request that a customer would require to interact with Charles Schwab can be satisfied via its web site. Of course, the company continues to offer a 1-800 service for customers who need additional assistance. And it continues to operate and even expand its network of branch offices to assist its customers in person.

The Charles Schwab E-business Web site has not replaced the company's traditional customer service mechanisms, but the web site has allowed Charles Schwab to grow its asset and customer base faster than it would have been able to do so using traditional means. The traditional way of servicing more customers would have meant the expansion of its network of branch offices and also the expansion of its network of branch offices and also the expansion of its telephone call center for handling customer service inquiries. The addition of each new customer would have required a certain investment in new staff and infrastructure to support that customer. In the E-business model, each additional customer requires only a modest incremental investment in new infrastructure and systems and some fractional new investment in call centers and branch offices. The required investment for the traditional model versus the E-business model is likely on the order of 100 : 1 or 1,000 : 1. These cost efficiencies and the ability to scale the operation are the driving forces behind the development of B2C E-business solutions.

Ⅰ. New Words and Expressions

ultimate	[ˈʌltɪmɪt]	(*a*.) 最后的,最终的
vendor	[ˈvendə]	(*n*.) 卖主
coin	[kɒɪn]	(*v*.) 杜撰
subset	[ˈsʌbset]	(*n*.) [数]子集
legacy	[ˈlegəsɪ]	(*n*.) 遗赠,遗产
hierarchical	[ˌhaɪəˈrɑːkɪkl]	(*a*.) 分等级的
real-time	[ˈriːlˈtaɪm]	(*a*.) 实时的
overview	[ˈəʊvəˌvjuː]	(*n*.) 概况,总结
fractional	[ˈfrækʃənəl]	(*a*.) 少量的,很少的
versus	[ˈvɜːsəs]	(*prep*.) 与……相对
deployment	[dɪˈplɒɪmənt]	(*n*.) 有效的使用
differentiate from		使……与……分开

Ⅱ. Fill in the blanks in the following sentences with the listed words or expressions.

place an order	by definition	rely on	therefore	via
differentiate from	apply for	in person	versus	coin

1. He ________ an entry visa.
2. He will be present at the meeting ________.
3. He is on the way to Pakistan ________ the Silk Route.
4. The big match tonight is England ________ Spain.
5. They cannot ________ to offer much support or advice.
6. He was very tired, and ________ he didn't give the market report.
7. He ________ several new technical words which are now widely used.
8. ________ the capital is the political and cultural center of a country.
9. The house ________ its neighbor by the shape of its windows.
10. As silk garment is in great demand, we do not usually grant any discount unless you ________ for more than $ 50,000.

Ⅲ. There are four choices marked A. B. C. and D. in the following questions. You should decide on the best choice and mark the corresponding letter with a circle.

1. It is ________ that first coined the term E-business.

   A. IBM　　B. Charles Schwab site

   C. Dell Computer　　D. Cisco

2. Which of the following is NOT true?

   A. E-business is the transformation of key business processes through the use of internet technologies.

   B. E-commerce is a subset of E-business.

   C. E-commerce is a necessary but not sufficient criterion for achieving E-business.

   D. The ultimate goal for organizations hoping to maximize the potential of the Web is E-commerce.

3. The achievement of E-business implies that _______.

   A. an enterprise has to give up its original customers

   B. an enterprise should focus on its customers on the web sites

   C. an enterprise may have to integrate its Web systems with its legacy hierarchical and client

   D. an enterprise must pay more attention to its costs

4. Those are the reasons why Charles Schwab consistently ranks at or near the top of online brokerage firms EXCEPT _______.

   A. customers can perform a wide range of functions and services through its Web site

   B. Charles Schwab has crossed the line from E-commerce to E-business

   C. Charles Schwab E-business Web site has replaced the company's traditional customer service mechanisms

   D. almost every transaction or request that a customer would require to interact with Charles Schwab can be satisfied via its web site

5. The key business processes may rely on _______.

   A. the Web system

   B. a variety of mission-critical legacy system

   C. legacy hierarchical

   D. client/server systems

6. The enterprise that has achieved E-business is in the _______ stage of web presence.

   A. upper　　B. third　　C. first　　D. advanced

7. The core commerce function of Charles Schwab, _______, is available on the Web.

   A. exchanging currency　　B. securities trading

   C. delivery of the goods　　D. import and export

8. Charles Schwab can grow its asset and customer base faster by _______.

   A. communication　　B. the web site

   C. the new technology　　D. cooperative spirit

9. The addition of each new customer would have required ________.
   A. enough intelligence
   B. more funds to do business
   C. investment in new staff and infrastructure
   D. nothing
10. ________ are the driving forces behind the deployment of B2C E-business solutions.
    A. The addition of each new customer
    B. Cost efficiencies and the ability to scale the operation
    C. A certain investment in new staff and infrastructure
    D. Some fractional investment in call centers

At some point, every small business must set up shop online. A website can serve as another sales channel, a place to feature products, or just a resource for more information about your business. But above all, it serves as a communication channel with your customer. Establishing an online presence doesn't have to break the bank or eat up your time. Here's a guide to help get you on your way.

1. The basics

1.1 Register a domain name

Dozens of online registry sites allow you to secure a domain name. Some of the most popular include Register.com, NetworkSolutions.com, and GoDaddy.com. They're all fairly similar, and the one you choose won't really affect anything else about your site, so the main difference is price. In general you can expect to pay an annual fee of about $15, but if you're inclined to comparison shop you can pay as little as $8 a year. Try to pick a domain name that's as simple and intuitive as possible — complicated URLs just make it harder for customers to find you. Most companies simply drop their name into the middle of www and com, as in: www.JetBlue.com.

1.2 Set up an e-mail account to receive customer feedback

One of the keys to your Web success is making sure your customers can always reach you. Once you have your domain set up, be sure to create an active e-mail address and post it on your site right away. As your site grows, this will become a key contact point for your customers, and it will allow you to get feedback on your business.

1.3 Hire a temp

You probably have better things to do than spend all day entering data for every item you intend to sell online. As you start assembling your site in earnest, hire someone else to help with the setup work.

2. Sources to turn to for easy solutions

Numerous Internet service providers (ISPs) offer e-commerce solutions that require little work on your part. Some of the most basic handle your Web hosting needs and provide standardized storefront templates. Many are capable of growing with your business, offering additional services and customizable options should you need them down the road. These companies can provide

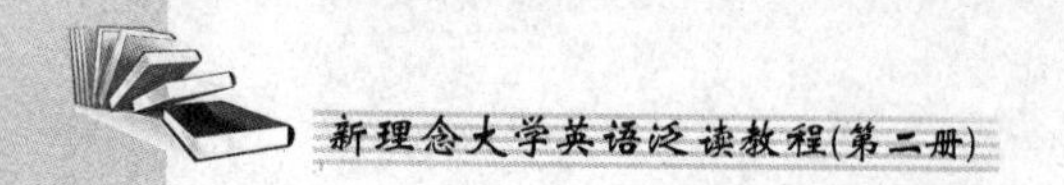

basic design templates and technology to process transactions, too.

Telecommunications company SBC offers an assortment of off-the-shelf set-up packages for individual merchants. Some key components to look for in such packages are shopping-cart software (allowing your customers to drop in items as they go through your site) and assistance with Web design. This last part is extremely important, as deciding how customers will flow your site is the same as directing them to merchandise. You have to get this part right.

You may have to go through your bank or through services like Verisign to set up a secure system to accept online payment for orders. For smaller operations, you can also explore services like PayPal, which make it easy to accept customer payments with an easily downloadable software package.

3. Think about affiliating with another site

Is it better to go it alone or join an existing online community? If you really need to differentiate your product or brand, particularly through site design, you may be better off building your own site. But if your needs are more basic and you want to keep costs down, it's probably to your benefit to pitch your tent in an existing online marketplace, which can provide more traffic than if you just open a shop and wait for customers to blow by. Sites like Ebay, Yahoo, and Amazon offer prepackaged storefront services with variety of options for individual merchants, often including free registration of your domain name.

Ebay offers your customers the chance to bid on items or buy them outright at a set price. The Ebay package also includes flexible listing options, limited customization tools, monthly sales reports, inventory search options, and the ability to cross-promote other items with ones you are selling. A mid-level Ebay store costs $49.95 per month, but options rage from $9.95 a month for a bare-bones storefront to $499.95 for a full-service store complete with marketing support.

Yahoo offers three basic levels of service, ranging from $39.95 a month to $299.95 a month, plus a $50 setup fee (sometimes the setup fee is waived during promotions) and transaction fees that range from 0.75 percent to 1.5 percent. It, too, offers a selection of services as well as simple step-by-step methods for listing your products online and software for accepting payment.

Depending on what kind of products you're selling, Amazon also offers several online options for third-party sellers. Amazon's Marketplace program charges a 15 percent commission, on top of a $39.99 monthly subscription cost (or $0.99 per item if you prefer), but leaves shipping and customer service to you. As another alternative, you can partner with Amazon and sell its goods on your own site for a commission.

4. The bottom line: Always focus on the benefits to your business

Be sure to keep your customers and your business goals in mind as you set up your site. Getting online is the easy part. Creating an online presence that adds value to your core business is what really matters.

Ⅰ. New Words and Expressions

register	[ˈredʒɪstə]	(*n.* & *v.*) 登记,注册
secure	[sɪˈkjʊə]	(*v.*) 获得,赢得
intuitive	[ɪnˈtjuːɪtɪv]	(*a.*) 直觉的
temp	[temp]	(*n.*) 临时雇员
assemble	[əˈsembl]	(*vt.*) 集合,聚集
assortment	[əˈsɔːtmənt]	(*n.*) 分类
merchandise	[ˈmɜːtʃəndaɪz]	(*n.*) 商品
pitch	[pɪtʃ]	(*v.*) 扎(营),搭(帐篷)
outright	[ˈaʊtˈraɪt]	(*adv.* & *a.*) 痛快地;直率的,完全的
waive	[weɪv]	(*v.*) 放弃
prepackage	[priːˈpækɪdʒ]	(*n.* & *v.*) 事先做好的包装;出售前预先包装
alternative	[ɔːlˈtɜːnətɪv]	(*n.* & *a.*) 二者选一,抉择;选择性的
differentiate	[ˌdɪfəˈrenʃɪˌeɪt]	(*v.*) 区别,区分
local web		本地网
targeted market		目标市场
discount rate		折扣率

Ⅱ. Fill in the blanks in the following sentences with the listed words or expressions.

be inclined to	eat up	keep in mind	in earnest	waive
be capable of	bid on	depend on	in general	range

1. The firm decided to ________ the new bridge.
2. His interests ________ from chess to canoeing.
3. Now he applied himself to the job ________.
4. They ________ overcoming any difficulty.
5. ________, people don't like to be made fun of.
6. Happiness does not ________ material possessions.
7. It is not easy to ________ what you have told me.
8. He was so hungry that he ________ his meal at a stretch.
9. As this offer ________, it is not binding upon us now.
10. In the first instance I ________ refuse, but then I reconsidered.

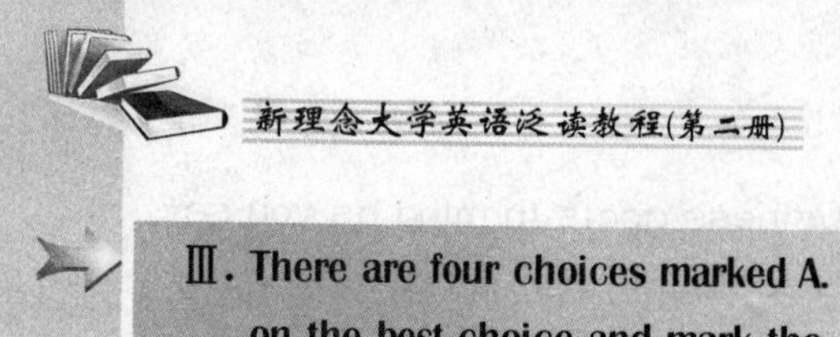

Ⅲ. There are four choices marked A. B. C. and D. in the following questions. You should decide on the best choice and mark the corresponding letter with a circle.

1. A website can serve as ________.
   A. a place to feature products
   B. just a resource for more information about your business.
   C. a communication channel with customers
   D. all above
2. Most companies simply ________ as their domain names.
   A. use their first letters
   B. make a new name
   C. choose some figures
   D. drop their name into the middle of www. and com.
3. One of the keys to your Web success is ________.
   A. to pay much money to your customers
   B. making many interesting advertisements
   C. making sure your customers can always reach you
   D. to focus on the important events
4. Which of the following is true?
   A. It is unnecessary for you to register a domain name.
   B. Once you have your domain set up, be sure to create an active e-mail address and post it on your site right away.
   C. Establishing an online presence have to break the bank.
   D. Most of enterprises wouldn't like to set up shop online.
5. Telecommunications company SBC offers ________ for individual merchants.
   A. much information
   B. some money
   C. an assortment of off-the-shelf set-up package
   D. designs of the web sites and sales information
6. You'd better build your own site ________.
   A. if you have enough money
   B. if you really need to differentiate your product or brand, particularly through site design
   C. if you hope to do business of import and export
   D. if you want to enlarge your size of the store
7. If your needs are more basic and you want to keep costs down, you should ________.
   A. open a shop and wait for customers to blow by
   B. make more advertisements in the media

C. build your store in an existing online market

D. look for some passive cooperative partners

8. Ebay offers your customers ________.

A. the chance to earn much money

B. various kinds of goods

C. information about the product discounts

D. the chance to bid on items or buy them outright at a set price

9. Yahoo offers ______.

A. three basic levels of service

B. a selection of services as well as simple step-by-step methods for listing your products online

C. software for accepting payment

D. above all

10. As you set up your site, you should ________.

A. put economic interests in the first place

B. focus on the newest technique and renovation

C. focus on developing customers

D. put the customers and business objectives in mind

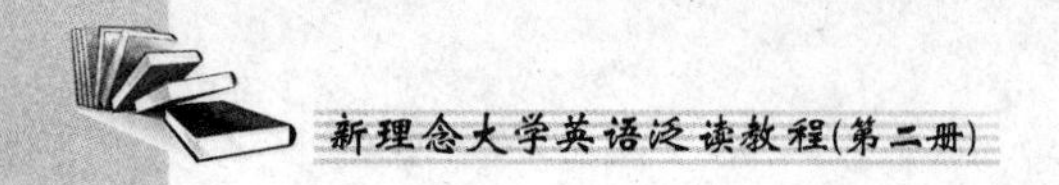

Passage 41

At the recent All Things D conference, Steve Jobs described Apple's culture as "that of a startup." Why?

Is it because he is nostalgic, yearning to rebuild the company he founded nearly 35 years ago? Is he reflecting a passion for the innovation and entrepreneurship so often inherent in startups? Or is he saying that a startup drives better products, velocity, and growth?

Guess what: all of the above. But what's perhaps more interesting is that by sharing this idea, Jobs also gave up a secret of what makes Apple successful. The essence of what causes Apple to win is the same thing that causes startups to innovate, the same thing that is at the root of all high-performance cultures. His description encapsulates the smart collaboration that underlies the creative acts of innovation throughout Apple and that exemplifies the company's culture.

Culture Drives Innovation

Culture is a shared set of norms. David Caldwell, professor of management at Santa Clara University, talks about "Culture as a shared understanding of assumptions and expectations among an organization's members, and it is reflected in the policies, vision, and goals of that organization."

In other words, culture informs success, not the other way around. Leadership drives a culture. Stephen Sadove, chairman and chief executive of Saks, says culture drives numbers: "Culture drives innovation and whatever else you are trying to accomplish within a company — innovation, execution, whatever it's going to be. And that then drives results," he said in a recent *New York Times* article. "When I talk to Wall Street, people really want to know your results, what are your strategies, what are the issues, what it is that you're doing to drive your business. Never do you get people asking about the culture, about leadership, about the people in the organization. Yet it's the reverse, because it's the people, the leadership, and the ideas that are ultimately driving the numbers and the results.

So culture might feel like a soft idea, but it's the stuff that formulates how you get things done. Thus it's a key driver of results and its importance should never be underestimated.

Apple as a Startup

Recently, Apple's market cap surpassed Microsoft's to make Apple the

most valuable technology company in the world. Yet as Jobs said at All Things D, Apple was near the brink of death only 10 years ago. It had $150 million in the bank, and its stock was trading at a few bucks a share.

Jobs could have focused on near-term fixes. Instead, he focused on building a high-performance culture by doing three things well.

1. He refocused the strategy to be about one thing. That meant he killed off even good things. I led server channel management at Apple when Jobs returned to the company in 1997, and I was there when he made the decision to shut down big portions of revenue-generating businesses (including my division) because they didn't fit with his vision for the company. Some people thought he was crazy. But he was being extremely clear, and in doing so, he "MurderBoarded" — eliminated many options to get one cohesive strategy — his way to greatness.

2. He eliminated passive aggressiveness and encouraged debate when new ideas were forming. When you are thinking about difficult problems together with exceptionally bright people, there are going to be disagreements. But it is through the tension of that creative conflict that new ideas get born, new angles get explored, and risks get mitigated. Thinking together means you deal with conflict up front, rather than have to counter passive aggressiveness on the back end.

3. He set up a cross-disciplinary view of how the company would succeed. This holistic vision means there is cohesion throughout the company, from concept to product to sales. For example, the retail strategy could have been a separate or disparate part of the whole, but Apple has made its retail strategy part and parcel of its overall promise of ease of use.

None of these three things is easy to do. It would be easy to count any revenue as good revenue, to allow a few people to stay even though they were rotting the culture, or to allow the different parts of a business to act in their silos. Apple's leadership doesn't accept easy. Executives believe that when the company wins, everyone wins. That belief drives the necessary behavior and tradeoffs necessary to achieve success. That's why Jobs has earned the respect of his peers. He has recreated a culture in which the company acts like all the best parts of a startup.

Your Turn

In the end, people create the culture of a company. And corporate culture ultimately separates the winners from the pack. Through culture, leaders can drive up the level of innovation, outcompete the market, and attract the best employees. Or not.

So here's a code-of-conduct question you can ask yourself: If yours were a startup culture, would you make a particular call the same way? If not, think about Steve Jobs and all he has achieved at Apple, and do what you need to do.

Ⅰ. New Words and Expressions

nostalgic	[nɒˈstældʒɪk]	(*a.*) 怀旧的
inherent	[ɪnˈhɪərənt]	(*a.*) 固有的,内在的
velocity	[vɪˈlɒsɪtɪ]	(*n.*) 速度;速率
encapsulate	[ɪnˈkæpsjʊˌleɪt]	(*v.*) 封装,压缩
exemplify	[ɪgˈzemplɪfaɪ]	(*v.*) 例示;作为……的例子
execution	[ˌeksɪˈkjuːʃən]	(*n.*) 执行,实施
formulate	[ˈfɔːmjʊleɪt]	(*v.*) 制定,规划
brink	[brɪŋk]	(*n.*) 边缘
cohesive	[kəʊˈhiːsɪv]	(*a.*) 有凝聚力的
mitigate	[ˈmɪtɪˌgeɪt]	(*v.*) 减轻,缓和
cross-disciplinary	[krɒsˈdɪsɪplɪnerɪ]	(*a.*) 交叉学科的
holistic	[həʊˈlɪstɪk]	(*a.*) 全部的
disparate	[ˈdɪspərɪt]	(*a.*) 不同的;异类的

Ⅱ. Fill in the blanks in the following sentences with the listed words or expressions.

in other words	shut down	give up	kill off	underestimate
together with	deal with	mitigate	drive up	nostalgic

1. I ________ the time we needed by 30%.
2. I have a huge pile of letters to ________.
3. The government is going to ________ interest rates.
4. He sent her some books, ________ a dictionary.
5. I get very ________ when I watch these old musicals on TV.
6. The government is trying to ________ the effects of inflation.
7. The workshop ________ and the workers are unemployed.
8. His wife is my daughter, ________, I am his mother-in-law.
9. The flood of hunters ________ most of the buffaloes in that area.
10. Many young workers ________ their days off to do voluntary labor.

Ⅲ. There are four choices marked A. B. C. and D. in the following questions. You should decide on the best choice and mark the corresponding letter with a circle.

1. Steve Jobs described Apple's culture as "that of a startup" because of the following reasons except ________.

A. he is nostalgic, yearning to rebuild the company he founded nearly 35 years ago

B. he is reflecting a passion for the innovation and entrepreneurship so often inherent in startups

C. he is saying that a startup drives better products, velocity, and growth

D. he is trying to keep the secret that makes Apple successful — the innovation

2. According to the author, which of the following is not the reason for Apple's success?

A. Creative act of innovation. B. High performance culture.

C. All things D conference. D. Leadership.

3. Which of the following statements is NOT true?

A. Culture creates leadership.

B. Culture is a shared set of norms.

C. Culture is a shared understanding of assumptions and expectations among an organization's members.

D. Culture is reflected in the policies, vision, and goals of that organization.

4. According to Stephen Sadove, people from Wall Street are not interested in ________.

A. company results

B. company culture

C. company issues which can drive business

D. company strategies

5. According to Stephen Sadove, which one of the following is not the ultimate reason for success?

A. People. B. Leadership.

C. Business strategies. D. Ideas.

6. How do you understand the importance of the culture to a company?

A. It's a soft idea.

B. It is reverse.

C. It formulates how people get things done.

D. It's a key driver of the results.

7. Which one of the four is the most valuable technology company in the world at the time when this article was written?

A. Apple. B. Wal Mart.

C. Microsoft. D. Samsung.

8. Jobs did the following things to build a high-performance culture except that ________.

A. he refocused the strategy to be about one thing by killing off even good things

B. he focused on near-term fixes

C. he eliminated passive aggressiveness and encouraged debate when new ideas were forming

D. he set up a cross-disciplinary view of how the company would succeed

9. Why can Jobs earn the respect of his peers?

A. Because he focuses on near-term fixes.

B. Because he allows a few people to stay even though they are rotting the culture.

C. Because he accepts easy.

D. Because he makes executives believe that when the company wins, everyone wins.

10. What cannot culture lead a successful company to do?

A. To create the winners from the pack.

B. To drive up the level of innovation.

C. To outcompete the market.

D. To attract the best employees.

I recently visited a business owner's facility. As our meeting ended, she turned to me and said, "Wouldn't it be great if you could run a business without employees?"

There were no employees around. I smiled and gave the perfunctory head nod — but it was a lying perfunctory head nod, if there is such a thing. I know that many people have commented on this very blog that they prefer, or would prefer, to run their businesses without employees. I don't feel that way, but let me state the obvious: employees can be a liability. Whether they are causing problems with customers, stealing, breaking things, suing you or doing something that gets you in trouble with a regulatory agency, employees can be trouble. And when trouble rears its ugly head, the owner cannot say, "I was only taking orders!"

Even if you weren't the one who personally hired the problem employees, you are responsible for them. That can be a tough pill to swallow. So tough, in fact, that many people choose not to hire anyone. In some businesses, you might be able to get away with working by yourself. Mine is not one of those businesses. I have 105 employees. I'm guessing that some of you may be cringing at the thought of managing that many people, but I do not. I have less grief today with 105 employees than I did when I had 10 employees. This is not a riddle. It is the law of averages, at least the way I define the phrase. If you have a bunch of average employees, you will end up with an average business. Probably not growing much. Probably not that profitable.

I have written about this before ("The Dirty Little Secret of Successful Companies"), but it bears repeating: It is a matter of having the right people — and enough of the right managers to deal with the occasional baloney. But it can go far beyond figuring out how to run the business without having everyone make you crazy. It starts with hiring the right people, then training them, and giving them direction until they can operate on their own or almost on their own. This could be someone you groomed to give customer service, to run the loading dock, or to be the vice president of your company.

The process can take months, a year, or many years. It can work with someone who came in at a young age with no experience or someone who has years of experience, maybe more than you do. Some companies promote mostly

from within, others hire "talent" from competitors. (And some think they are hiring talent from competitors when they are really hiring someone else's problem. I've been both the giver and the taker in that equation.) There is an almost magical time after you have hired and groomed people who take over a part of the business. They do a great job. They develop confidence and the respect of others, and they earn a raise. They become a valuable part of your company. But there is more. At least to me.

I don't pretend to speak for all business owners, but I know I am not the only one who regularly appreciates, respects, feels good about, and enjoys the fact that we have found and developed people who have not only done great jobs but have signed on to our adventure. This goes beyond the business. It gets personal. It's about people buying houses, sending their kids to college, or even just providing for themselves or their family in a way that exceeds their expectations. I know pride is one of the seven deadly sins, but I am not sure why. Is it a sin to be proud of your people? Or is it a sin not to be?

Do you get a sense of satisfaction from knowing that you've given people opportunities, and they have succeeded — which benefits everybody? Does this make up for the employees who don't succeed along the way, including the ones who do serious damage to your business or your psyche? Maybe. I hope so. It does in my case. Failure is fixable. Success can last for years. But it doesn't happen on its own.

Ⅰ. New Words and Expressions

facility	[fəˈsɪlɪtɪ]	(*n*.) 办公场所
perfunctory	[pəˈfʌŋktərɪ]	(*a*.) 敷衍的,马虎的
rear	[rɪə]	(*v*.) 抬起;(马)直立
cringe	[krɪndʒ]	(*v*.) 畏缩;蜷缩
baloney	[bəˈləʊnɪ]	(*n*.) 愚蠢或夸大的言行;胡扯
groom	[gruːm]	(*v*.) 训练,推荐
equation	[ɪˈkweɪʃən]	(*n*.) 方程式,等式
fixable	[ˈfɪksəbl]	(*a*.) 可补救的
psyche	[ˈsaɪkɪ]	(*n*.) 灵魂;精神

Ⅱ. Fill in the blanks in the following sentences with the listed words or expressions.

be responsible for	get away with	comment on	end up with	figure out
on one's own	make up for	perfunctory	take over	cringe

1. The dog ________ at the sight of a snake.

2. If you do that, you'll ________ egg on your face.
3. He's trying to ________ a way to solve the problem.
4. If you cheat in the exam you'll never ________ it.
5. It's easy to say sorry, but who will ________ the loss?
6. The police ________ the enforcement of the law.
7. The operator answered the phone with a ________ greeting.
8. When she fell ill her daughter ________ the business from her.
9. The minister refused to ________ the rumors of his resignation.
10. Some men ________ will live out of tins rather than cook meals for themselves.

Ⅲ. There are four choices marked A. B. C. and D. in the following questions. You should decide on the best choice and mark the corresponding letter with a circle.

1. Why did the author give a perfunctory head nod?
   A. He agreed with the business owner's opinion.
   B. He wanted to run his business without employees.
   C. He has his own understanding towards hiring employees.
   D. He wanted to please the business owner.
2. Employees can be a liability, which can be proved by following behaviors except ________.
   A. causing problems with customers
   B. stealing
   C. suing you
   D. rear owner's head
3. What does the owner mean by saying, "I was only taking orders."?
   A. I am a good waiter.
   B. I take orders for the company.
   C. It's not my fault.
   D. I don't care.
4. "A tough pill" in the sentence "That can be a tough pill to swallow." means ________.
   A. something very unpleasant that you must accept
   B. good medicine pills comfortable
   C. the problem employees
   D. a tough employee
5. How can you run the business without having everyone make you crazy?
   A. Offer them high salary.
   B. Give them more bonuses.
   C. Punish them without mercy.

D. Choose the right people and train them properly.

6. "I've been both the giver and taker in that equation", this sentence can be understood as ________.

   A. I first receive salary and then pay salary to employees

   B. I employed unsatisfactory employees and also let them leave to work for other companies

   C. I work on the equation by giving and taking numbers

   D. I borrow money from others and also lend money to others

7. "A magic time" comes when ________.

   A. your employees become a valuable part of your company

   B. you make a lot of money

   C. once you hire the right employee

   D. the employee gets a raise in his or her salary

8. Which kind of pride is regarded as sin?

   A. Company owners looked down upon competitors.

   B. Family is proud of one of the important members.

   C. Company owners feel happy about employees' development.

   D. Company owners feel proud of their employees.

9. Why did the author say, "Failure is fixable"?

   A. The damage caused by employees can be repaired by workers.

   B. Your psyche damage can be cured by doctors.

   C. Your will forget about the damages when you see success of employees.

   D. Without failures, there is no success.

10. The main idea of this passage is ________.

    A. your business would be better without employees

    B. your business would be better with few employees

    C. if you use the right people, your business will be better

    D. if you give people opportunities and they have succeeded, business success can last long

Building a "Googley" Workforce

— Corporate Culture Breeds Innovation

By Sara Kehaulani Goo

Washington Post Staff Writer

Saturday, October 21, 2006

MOUNTAIN VIEW, Calif. — To understand the corporate culture at Google Inc., take a look at the toilets.

Every bathroom stall on the company campus holds a Japanese high-tech commode with a heated seat. If a flush is not enough, a wireless button on the door activates a bidet and drying.

Yet even while they are being pampered with high-tech toiletry, Google employees are encouraged to make good use of their downtime: A flier tacked inside each stall bears the title, "Testing on the Toilet, Testing code that uses databases." It features a geek quiz that changes every few weeks and asks technical questions about testing programming code for bugs.

The toilets reflect Google's general philosophy of work: Generous, quirky perks keep employees happy and thinking in unconventional ways, helping Google innovate as it rapidly expands into new lines of business.

Maintaining Google's culture of innovation is a hot internal topic as the Internet search king turns eight this fall and marches around the world, opening new offices in such cities as Beijing, Zurich and Bangalore. In the past three years, Google's workforce has more than tripled in size, to 9,000 employees, and the company has launched a new product nearly every week, including some widely regarded as flops. When its own offerings don't catch on, Google isn't shy about snapping up the competition, as it did this month when it agreed to acquire online video-sharing site YouTube for $ 1.65 billion in stock.

While Google places a premium on success, it appears to shrug off failure. The resulting culture of fearlessness permeates the 24-hour Googleplex, a collection of interconnected low-rise buildings that look more like some new-age college campus than a corporate office complex. The colorful, glass-encased offices feature upscale trappings — free meals three times a day; free use of an outdoor wave pool, indoor gym and large child care facility; private shuttle bus service to and from San Francisco and other residential areas — that are the envy of workers all over Silicon Valley.

Google employees are encouraged to propose wild, ambitious ideas often. Supervisors assign small teams to see if the ideas work. Nearly everyone at Google carries a generic job title, such as “product manager”. All engineers are allotted 20 percent of their time to work on their own ideas. Many of the personal projects yield public offerings, such as the social networking Web site Orkut and Google News, a collection of headlines and news links.

The corporate counterculture explains a lot about why the search company rolls out such a wide range of products in its self-proclaimed mission to organize the world’s information. Despite objections by publishers and authors, Google is attempting to copy every book ever published and make snippets available online. It plans to launch a free wireless Internet service in San Francisco. It also hopes to shake up the advertising world by using the Internet to sell ads in magazines, newspapers and on radio.

Philip Remek, an analyst who follows Google for Guzman and Co., sees the many initiatives as a series of lottery cards.

“A lot of them aren’t going to work,” Remek said. “Maybe there will be a few that take off spectacularly. And maybe they’re smart enough to realize no one is smart enough to tell which lottery card is the winner five years out.”

While Google often launches products before they are ready for prime time, even the premature ones instill fear in competitors, who know that the search leader has the patience and money — a market value of about $ 140 billion and $ 2.69 billion in quarterly revenue — to keep trying.

That’s also a message Google sends employees.

Ⅰ. New Words and Expressions

stall	[stɔːl]	(*n.*) 小隔间
commode	[kəˈməud]	(*n.*) 抽水马桶
activate	[ˈæktɪveɪt]	(*v.*) 使(某事物)活动
bidet	[biːˈdeɪ]	(*n.*) 坐浴盆
pamper	[ˈpæmpə]	(*v.*) 悉心照料
flier	[ˈflaɪə]	(*n.*) 小张广告传单
tack	[tæk]	(*v.*) 用钉钉住
bug	[bʌg]	(*n.*) 机器故障(尤指计算机的)
quirky	[ˈkwɜːkɪ]	(*a.*) 古怪的,不一般的
perk	[pɜːk]	(*n.*)(工作、职位等带来的)好处,特权
unconventional	[ˈʌnkənˈvenʃənəl]	(*a.*) 非传统的
flop	[flɒp]	(*n.*) 彻底失败
permeate	[ˈpɜːmɪeɪt]	(*v.*) 充满;遍布
complex	[ˈkɒmpleks]	(*n.*) 相关联或相似的综合事物
encase	[ɪnˈkeɪs]	(*v.*) 将某物置于箱、盒、套等之中

upscale	[ˈʌpˌskeɪl]	(*a.*)高消费的
generic	[dʒɪˈnerɪk]	(*a.*)一般的，普通的，共有的
allot	[əˈlɒt]	(*v.*)分配
snippet	[ˈsnɪpɪt]	(*n.*)片断
spectacular	[spekˈtækjʊlə]	(*a.*)引人注目的；出色的；与众不同的
place a premium on		高度重视
shrug off		不予理会

Ⅱ. Fill in the blanks in the following sentences with the listed words or expressions.

place a premium on	expand into	shrug off	snap up	roll out
make good use of	shake up	catch on	take off	feature

1. When do you guess the airplane will ________?
2. The new chairman will ________ the company.
3. It is a nice song and I think it will ________ quickly.
4. The latest popular actor ________ in this new film.
5. The company is eager to ________ new markets.
6. The cheapest articles at the sale ________ quickly .
7. You should ________ every precious minute to study.
8. I really admire the way she is able to ________ unfair criticism.
9. They ________ the red carpet for the visiting president and his party.
10. In the army we ________ bravery, courage and wisdom, while cowards are looked down upon.

Ⅲ. There are four choices marked A. B. C. and D. in the following questions. You should decide on the best choice and mark the corresponding letter with a circle.

1. How does Google make good use of their employees' downtime?

   A. Every bathroom stall on the company campus holds a Japanese high-tech commode with a heated seat.

   B. If a flush is not enough, a wireless button on the door activates a bidet and drying.

   C. It features a geek quiz and asks technical questions about testing programming code for bugs.

   D. They need to do a test on the toilet about its high-tech functions.

2. What is Google's general philosophy of work?

   A. The toilet. B. Be happy.

   C. Be comfortable. D. Innovative thinking.

3. The Internet search king turns eight this fall and marches around the world. It means: ________.
   A. Google is 8 years old
   B. Google has eight new offices
   C. Google failed eight times
   D. Google has expanded 8 time in size
4. How many people did the workforce of Google make up three years ago?
   A. 3,000　　B. 6,000　　C. 9,000　　D. 1,000
5. Among the following four, which is not the upscale trapping for workers all over Silicon Valley?
   A. Free meals three time a day.
   B. Free use of an outdoor wave pool, indoor gym and large child care facility.
   C. Private shuttle bus service to and from San Francisco and other residential areas.
   D. The 24-hour Googleplex, a collection of interconnected low-rise buildings.
6. What is Google's attitude towards failure?
   A. Objective.　　B. Supportive.
   C. Shrug off.　　D. Sensitive.
7. Which of the following is NOT mentioned in the passage?
   A. Maintaining Google's culture of innovation is a hot internal topic.
   B. Google makes a large profit by advertising.
   C. Google employees are encouraged to propose wild, ambitious ideas often.
   D. The corporate counterculture explains the reason for Google's success.
8. Many initiatives at Google can be seen as a series of lottery cards, because ________.
   A. a lot of cards aren't going to work
   B. no one is smart enough to tell which idea will generate the company progress in the future
   C. google often launches products at the prime time
   D. many employees at Google like playing the game of lottery cards
9. Which one of the following is not Google's strength?
   A. Patience.　　B. Creative thinking.
   C. Fearless spirit.　　D. Conventional ideas.
10. We can understand Google's corporate culture as ________.
   A. Google is not a conventional company, and Google intends to become one
   B. getting the right answer is necessary to every one of the company
   C. the innovation culture at Google is all about coming up with an idea, getting it out there for people to use as quickly as possible
   D. high welfare can lead to high performance

Culture affects everything we do. This applies to all areas of human life from personal relationships to conducting business abroad. When interacting within our native cultures, culture acts as a framework of understanding. However, when interacting with different cultures this framework no longer applies due to cross cultural differences.

Cross cultural communication aims to help minimize the negative impact of cross cultural differences through building common frameworks for people of different cultures to interact within. In business, cross cultural solutions are applied in areas such as HR, team building, foreign trade, negotiations and website design.

Cross cultural communication solutions are also critical to effective cross cultural advertising. Services and products are usually designed and marketed at a domestic audience. When a product is then marketed at an international audience, the same domestic advertising campaign abroad will in most cases be ineffective.

The essence of advertising is convincing people that a product is meant for them. By purchasing it, they will receive some benefit, whether it be life-style, status, convenience or financial. However, when an advertising campaign is taken abroad, different values and perceptions as to what enhances status or gives convenience exist. These differences make the original advertising campaign defunct.

It is therefore critical to any cross cultural advertising campaign that an understanding of a particular culture is acquired. By way of highlighting areas of cross cultural differences in advertising a few examples shall be examined.

Language in Cross Cultural Advertising

It may seem somewhat obvious to state that language is key to effective cross cultural advertising. However, the fact that companies persistently fail to check linguistic implications of company or product names and slogans demonstrates that such issues are not being properly addressed.

The advertising world is littered with examples of linguistic cross cultural blunders. Of the more comical was Ford's introduction of the "Pinto" in Brazil. After seeing sales fail, they soon realized that this was due to the fact that Brazilians did not want to be seen driving a car meaning "tiny male geni-

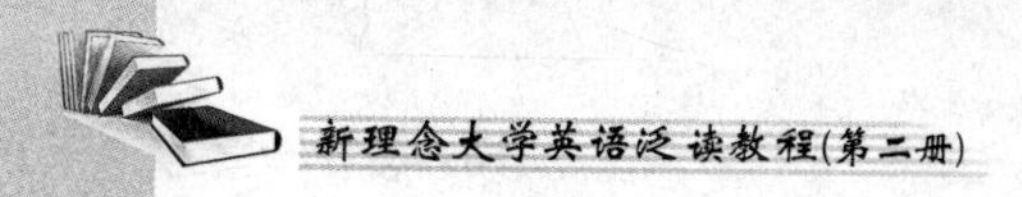

tals".

Language must also be analyzed for its cultural suitability. For example, the slogan employed by the computer games manufacturer, EA Sports, "Challenge Everything" raises grumbles of disapproval in religious or hierarchical societies where harmonious relationships are maintained through the values of respect and non-confrontation.

It is imperative therefore that language be examined carefully in any cross cultural advertising campaign.

Communication Style in Cross Cultural Advertising

Understanding the way in which other cultures communicate allows the advertising campaign to speak to the potential customer in a way they understand and appreciate. For example, communication styles can be explicit or implicit. An explicit communicator (e.g. USA) assumes the listener is unaware of background information or related issues to the topic of discussion and therefore provides it themselves. Implicit communicators (e.g. Japan) assume the listener is well informed on the subject and minimize information relayed on the premise that the listener will understand from implication. An explicit communicator would find an implicit communication style vague, whereas an implicit communicator would find an explicit communication style exaggerated.

Colors, Numbers and Images in Cross Cultural Advertising

Even the simplest and most taken for granted aspects of advertising need to be inspected under a cross cultural microscope. Colors, numbers, symbols and images do not all translate well across cultures.

In some cultures there are lucky colors, such as red in China and unlucky colors, such as black in Japan. Some colors have certain significance; green is considered a special color in Islam and some colors have tribal associations in parts of Africa.

Many hotels in the USA or UK do not have a room 13 or a 13th floor. Similarly, Nippon Airways in Japan do not have the seat numbers 4 or 9. If there are numbers with negative connotations abroad, presenting or packaging products in those numbers when advertising should be avoided.

Images are also culturally sensitive. Whereas it is common to see pictures of women in bikinis on advertising posters on the streets of London, such images would cause outrage in the Middle East.

Cultural Values in Cross Cultural Advertising

When advertising abroad, the cultural values underpinning the society must be analyzed carefully. Is there a religion that is practiced by the majority of the people? Is the society collectivist or individualist? Is it family orientated? Is it hierarchical? Is there a dominant political or economic ideology?

All of these will impact an advertising campaign if left unexamined.

For example, advertising that focuses on individual success, independence and stressing the word "I" would be received negatively in countries where teamwork is considered a positive quality. Rebelliousness or lack of respect for authority should always be avoided in family orientated or hierarchical societies.

By way of conclusion, we can see that the principles of advertising run through to cross cultural advertising too. That is — know your market, what is attractive to them and what their aspirations are. Cross cultural advertising is simply about using common sense and analyzing how the different elements of an advertising campaign are impacted by culture and modifying them to best speak to the target audience.

Ⅰ. New Words and Expressions

interact	[ˌɪntəˈrækt]	(v.) 互相作用；互相影响
audience	[ˈɔːdɪəns]	(n.) 观众，听众
defunct	[dɪˈfʌŋkt]	(a.) 无效的
premise	[ˈpremɪs]	(n.) 前提，假设
outrage	[ˈaʊtreɪdʒ]	(n.) 义愤，愤慨；暴怒

Ⅱ. Fill in the blanks in the following sentences with the listed words or expressions.

be unaware of	by way of	act as	as to	whereas
interact with	apply to	no longer	due to	imperative

1. He ________ his mistakes.
2. The two ideas ________ each other.
3. Sex is ________ the taboo subject as it used to be.
4. Some people like coffee, ________ others like tea.
5. The forest will ________ a defense against desert dust.
6. It's ________ that he apologize to her immediately.
7. It is a good idea for children to learn to read ________ pictures.
8. The law ________ everyone irrespective of race, religion or color.
9. ________ intelligence, the boy has more than he can possibly make use of.
10. The two countries were on the point of war ________ the diplomatic disputes.

Ⅲ. There are four choices marked A. B. C. and D. in the following questions. You should decide on the best choice and mark the corresponding letter with a circle.

1. The passage centers on ________ in cross cultural advertising.

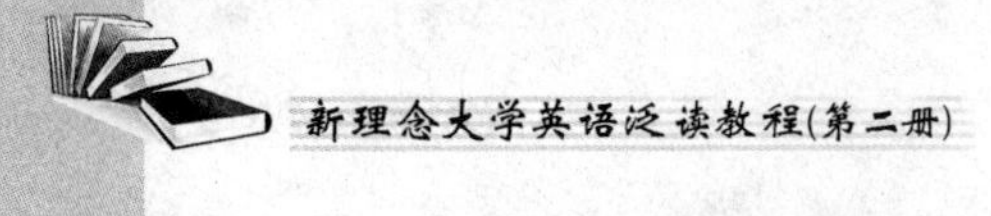

A. cultural differences B. languages

C. communication styles D. cultural values

2. Culture can't act as a framework of understanding when interacting with different cultures because of ________.

A. international audience

B. foreign trade

C. advertising campaign

D. cross cultural differences

3. ______ is key to effective cross cultural advertising.

A. Moral B. Value C. Culture D. Language

4. What do we learn about the "Pinto" made by Ford ?

A. It sells well in Brazil.

B. It met its Waterloo in Brazil.

C. It should be given another name.

D. It failed to be reputed as expected.

5. What should advertisers take into consideration in cross cultural advertising?

A. Language and communication style.

B. Colors, numbers and images.

C. Cultural values.

D. All of the above.

6. Which of the following statements is true according to the passage?

A. An implicit communicator assumes the listener is unaware of background information or related issues to the topic of discussion.

B. Explicit communicators assume the listener is well informed on the subject.

C. An explicit communicator finds an implicit communication style vague, whereas an implicit communicator finds an explicit communication style exaggerated.

D. Americans are implicit communicators while Japanese are explicit communicators.

7. Which number appears to be the most undesirable in UK?

A. 8 B. 4 C. 13 D. 9

8. Which of the following will be regarded as improper in the Middle East?

A. Packaging products in number 4 or 9.

B. Women in bikinis on advertising posters.

C. Wearing in red.

D. Green is forbidden.

9. All of these will impact an advertising campaign if left unexamined EXCEPT ______.

A. religion B. social pattern

C. team spirit D. economic ideology

10. What is wrong with cultural values in cross cultural advertising?

    A. The cultural values must be looked into carefully when advertising abroad.

    B. Advertising that focuses on teamwork would be received negatively in countries where individual success, independence and stressing the word "I" are considered positive qualities.

    C. Individual success, independence and stressing the word "I" are considered positive qualities when advertising abroad.

    D. Lack of respect for authority should always be avoided in hierarchical societies.

Passage 45

—How to Create Effective Billboard Ads

Billboards surround us. We probably see hundreds of billboard ads every single week, but remember just a handful. With outdoor advertising upping the stakes and becoming increasingly more competitive, it's important to know how to make your advertising count. Here are six strategies to ensure your billboard has the highest chance of being noticed, and more importantly, remembered.

1. For Billboards, Six Words or Less Is Ideal.

Considering we're on the move when we read billboards, we don't have a lot of time to take them in. Six seconds has been touted as the industry average for reading a billboard. So, around six words is all you should use to get the message across. You can push this to a few more words depending on their length and ease of reading, but as a rule of thumb, less is more here. Concision is tough, but headlines that are small paragraphs will not get read. And that means, if you have a complex brand, product or service, you should stay away from billboards completely.

2. Get Noticed, But Don't Make Your Billboards a Huge Distraction.

Most of the time, billboards are aimed at drivers, bikers, cyclists or pedestrians (which is why you have just a few seconds to get a message across). This causes an interesting dilemma for the advertiser; you want to get noticed, but you don't want to be responsible for major, or even minor, accidents. The iconic "Hello Boys" Wonderbra ads were guilty of this. Drivers were so fascinated by Eva Herzigova's cleavage that they were crashing into poles, medians and even each other. So, while being distracting is paramount in many mediums, it's a fine balance with the billboard.

3. This Is Not the Time for Direct Response.

I've seen billboards covered in phone numbers and website addresses, knowing without a doubt that 99.9% of the people who actually read the billboard would not have called or logged on. A billboard is a secondary advertising medium, which means that it's ideal for brand-building and supporting a campaign, but it just cannot do the heavy lifting. If you want a more intimate conversation with your target audience, use print advertising, television, radio, flyers, websites and direct mail. But billboards, they are the wrong medium for anything other than a quick message. However, if your website or phone number is the headline, and makes sense, then you have an out.

4. Billboards Should Be Smart, But Not Too Clever.

A boring billboard will be ignored. A smart billboard will grab the attention and leave a lasting impression. A billboard that's trying to be too clever, well, it will get lost on the audience. As a rule, you don't want billboards to make people scratch their heads and wonder what is going on. Complex visual metaphors are no good here. They say advertising should be like a puzzle to solve, it gives the audience a sense of fulfillment to know they figured it out. But billboards should be much simpler than that. Be smart, have fun, but don't give people puzzles that Einstein would have trouble solving. You're in the business of advertising, not showing off how clever you are.

5. The More Billboards, The Better.

One billboard is not cheap. But it's also not very effective either. Billboards are a mass market medium, but they need support. So, you want more than one, and you want as many eyes on them as possible. Every billboard has a rating, called Gross Ratings Points (GRP). It's based on traffic, visibility, location, size and so on. This rating gives you a showing score between 1 and 100. If it's 50, it means that at least 50% of the population in the area would see one of your boards at least once a day. If you have only one board, your impact chances are obviously less than if you have four or five. You really want a 100 showing, but that's not going to be cheap. You can expect to pay tens of thousands of dollars for a 50 showing for one month. In a major area like New York, the price shoots up.

6. Don't Say It, Show It.

Get creative with your billboard ideas. A flat billboard is the standard, but it doesn't have to be the norm. You can go 3D, have moving parts, have people interacting with it and even have your billboard animate. There is no reason that it just has to be a large, simple print ad. This is your opportunity to do something eye-catching and memorable, so go for it. The upside to this is it can create additional press, for free. A recent example of that is this simulated crash billboard that got major coverage from multiple news stations. The price of the 3D board was more than the cost of regular artwork, but it paid for itself many times over with PR impressions.

Ⅰ. New Words and Expressions

count	[kaʊnt]	(*v.*) 有价值
tout	[taʊt]	(*v.*) 宣扬
distraction	[dɪ'strækʃən]	(*n.*) 分散注意的事物

pedestrian	[pɪˈdestrɪən]	(*n.*) 步行者,行人
iconic	[aɪˈkɒnɪk]	(*a.*) 画像的,肖像的
cleavage	[ˈkliːvɪdʒ]	(*n.*) 劈开,乳沟
pole	[pəʊl]	(*n.*) 柱子
paramount	[ˈpærəmaʊnt]	(*a.*) 最重要的
intimate	[ˈɪntɪmɪt]	(*a.*) 亲密的
grab	[græb]	(*v.*) 抓住,攫取
mass	[mæs]	(*n.*) 大众,民众
animate	[ˈænɪˌmeɪt]	(*a.*) 有活力的,有生命的
stimulate	[ˈstɪmjʊleɪt]	(*v.*) 刺激,激励,促使

Ⅱ. Fill in the blanks in the following sentences with the listed words or expressions.

stay away from	paramount	crash into	surround	take in
be guilty of	show off	shoot up	as a rule	log on

1. The house ________ by high walls.
2. The naval officer asked him to ________ the base.
3. The kind old lady offered to ________ the poor homeless boy.
4. He was sentenced to ________ intrusion upon my privacy.
5. The truck spun out on the icy road and ________ the fence.
6. The child ________ out of the chair as soon as he heard the doorbell ring.
7. Mike has only driven to the pub to ________ his new car — he usually walks!
8. ________, it's the gentleman that holds out his hand to invite a lady to dance.
9. The reduction of unemployment should be ________ in the government's economic policy.
10. The two-year study showed that even people who spent just a few hours a week on the Internet experienced more depression and loneliness than those who ________ less frequently.

Ⅲ. There are four choices marked A. B. C. and D. in the following questions. You should decide on the best choice and mark the corresponding letter with a circle.

1. Which statement is true about billboard advertising?

   A. Concision is important, so we have to make long paragraphs into small ones in billboard headlines.

   B. If you have a complex brand, product or service, a billboard is the best choice for advertising.

   C. Six words on the billboardare enough to convey information clearly.

D. It takes us at least six seconds to read a billboard.

2. What can we learn from the example of "Hello Boys" Wonderbra ads?

A. Sexy images make the advertising attractive and fascinating, therefore they're highly recommended in advertising.

B. As the billboard aims to catch people's eyeballs, it should be as attractive as possible.

C. Because billboards may cause traffic accidents, they shouldn't become a distraction but be neglected.

D. Being distracting is not necessarily the most important factor in billboard advertising.

3. Which of the following mediums is NOT suitable for direct contact?

A. Television. B. Billboards. C. Websites. D. Flyers.

4. What does "heavy lifting" in the sentence "A billboard is a secondary advertising medium, which means that it's ideal for brand-building and supporting a campaign, but it just cannot do the heavy lifting" mean?

A. Tough or serious work. B. Weight lifting.

C. Successful work. D. Trying activity.

5. A billboard with its website or phone number as the headline _______.

A. won't get noticed at all

B. will build its brand and support its campaign

C. may probably have people logged on or called

D. is the wrong medium for direct response

6. Complex visual metaphors in billboard advertising may _______.

A. grab the attention and leave a lasting impression

B. lose the audience

C. give the audience a sense of fulfillment

D. give the audience much fun

7. The phrase "shoot up" in the sentence "In a major area like New York, the price shoots up" is closest in meaning to _______.

A. decrease a little B. decrease a lot

C. increase a little D. increase a lot

8. Why we should have more billboards?

A. Because we want a high GRP.

B. Because they're effective.

C. Because they're less expensive in small cities.

D. Because we can show off how strong we are.

9. The sentence "There is no reason that it just has to be a large, simple print ad" means _______.

A. we can't explain why it has to be a large, simple print ad

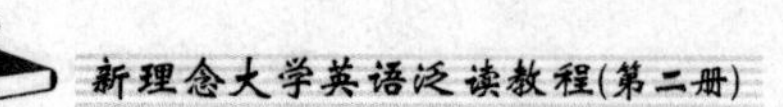

B. we can explain why it has to be a large, simple print ad

C. it has by no means to be a large, simple print ad

D. it doesn't have to be a large, simple print ad at all times

10. The following tips are critical and indispensable for effective advertising except ________.

A. make billboards creative and impressive

B. try the best to catch the audience's whole attention

C. have more than one billboard

D. be simple and concise

1. ZIP IT.

Learn to think before you speak. Bite your tongue before that provocative remark comes out of your mouth and you find yourself embroiled in a fight.

2. SIT, WAIT, THINK AND ACT WHEN CORRECT.

Whenever you have issues in the workplace, you're better off thinking through your words before you voice complaints, thoughts or suggestions. Whether you're a business owner, supervisor, manager or employee, the workplace can sometimes become a tinderbox for conflict.

3. LISTEN, DON'T DISPUTE.

Sometimes your manager needs to tell you how disappointed he is with you. Sometimes your co-worker needs to go on a diatribe about how you "neglect" him. Sometimes your employee needs to express his or her resentment about the way you've treated them. You can't argue with feelings. Listen when your co-workers, managers, or employees express strong feelings. Rather than argue and try to insist that they shouldn't be feeling what they're feeling, understand that they are feeling that way and simply say, "I'm sorry you feel that way." Try to put yourself in their shoes and give them the empathy that you would want yourself. Arguing may only make a situation worse.

4. DOCUMENT, DOCUMENT AND DOCUMENT AGAIN.

Rule No. 3 having been followed, make sure you protect yourself with thorough documentation of any potentially volatile situation. This rule applies to people on both sides of the power structure. A smart employee as well as a smart manager will document issues that relate to self-preservation and the protection of job security.

5. GOOD FENCES MAKE FOR GOOD WORK RELATIONSHIPS

Create boundaries and set limits in the workplace. Know how much contact you can take and how much will ignite your internal nuclear bomb. Also, keep in mind that you don't know which one of your co-workers will be easily ignited, offended or wounded; another reason why keeping clear, but cordial, boundaries is another way of protecting and preserving yourself.

6. CORDIALITY AND FRIENDLINESS

Having vowed to create appropriate boundaries, make every effort to be cordial and friendly. Ask co-workers and supervisors about how they are; notice changes in their appearance in a complimentary way; comment upon the quality of their (good) work. Being popular can only make work life easier.

7. THOU SHALT NOT OVERREACT. EVER.

When co-workers feel neglected, they often will create a scenario that invites your overreaction. Overreactions cause all out wars and can get you fired. Don't do it! Assess a dispute with your co-worker. Is it really worth fighting over? Repeat to yourself, "They're only words and I WANT my job."

8. PLAY WELL WITH OTHERS.

If you want to win the war (keep your job and progress up the career ladder), sometimes it's strategically advantageous to lose the battle. Assess a work situation carefully. Strategize and assess your gains and losses in a situation. If your supervisor or manager needs to act as if he or she came up with an idea that was actually yours, don't argue with them.

9. LET BREVITY AND PAUCITY BE YOUR MOTTO.

In the workplace, if you keep contact limited and utilize a cordial and polite silence to avoid fights, you can often extinguish flames that are being directed your way. Supervisors and managers appreciate a cooperative employee who gets to the point succinctly.

10. WHAT YOU SEE IS WHAT YOU GET.

Do not ever try to change your co-workers, especially those who are above you in the hierarchy of the workplace. It is a cardinal rule that people can change themselves, but none of us can change another. You are doomed to failure if you try to get your supervisor to see their flaws and change their ways. Learn to change what you can and accept what you cannot change.

11. STAY IN THE DRIVER'S SEAT.

Take control of potentially volatile work situations and take charge of managing them. For example, if you work for an individual who needs ample amounts of admiration and appreciation, give it to them. Work actively to make your work life smoother and to protect your employment and chances of rising on the career ladder. Remember that the best defense is a good offense. Strategize and evaluate the personalities you contend with and apply good people management techniques to the cast of characters you live with during your workday.

Ⅰ. New Words and Expressions

embroil	[ɪmˈbrɒɪl]	(v.) 使卷入;使陷入
diatribe	[ˈdaɪətraɪb]	(n.) 苛评,漫骂,争论
tinderbox	[ˈtɪndəˌbɒks]	(n.) (旧时用的)引火盒
volatile	[ˈvɒlətaɪl]	(a.) 易变的,无定性的,无常性的
ignite	[ɪgˈnaɪt]	(v.) (使)燃烧,着火;点燃
cordial	[ˈkɔːdjəl]	(a.) 热情友好的,和蔼可亲的

brevity	[ˈbrevɪtɪ]	(*n*.)(讲话、记述等的)简洁,简练
paucity	[ˈpɔːsɪtɪ]	(*n*.)少数;少量;缺乏
succinctly	[səkˈsɪŋktlɪ]	(*adv*.)简洁地;简便地
better off		(在某种情况下)更幸福,更满意

Ⅱ. Fill in the blanks in the following sentences with the listed words or expressions.

make every effort	take charge of	be embroiled in	make sure	fight over
take control of	be doomed to	contend with	argue with	worth

1. Have you ________ of the time of the train?
2. It's a trivial matter and not ________ fighting about.
3. Don't try to ________ him till he's cooled down.
4. I have a feeling that this project ________ fail.
5. I will ________ (ie do all I can) to arrive on time.
6. It's no easy task to ________ a class of young children.
7. The two boys ________ a game and then made friends again.
8. He had to ________ many difficulties when he was a young man.
9. Michael ________ all the arrangements for the Christmas party.
10. John and Peter were quarreling, but Mary refused to get ________ it.

Ⅲ. There are four choices marked A. B. C. and D. in the following questions. You should decide on the best choice and mark the corresponding letter with a circle.

1. How do you understand "bite your tongue"?
   A. Think before saying.
   B. Use teeth to cut the tongue.
   C. Stop oneself from speaking.
   D. Interrupt others when they speak.
2. When you have issues in the workplace, what will you do?
   A. To keep silent.
   B. To think before acting.
   C. To fly into rage.
   D. To report them to the manager.
3. In your workplace, when others make complaints about you, how will you deal with it?
   A. Listen to them. B. Argue with them.
   C. Fight with them. D. Feel sorry for them.

4. According to the passage, how can you be on good terms with others in your workplace?
   A. You can often invite them to eat outside.
   B. You can frequently communicate with them.
   C. You can tell them how you are feeling.
   D. You cannot offend anyone you are working with.
5. According to the passage, how to make efforts to be friendly to your co-workers?
   A. Having smart appearance.
   B. Dressing fashionably.
   C. Speaking formally.
   D. Being popular among them.
6. How do you understand "They're only word and I want my job." in the 7th point?
   A. Quarrelling with others in the workplace.
   B. Repeating the words to them.
   C. React in anger.
   D. Not care about what others say.
7. What does "Play well with others" mean?
   A. To play with others after work.
   B. To cooperate with others while working.
   C. Losses don't mean you will never go up the career ladder.
   D. To argue with others in a humorous way.
8. What can you change according to the passage?
   A. One's thoughts.   B. One's appearance.
   C. One's dressing style.   D. Nothing.
9. What seems important in dealing with others in the workplace?
   A. Keep silent.
   B. Never argue with the boss.
   C. Give in for ever.
   D. Be cordial.
10. If the title can be changed, which of the following will you choose?
    A. How to protect yourself in the workplace.
    B. How to avoid arguing with your employees.
    C. How to become a popular person in the workplace.
    D. How to avoid arguing with your employees.

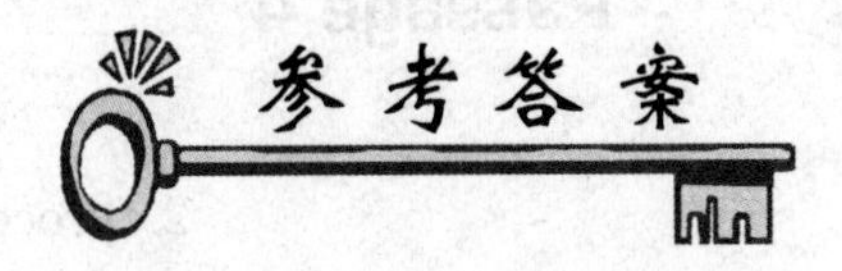

Passage 1

Ⅱ.

1. controlling
2. make contact
3. compare
4. courageous
5. cut... out
6. make a profit from
7. precious
8. get... to
9. similarity
10. in the quality of

Ⅲ.

1. B 2. C 3. D 4. D 5. B

Passage 2

Ⅱ.

1. couple ... with
2. development
3. forecasts
4. favorable
5. evaluate
6. Motivation
7. quantity
8. pattern
9. relates to
10. utilize

Ⅲ.

1. A 2. B 3. D 4. B 5. A

Passage 3

Ⅱ.

1. go up
2. put into
3. return
4. Suppose
5. risk
6. own
7. decrease
8. gain
9. invest
10. convert

Ⅲ.

1. C 2. B 3. A 4. B 5. C

Passage 4

Ⅱ.

1. variables
2. procedure
3. tailor
4. rejection
5. challenged
6. converge
7. cope with
8. critical
9. deals with
10. in some cases

Ⅲ.

1. C 2. A 3. C 4. D 5. B

Passage 5

Ⅱ.

1. do nothing with
2. take care
3. cure
4. predicted
5. succeed in
6. brought... to
7. solved
8. At present
9. spanning
10. came out

Ⅲ.

1. B 2. C 3. A 4. D 5. C

Passage 6

Ⅱ.

1. are faced with
2. claimed
3. led to
4. as far as... is concerned
5. contribute to
6. experimenting with
7. rather than
8. succeed in
9. neither... nor
10. no doubt

Ⅲ.

1. D 2. A 3. D 4. B 5. C

Passage 7

Ⅱ.

1. come from
2. at large
3. am unwilling to
4. on a smaller scale
5. come to
6. developed

7. create
8. agree to
9. seek to
10. depend on

Ⅲ.

1. D 2. B 3. C 4. B 5. C

Passage 8

Ⅱ.

1. apply to
2. build up
3. in this case
4. deals in
5. is tied up
6. try to
7. For example
8. a range of
9. spread
10. expand

Ⅲ.

1. C 2. B 3. D 4. A 5. B

Passage 9

Ⅱ.

1. has gained wide recognition
2. specializing in
3. to learn about
4. instead of
5. is taken for granted
6. to compare with
7. at the heart of
8. turn to
9. imitate
10. adapt

Ⅲ.

1. A 2. B 3. C 4. C 5. C

Passage 10

Ⅱ.

1. go online
2. free trial
3. tedious
4. First off
5. as well
6. doing his research
7. do business
8. look for
9. offered
10. was set up

Ⅲ.

1. A 2. B 3. A 4. D 5. C

Passage 11

Ⅱ.

1. is noted for
2. argued
3. tend to
4. bring on
5. on his behalf
6. be resolved
7. are interested in
8. is bad at
9. expand on
10. toot his own horn

Ⅲ.

1. C 2. C 3. B 4. D 5. B

Passage 12

Ⅱ.

1. announces
2. finance
3. got lost
4. start
5. turned to
6. launch
7. by instinct
8. meet their needs
9. chosen among
10. calculate

Ⅲ.

1. C 2. B 3. C 4. A

Passage 13

Ⅱ.

1. in the case of
2. drawing to
3. convey
4. employed
5. inspiring
6. is/was communicated
7. stretching back
8. is/was proved
9. Imagine
10. pay off

Ⅲ.

1. A 2. B 3. C 4. D 5. C

Passage 14

Ⅱ.

1. end up
2. embodies
3. one-way
4. aim at
5. reflected
6. turned out

7. approach
8. target
9. engage with
10. interact

Ⅲ.

1. D 2. C 3. C 4. D 5. A

Passage 15

Ⅱ.

1. at length
2. authenticity
3. commitment
4. candidates
5. dodgy
6. monster
7. gaga
8. Celebrity
9. old-fashioned
10. brought up

Ⅲ.

1. B 2. D 3. A 4. D 5. B

Passage 16

Ⅱ.

1. obsolete
2. impose on
3. exempt
4. round-trip
5. practice
6. hovering
7. itinerary
8. inconsistent
9. surcharged
10. dodge

Ⅲ.

1. D 2. D 3. B 4. D 5. A

Passage 17

Ⅱ.

1. probe
2. consider
3. on the table
4. on the spot
5. deal with
6. Find out
7. due to
8. By virtue of
9. gain
10. encountered

Ⅲ.

1. D 2. B 3. C 4. D 5. C

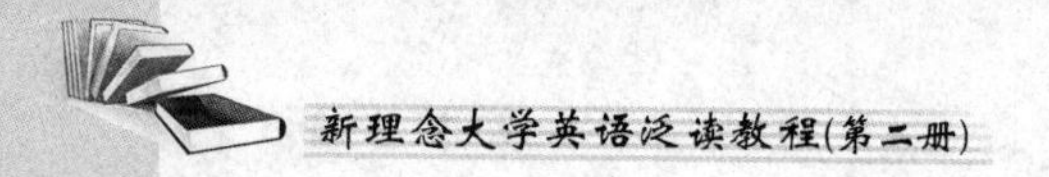

Passage 18

Ⅱ.

1. in order to
2. worth
3. be able to
4. is equipped with
5. are capable of
6. A variety of
7. because of
8. maintain
9. befall
10. attempt to

Ⅲ.

1. D 2. A 3. C 4. B 5. D

Passage 19

Ⅱ.

1. was familiar with
2. come with
3. entertaining
4. tend to
5. go window shopping
6. take a look at
7. pop up
8. combine
9. in stock
10. shows up

Ⅲ.

1. B 2. D 3. B 4. A 5. C

Passage 20

Ⅱ.

1. return to
2. place an order
3. have access to
4. represents
5. add... to
6. out of business
7. forecast
8. due to
9. shop online
10. worth noting

Ⅲ.

1. D 2. A 3. D 4. B 5. A

Passage 21

Ⅱ.

1. intense
2. maintain
3. pick up
4. check out
5. adopted
6. blow off

7. is reserved
8. erupted
9. hold... back
10. grab

Ⅲ.

1. D 2. C 3. D 4. B 5. A

Passage 22

Ⅱ.

1. episode
2. Division
3. weave
4. impeded
5. figure out
6. folks
7. be argued
8. focus
9. excelled
10. thrive

Ⅲ.

1. A 2. B 3. D 4. D

Passage 23

Ⅱ.

1. make a contribution to
2. mass market
3. accomplish
4. consumer goods
5. come in for
6. tend to
7. derive... from
8. made a difference to
9. perform
10. gaze at

Ⅲ.

1. C 2. A 3. A 4. C 5. C

Passage 24

Ⅱ.

1. amount to
2. a double-edged sword
3. pop up
4. release
5. make a purchase
6. show up
7. within reach
8. transform
9. based on
10. socialize with

Ⅲ.

1. D 2. C 3. C 4. C 5. C

Passage 25

Ⅱ.

1. getting into
2. pass by
3. has been bothering
4. can go a long way
5. knocked into
6. No matter how
7. bet
8. is thought of as
9. melted away
10. turned around

Ⅲ.

1. D 2. C 3. B 4. A 5. D

Passage 26

Ⅱ.

1. rest on
2. to be aware of
3. come across
4. indicate
5. based on
6. deal with
7. receptive
8. account for
9. is of no importance
10. pay attention to

Ⅲ.

1. B 2. D 3. A 4. B 5. C

Passage 27

Ⅱ.

1. yielded
2. rest on
3. stood out
4. look to
5. expect of
6. came up with
7. keep abreast of
8. is involved in
9. off-balance
10. in the shoes of

Ⅲ.

1. D 2. D 3. A 4. A 5. D 6. A 7. C 8. C
9. D 10. B

Passage 28

Ⅱ.

1. on the side of
2. make up for
3. vulnerable
4. has slashed

5. follows suit
6. are likely to
7. A flurry of
8. were loading up on
9. a grand gesture
10. have deteriorated

Ⅲ.

1. B 2. D 3. A 4. C 5. B 6. A 7. B 8. C
9. A 10. C

Passage 29

Ⅱ.

1. along with
2. engage in
3. as well as
4. No matter what
5. assessed
6. be adapted to
7. fluctuation
8. was enhanced
9. are familiar with
10. put... out of business

Ⅲ.

1. B 2. A 3. C 4. D 5. C 6. B 7. A 8. D
9. C 10. D

Passage 30

Ⅱ.

1. came in contact with
2. were aware of
3. in terms of
4. were imposed on
5. discouraged... from
6. ended up
7. undersell
8. dilemma
9. cool his heels
10. amounts to

Ⅲ.

1. D 2. D 3. C 4. D 5. B 6. D 7. A 8. C
9. C 10. D

Passage 31

Ⅱ.

1. as a result
2. hold back
3. plays a... role in
4. abated
5. bankrupt
6. Superficially
7. has resulted in
8. was compensated

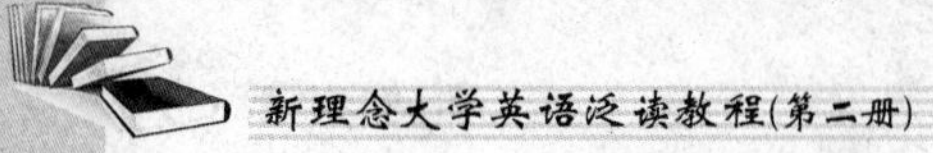

9. come forth 10. soared

Ⅲ.

1. C 2. B 3. B 4. D 5. A 6. D 7. D 8. A
9. D 10. A

Passage 32

Ⅱ.

1. The odds 2. take account of
3. prevails 4. in spite of
5. apace 6. was called off
7. suffer from 8. is referred to
9. take your time 10. hang around

Ⅲ.

1. A 2. B 3. A 4. A 5. C 6. C 7. C 8. B
9. D 10. C

Passage 33

Ⅱ.

1. adopt 2. is comprised of
3. account for 4. has been put up
5. was traced to 6. In response to
7. were undermined 8. eliminate
9. are subject to 10. furthermore

Ⅲ.

1. C 2. C 3. D 4. A 5. D 6. B 7. D 8. A
9. C 10. A

Passage 34

Ⅱ.

1. is sold out 2. a bunch of
3. Despite 4. on the road to
5. work out 6. in place
7. met up with 8. got ready to
9. have been committed to 10. earn his trust

Ⅲ.

1. D 2. B 3. C 4. A 5. C 6. B 7. D 8. B

9. D 10. A

Passage 35

Ⅱ.

1. react to
2. is critical to
3. was derived from
4. As long as
5. at your peril
6. begin with
7. optimize
8. a host of
9. was focused on
10. in between

Ⅲ.

1. A 2. B 3. A 4. D 5. A 6. C 7. D 8. A
9. D 10. C

Passage 36

Ⅱ.

1. went through
2. is based on
3. get caught up
4. speed up
5. vary
6. slowed down
7. jot down
8. be applied
9. Armed with
10. entrepreneur

Ⅲ.

1. B 2. D 3. A 4. D 5. A 6. B 7. B 8. D
9. B 10. A

Passage 37

Ⅱ.

1. sank into
2. pick up
3. by means of
4. competed with
5. undoubtedly
6. So far
7. has gone up
8. in case of
9. favorably
10. dozens of

Ⅲ.

1. D 2. B 3. C 4. C 5. B 6. A 7. D 8. A
9. B 10. C

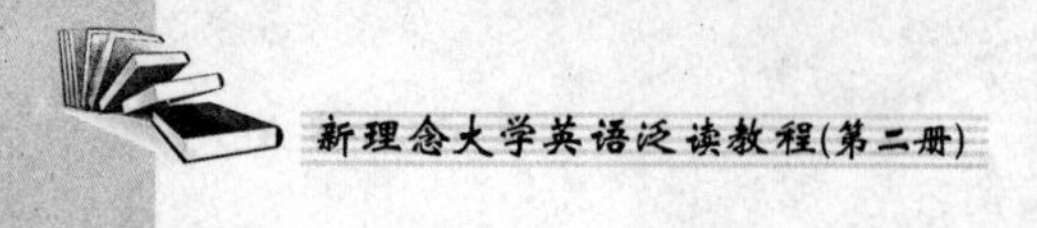

Passage 38

Ⅱ.

1. is made up of
2. oversee
3. abide by
4. are intended to
5. is empowered
6. called for
7. sort out
8. call off
9. in charge of
10. conducted their business

Ⅲ.

1. B 2. C 3. C 4. C 5. B 6. A 7. D 8. B
9. B 10. D

Passage 39

Ⅱ.

1. has applied for
2. in person
3. via
4. versus
5. be relied on
6. therefore
7. has coined
8. By definition
9. is differentiated from
10. place an order

Ⅲ.

1. A 2. D 3. C 4. C 5. B 6. B 7. B 8. B
9. C 10. B

Passage 40

Ⅱ.

1. bid on
2. ranged
3. in earnest
4. are capable of
5. In general
6. depend on
7. keep in mind
8. ate up
9. has been waived
10. was inclined to

Ⅲ.

1. D 2. D 3. C 4. B 5. C 6. B 7. C 8. D
9. D 10. D

Passage 41

Ⅱ.

1. underestimated
2. deal with
3. drive up
4. together with
5. nostalgic
6. mitigate
7. has shut down
8. in other words
9. killed off
10. gave up

Ⅲ.

1. D 2. C 3. A 4. B 5. C 6. C 7. A 8. B
9. D 10. A

Passage 42

Ⅱ.

1. cringed
2. end up with
3. figure out
4. get away with
5. make up for
6. are responsible for
7. perfunctory
8. took over
9. comment on
10. on their own

Ⅲ.

1. C 2. D 3. C 4. C 5. D 6. B 7. A 8. A
9. C 10. D

Passage 43

Ⅱ.

1. take off
2. shake up
3. catch on
4. is featured
5. expand into
6. were quickly snapped up
7. make good use of
8. shrug off
9. rolled out
10. place a premium on

Ⅲ.

1. C 2. D 3. A 4. A 5. D 6. C 7. B 8. B
9. D 10. C

Passage 44

Ⅱ.

1. was unaware of
2. interact with
3. no longer
4. whereas
5. act as
6. imperative
7. by way of
8. applies to
9. As to
10. due to

Ⅲ.

1. A 2. D 3. D 4. B 5. D 6. C 7. C 8. B
9. C 10. C

Passage 45

Ⅱ.

1. was surrounded
2. stay away from
3. take in
4. be guilty of
5. crashed into
6. shot up
7. show off
8. As a rule
9. paramount
10. logged on

Ⅲ.

1. C 2. D 3. B 4. A 5. C 6. B 7. D 8. A
9. D 10. B

Passage 46

Ⅱ.

1. made sure
2. worth
3. argue with
4. is doomed to
5. make every effort
6. take control of
7. fought over
8. contend with
9. takes charge of
10. embroiled in

Ⅲ.

1. A 2. B 3. A 4. D 5. D 6. D 7. C 8. C
9. D 10. A

参考文献

[1] 王洗薇,任奎艳.世纪商务英语阅读教程基础篇 I(第四版).大连:大连理工大学出版社,2009

[2] 虞苏美,吴长镛.新编商务英语泛读 2.北京:高等教育出版社,2004

[3] 宋梅.电子商务英语.北京:科学出版社,2006

[4] 教育部《实用英语》教材编写组.实用英语 3 综合教程(第二版).北京:高等教育出版社,1999